Quiet

Sarah Ward is a critically acclaimed crime and gothic thriller writer. Her book, *A Patient Fury*, was an Observer book of the month and *The Quickening*, written as Rhiannon Ward, was a Radio Times book of the year. Sarah is a former Vice-Chair of the Crime Writers Association, Trustee of Gwyl Crime Cymru Festival and an RLF Fellow at Sheffield University.

Also by Sarah Ward

A Mallory Dawson Crime Thriller

The Birthday Girl
The Sixth Lie
The Vanishing Act

Carla James Crime Thrillers

Death Rites
Quiet Bones

SARAH WARD

QUIET BONES

First published in the United Kingdom in 2025 by

Canelo Crime, an imprint of
Canelo Digital Publishing Limited,
20 Vauxhall Bridge Road,
London SW1V 2SA
United Kingdom

A Penguin Random House Company
The authorised representative in the EEA is Dorling Kindersley Verlag GmbH.
Arnulfstr. 124, 80636 Munich, Germany

Copyright © Sarah Ward 2025

The moral right of Sarah Ward to be identified as the creator of this work has been asserted in accordance with the Copyright, Designs and Patents Act, 1988.
All rights reserved. No part of this publication may be reproduced or transmitted in any form or by any means, electronic or mechanical, including photocopy, recording, or any information storage and retrieval system, without permission in writing from the publisher.
No part of this book may be used or reproduced in any manner for the purpose of training artificial intelligence technologies or systems. In accordance with Article 4(3) of the DSM Directive 2019/790, Canelo expressly reserves this work from the text and data mining exception.

A CIP catalogue record for this book is available from the British Library.

Print ISBN 978 1 80436 676 9
Ebook ISBN 978 1 80436 677 6

This book is a work of fiction. Names, characters, businesses, organizations, places and events are either the product of the author's imagination or are used fictitiously. Any resemblance to actual persons, living or dead, events or locales is entirely coincidental.

Cover design by Kid-ethic

Cover images © Shutterstock

Printed and bound in Great Britain by Clays Ltd, Elcograf S.p.A.

Look for more great books at
www.canelo.co | www.dk.com

For Heulwen

Chapter 1

Article from the *Jericho Tribune*
2nd May 2024

> Jericho Police Department is appealing for the mother of a baby girl found deceased in local woodland to come forward. The preterm baby was abandoned next to a dumpster in Shining Cliff Wood, three miles northeast of Jericho, its remains discovered by two dog walkers late on Saturday afternoon. It is thought the baby had been outside for some considerable time and doctors believe the mother may be in need of urgent medical aid.
>
> A spokesperson for Jericho PD said, 'We ask for the community's thoughts and prayers for the soul of this little one and would appreciate any information as to the welfare of the mother as soon as possible. We remind our citizens to avail themselves of the safe havens available in this county.'

Every State has a Safe Haven Law

All US states have a so-called Safe Haven law which allows mothers to relinquish their unharmed baby to a state-agreed safe place without fear of prosecution. In many states, fire stations and police precincts are designated safe havens with very few requiring the parent to drop the child at a hospital or medical services provider. Safe Haven laws allow the parent to remain anonymous. It is usually considered abandonment if a parent does not hand their child in to a Safe Haven location.

Chapter 2

It was the fourth poster Professor Carla James had seen on her way home from the college. It was a warm May afternoon, something Carla hadn't expected after the vicious snow over the winter months that had sent her trudging to the hardware store for a shovel to clear the path to her car so she could get to work each day. That now felt like a different age. A week of clear skies and spring sunshine had warmed Carla's chilly flat and she'd finally left her car at home to enjoy the fresh air on the way to and from lectures. It appeared someone was taking advantage of the kind weather to try to jog memories. The image of Lucie Tandy stared down from the colour photo, taken according to news reports during her first week of term. Carla reached out to flatten the photo to get a closer look at the girl.

Lucie had long fair hair that had been pulled over one shoulder, probably to pose for whoever had taken the snap. She was smiling broadly into the camera, revealing a row of even white teeth, and was sporting a pair of wide black glasses. 'Joe 90' her mother would have called them, but Carla noticed that many of her students adopted the same look. It gave Lucie's soft, pretty features a more bluestocking look; she had been a striking girl who Carla had occasionally glimpsed across campus. Carla, a little self-conscious about her own lack of height, admired any female who was tall and Lucie had been five foot nine inches. Carla knew this because it was written on the poster: *Lucie Tandy, missing since 3 April. Age twenty, height five nine, last seen wearing a yellow raincoat. Greatly missed by her family and friends.*

Carla had been following the story of Lucie's disappearance and it had been discussed extensively at departmental meetings. She didn't like it when students took themselves off and she'd been paranoid about women's safety after a serial killer had been unmasked the previous year as a member of the archaeology department's staff. But the view of the police, the college and Lucie's friends was that her disappearance was voluntary, something that Carla had reluctantly come around to agreeing with after untangling the scant information available.

Lucie had been living in female-only second-floor accommodation in the halls of residence with three other students she'd not known before arriving at the college. At first, she'd thrown herself into student life but, according to her dormmates, had become a little disillusioned with the realities of studying within a hothouse institution. She'd returned from the Christmas break more thoughtful and downbeat than she had been the previous term and had become secretive over her comings and goings. The girls had asked individually and over dinner one night what the issue was but Lucie had said she was feeling stressed by the course. She was majoring in anthropology and struggling to keep up with her grades. This, it subsequently turned out, had not been true. Lucie had been consistently getting As for her assignments and, if she'd been struggling with the volume of work, it had not affected the quality of the papers she was handing in. So, perhaps Lucie had been lying and there was something else that had been bothering her.

On the day in April when she went missing, Lucie had attended classes as usual and none of her fellow students had noticed anything untoward. The only sign of something amiss was when Lucie didn't turn up for a coffee appointment with Anika, a friend from the Student Ethical and Environment Club, known as SEEC. The girls had known each other since the first week of term when they'd joined the society, but as Anika was majoring in accounting and they didn't share any classes, they liked to catch up regularly in the campus coffee shop. When Lucie failed to show, Anika texted her and received a reply. *Just need some time out.* Other than being a little put out at being stood up, Anika thought nothing more of it. Clearly something had come up.

Meanwhile, Lucie's three dormmates – Daria, Ali and June – had thought it strange when Lucie hadn't come home. They were all busy with their studies and extra-curricular life but had gathered in the dorm by seven that night. Although the girls often cooked each other meals, they were doing their own thing that evening. Daria and June went to a nearby diner while Ali ate a salad at the table in the shared kitchen. By nine, Lucie hadn't returned and the girls began to ring round friends to see if anyone had spoken to her. Through a friend they contacted Anika who told them about Lucie's no-show in the cafe and her message. The girls left it three days, wondering how much time out would be acceptable to the college mid-term, until they were contacted by the tutor of a class where Lucie was supposed to be giving a presentation. The skipped talk would mean a deduction in Lucie's marks which she'd never ordinarily countenance, and Carla had been drawn into the departmental alarm when it became clear that the three p.m. class with her colleague Jack Caron on 3 April was the last time Lucie had been seen.

'Pretty girl.'

Carla's reverie was broken by the voice of a woman who was squinting up at the poster.

'Who is she?' the woman asked Carla.

'Lucie Tandy, a missing Jericho student. It looks like a member of her family or perhaps a friend is having another push to see if anyone has information. It's been over a month now.'

'Probably run off with a guy, if you ask me. That's what young girls do. They always have.'

Carla shook her head but remained silent. Whatever Lucie had done, she hadn't run off with a guy. After an initial search of Lucie's rooms by college security, Jericho police had been called in. Lucie's love life had been the first line of questioning, according to feedback given at the last department update. June, the dormmate friendliest with Lucie, said that the missing girl had confided to her that she was gay. June had been sworn to secrecy and had only revealed Lucie's sexual orientation under police questioning. Neither Lucie's other dormmates nor Anika had known anything about Lucie's love affairs. Naturally, the police had then looked closer at Lucie's circle of friends but had been unable to uncover a relationship. There was no evidence of a struggle or kidnap, nor any reports of a woman being forced into a vehicle between the time of her class finishing and her scheduled coffee with Anika at five p.m. Furthermore, Lucie's parents, who lived in the Seattle area, said that Lucie occasionally liked to take herself off when things became too much for her, which added to the sense that the pressured Jericho environment had not suited this particular student. That had been that. Lucie's 'time out' continued indefinitely.

Carla left the woman still peering up at the photo and hurried to her flat. The warmth of a long day of teaching students, some of whom had begun to panic about their grades, had left her tired and scratchy and she needed a shower. As she went up the steps of her building, she could hear music playing from the downstairs flat. It was occupied by a woman in her early fifties who had some kind of corporate job. Carla often saw her leaving early in the morning in a pinstripe trouser suit always teamed with high heels. The flat would be left silent until the sound of a car door shutting at around nine each evening. A long day, but it looked as if the resident was having a day off as the sounds of Joni Mitchell wafted in the summer air.

Carla put her key in the lock and after depositing her bag, stripped off and stood under the pulsating shower. The noise of the water masked the sound of her phone ringing and Carla only saw she had missed two calls from Erin Collins as she was towel-drying her hair. She pressed the call button and Erin picked up immediately.

'Caught ya. I was beginning to think I'd have to drive over to yours to track you down.'

Carla picked up her watch. Just gone five. 'Is everything all right?'

'Not really. I'd like you down here because there's someone I need you to look at in a professional capacity. I can't tell you over the phone as there's enough noise about it already. Can you come down now?'

Carla swallowed, her first thought of the photos of Lucie she'd just been studying. 'Don't tell me they've found her.' Erin was a pathologist and state medical examiner. The fact she was calling Carla in a professional capacity was not a good sign. An archaeologist in the anthropology department of Jericho College, Carla had been called in to assist a police investigation into the death of a woman found burnt to death. Working alongside Erin, Carla had uncovered a series of linked deaths and nearly lost her life because of her involvement.

'Who?' said Erin, her voice sharp. 'Who is supposed to have been found?'

'I thought... sorry, I was looking at a poster of Lucie Tandy, you know the missing student, on the way home. Someone's making a renewed effort to find her.'

'That's not the reason I called. I can categorically tell you it's not about her but I would like your professional opinion on something.'

'Can't you give me a clue what this is about?'

'Nope. Just get down here as soon as you can.'

Chapter 3

'I've called her Fionnuala.'

Carla swallowed, wondering how official her presence was in this most brutal of rooms. She and Erin were dressed in scrubs, face masks and oversized caps to cover their hair. On the statuesque Erin, the outfit looked as if she was starring in a TV show, but Carla felt claustrophobic and uncomfortable. Although immaculately clean, the autopsy room had a faint metallic tang combined with an earthy scent. It must be a legacy of a previous patient as the remains she was looking at were pitiful in their meagreness. The baby girl's skin was stretched taut across her bones, the process of mummification begun. Carla's rudimentary knowledge of the phenomenon suggested that the baby had been kept somewhere warm and dry.

'Is this the baby I read about in the newspaper? The child who was found abandoned by the dumpster?'

'Sure is. Not what I was expecting when it was brought in for me to autopsy. A child left exposed to the elements shouldn't look like this.'

'No, I can see that. Do you have any ideas where the body might have been kept?'

'Nowhere near the woodland where she was found, I don't think. It was a wet spring, remember. Maybe the mother kept it in their house – these things do happen –

and then, for whatever reason, decided to bring the death out into the open, figuratively and literally.'

'Why have you called her Fionnuala?' asked Carla who was aware of Erin's Irish heritage. She understood the need to humanise this nameless child. Abandoned and left to die it could be as much an act of hate as one of desperation, and here was a demonstration of humanity from a professional tasked with ascertaining the cause of death.

Erin didn't immediately reply, covering up the child with a facility branded blanket. 'I just wanted you to see Fionnuala so you can have an idea of what she looks like. It might be important when I explain why I've called you in here. The autopsy was straightforward. There is no obvious skeletal damage although there is bruising on the head and face. I'm no expert, but it looks like what I'd expect from a difficult vaginal birth.'

'Was she born alive?' asked Carla, following Erin to the hazards bin and taking off her mask. She thought it might matter very much when the baby's mother was found.

Erin sighed. 'I'm not sure. We tend to work backwards when it's not immediately clear if a child has taken a breath. We look for indicators that would absolutely preclude a live birth – the stage of gestation, for example, too early for extrauterine life or a lethal malformation that would rule out independent existence.'

'The baby – I mean Fionnuala – looks perfect.'

Erin sighed. 'I know. She was pre-term and I'm guessing maybe thirty-four weeks when born so that may have been a factor in her death. I looked at the lungs which appeared aerated suggesting Fionnuala took a breath. The problem is that it's not a definitive indicator. Some stillborn lungs can appear similar and those from live births can be devoid of air. However, the lungs' condition alongside the presence of gas when Baby F, Fionnuala's official name, was imaged post-mortem suggests a live birth.'

'Christ.' Carla ripped off her paper cap and threw it into the trash. 'What potential charges is the mother facing when she's found – or maybe I should say if she's found.'

Erin opened the door of the facility and nodded towards the office. 'Reckless abandonment, cruelty to children in the first degree, murder possibly if the prosecution can prove the baby was left to die. What I don't understand is why the mother didn't use a safe haven. There are three in Jericho – one of them at a medical facility – so she wouldn't have had to go anywhere near the police precinct.'

Carla shut the door behind her and took the chair next to Erin's desk. 'What am I doing here, Erin?'

Erin folded her arms across her chest. They were muscular, suggesting frequent gym workouts and in the warmth of the day, a sheen of sweat glistened on the tanned limbs despite the air conditioning.

'The baby, as the press articles have suggested, was found by a dumpster at Shining Cliff Wood. Two dog walkers, both females in their early sixties, saw what they thought was a dead animal and one of their dogs was pulling on the leash to get at it. They unwrapped the covering and saw the baby more or less as you see it now.'

'Christ. It must have been a horrible shock.'

'I'm sure it was. To answer your question, the reason I called her Fionnuala was due to an Irish story that my grandmother used to tell me. It's about the Children of Lir who had to spend nine hundred years as swans due to a jealous stepmother. There were three boys and a girl called Fionnuala.'

'What relevance does that have to our baby's death?' asked Carla.

Erin shook her head. 'To Fionnuala's death, possibly nothing. It's how she was found that brought swans to mind.'

'Swans?' Carla's head began to thump, and she reached down to retrieve the bottle of water from her rucksack.

'I want to show you something.' Erin pushed a metal tray towards Carla and pulled off a piece of plastic sheeting. Underneath there was a mass of organic matter although it was difficult to distinguish its origin. There were some dried twigs, brown-white feathers and what looked like shards of bone. This was the earthy smell Carla had detected in the autopsy room.

'What's this?' asked Carla, drawn to the mass despite her confusion.

'It's the wrapping the baby was found within. At first, I thought it was detritus swept from the forest floor. The mother might have made an attempt to make a rudimentary grave for her child although that wouldn't account for the mummification. I asked a colleague from the college to come and take a look at the feathers – she's an expert in birds – and she told me what in fact we're looking at is a swan's wing.'

'The baby was buried in a swan's wing?' asked Carla, shocked. 'Like the Vedbaek burial?'

Erin turned her face towards her, a spiral of hair falling in front of her eyes. 'Exactly like the Vedbaek burial. It was one of the top hits I got when I did an online search for babies and swans' wings. My mind was filled with the Children of Lir and swan mythology but I saw something about an archaeological dig and looked it up.'

Carla rubbed her head, trying to remember what she knew about the Danish Stone Age burial site. There had been other graves excavated, she was sure, but it was the discovery of the mother and newborn child that remained in the mind because of the careful placing of the baby within the swan's wing. 'So that's why you called me. You want to know if the Vedbaek burial offers any clues into this death.'

'That's about the size of it,' said Erin, her expression grim. 'I'm not expecting you to reel off all the facts without looking it up yourself. Let's get out of here and talk over a drink.'

Chapter 4

They escaped to Morrell's, the busy bar favoured by academics, office workers and tourists. Erin had suggested talking over a drink after she'd looked at Carla's wan expression and decided it would be a good idea to lift the atmosphere a little. Erin had forgotten how inured she'd become to death. The child lying on the cold slab had represented a mystery, or perhaps more specifically, a professional conundrum. Naming the baby Fionnuala hadn't obscured the fact that Erin's primary role was to concentrate on unravelling the sequence of events responsible for extinguishing her life. Extinguishing, Erin thought. It sounded so matter-of-fact, although surely Carla had her own jargon she used in relation to the people she unearthed. The problem was this was no prehistoric child, but a twenty-first-century death.

She ordered them a gin fizz each despite Carla's protestations she'd prefer a beer. Erin's grandmother had always said that gin was a drink to weep into and Carla looked like that was exactly what she wanted to do. As they were waiting for the drinks to arrive, Carla pulled out her phone and said she was going to refresh her memory of Vedbaek. Erin, impatient to get on with things, looked around the room to see if there was anyone she knew. Things had been shaken up earlier in the year with the arrest of Carla's colleague Max Hazen on the charge of multiple homicides, and some of the places such as Morrell's and the Greek cafe close to campus that Max had liked to frequent held unpleasant memories for those who had been involved in the case. Morrell's, however, was crowded and Erin could see little beyond the adjoining tables.

Finally, Carla put down her phone. 'I've looked at articles from the more respectable archaeology websites. I really could do with getting to the library and looking at some journal papers but I've basically managed to refresh myself of the facts. You want me to summarise it for you?'

'Please. I'd like fact separated from fiction which I suspect the websites I was looking at weren't so bothered about.'

Carla waited as two tall glasses were set in front of them before giving Erin's a light clink. 'There was a dig in the 1980s of a Mesolithic period settlement at Vedbaek, now a suburb of Copenhagen.'

'Mesolithic period being…'

Carla flushed. 'Sorry, about seven thousand years ago. During the excavation, pits and graves were found where adults and children had been buried or cremated. In one grave, the bones of a woman, aged around twenty, were found cradling a newborn baby. The inference is that she died in childbirth which, of course, was not uncommon even until fairly recently. What was unusual was that the child was cradled in a swan's wing which, I think, is unique in terms of finds.'

'Why a swan's wing?'

'Well, we don't know. It was part of a wider burial site but this grave was unique. Swans may represent purity, majesty even. Or there might be a symbolism about soaring to another place upon death. It's almost impossible to theorise, which doesn't stop us from trying. What I'm interested in though is the archaeology of emotion. What the feelings were behind the burial.'

'And?' Erin was impatient to get to the crux of the symbolism. There were too many questions around the discovery – where the fuck did you find a swan's wing in Jericho for a start – but Carla, she could see, was about to go off on a tangent.

'Grief, obviously, but also celebration. The woman found next to her child had been buried with snail-shell beads and her face dusted with red ochre which suggest a woman of status. There's a pride in her death, a celebration of life, although we need to be careful not to assume that these types of burials were the norm.'

'Lots of riders on your theories. Sounds a bit like my profession too, come to think of it. I'm looking for something concrete to connect Vedbaek to the baby found at Shining Cliff Wood. You don't think, for example, that maybe Fionnuala's mother was an archaeologist who decided to adopt the ritual for her own child?'

Carla made a face. 'I'm not sure. I mean, the story is readily available on the internet, so you don't need to be a student of archaeology to read up about it.'

'I suppose I was thinking about your missing student.'

'Lucie?' Carla looked surprised. 'Lucie was gay and as far as we know not in a relationship. There's also no suggestion of her having been pregnant. What made you think of her?'

'Despite the details being on the internet, I still think the Vedbaek burial is pretty niche.'

'There are lots of infant burials an archaeologist could reference, it's the swan's wing that's so unusual. That's what you should focus on. Why the baby was wrapped in the wing.' Carla stopped. 'You don't think the mother's body might be nearby? Has the site been searched?'

'Of course. It was the first thing I asked Detective Baros when I discovered what the child had been wrapped in. He said there's no evidence of any burial, but the wood is a huge site to search. In any case, Fionnuala wasn't buried, was she? Just placed next to the dumpster.'

'Maybe I was being too literal. Let me have a think about it, although maybe we're looking for a message that isn't there.' Carla looked glum.

Erin shrugged. 'Don't write yourself off yet. I have a feeling I'll be calling you again about this.'

But Carla wasn't listening, her attention fixed across the room. A man and a woman had come into the bar and were making their way towards a couple sat at a window table. The woman was wearing spiked heels with slim cigarette trousers and had a whiff of Seventies chic about her. Erin would never have recognised her if she hadn't caught sight of the woman's partner – Jack Caron.

'Jack and Anna. I'd heard they'd got back together again.' She kept her gaze on Carla. While the couple had tested out a trial separation, Carla and Jack had become close although Carla had professed to be ambivalent about the relationship.

Carla shrugged. 'They make an attractive couple.'

Carla's voice was cool, so why the hell was her attention riveted to the table? Erin reached for her eyeglasses and put them on to get a closer look at the Carons' dinner companions.

'Well, fuck me.' Carla's former boss Albert Kantz and his wife, disgraced police chief Viv, were rising to greet their drinking partners. 'That's pretty out there, isn't it? I mean they're both supposed to be lying low and yet they're sitting in Morrell's at a window table on a Thursday night.'

'Hmm. I wasn't aware they were in touch. Who do you think instigated the meeting?'

'Instigated?' Erin frowned. 'What do you mean?'

'It's just that you're right – it is a strange place to meet and there seems to be some urgency to it.'

Erin looked across and saw Jack and Albert engaged in a heated discussion, their conversation looked urgent and forthright. 'Do you think it's about the department?' she asked Carla.

'I'm not sure.' Carla picked up her glass. 'But I'd love to be a fly on the wall.'

Chapter 5

The following morning, Carla walked to work with a banging head from the gin and a night full of images of the two couples laughing as they'd drunk their cocktails at Morrell's. Carla had assumed at least Viv was keeping a low profile after her fall from grace. Six months earlier had come the revelation, discovered by Carla, that when Viv was a younger officer, she'd been involved in a car accident where Max Hazen's wife had died. Viv had been over the legal limit for alcohol and an older colleague had sworn that it was him who'd been driving, setting off a catastrophic chain of events that had led to the death of six women. Viv was currently on suspension which must surely be a blow for the ambitious officer. Maybe now, seven months later, she'd decided to rehabilitate herself and what better public place to do so than Morrell's. She hadn't realised that Albert and Jack were such pals – they'd shown little sign of it when Albert had been working in the department.

Carla shook the thoughts away as she entered the college and pushed open the panelled door that led into the meeting room. It was a beautiful space, the artichoke-green walls adorned with paintings of previous heads of departments and the herringbone parquet flooring buffed to a golden brown. Carla saw with a jolt that Jack was already there, sitting under Albert's portrait while flicking through his phone. He was wearing his customary black clothes, his only concession to the heat a short-sleeved polo shirt.

'Morning,' Carla said to him, taking a chair opposite. 'Did you enjoy Morrell's?'

Jack started. 'Were you there? I didn't see you.'

Carla wasn't going to admit that she'd persuaded Erin to slink out of the side entrance when they'd finished their drinks, dreading a social encounter with her former boss and the woman whose downfall she'd had a hand in orchestrating. And that was before the thorny issue of her place within Jack and Anna's on–off relationship.

'I was just catching up with Erin.'

Carla was saved from further explanations by the arrival of Professor Sabine Bauer. Albert's temporary replacement was a well-regarded academic in her fifties who had a collegiate approach to decision making, a contrast from Albert's previous dictatorial style. The room fell silent as she took the seat at the head of the table and pulled a sheaf of papers out of her bag. Next to Carla, a woman with sandy hair that was on its way to becoming white folded her arms and let out a long sigh. Doctor Jeanette Lavigne had been at Jericho for twenty years and was part of the furniture. She'd made little impression on Carla the previous term, but poor Jeanette had been at her wits' end the last month or so after a series of incidents on a dig. In fact, it was the first item on the agenda and, once everyone was settled, Jeanette took a deep breath.

'The site's been tampered with again. When Ashley and I returned after the weekend break it was clear that someone had tried to extend the trench near the north wall of the house. A right mess of it they made, too. Amateurs.'

Carla could understand her colleague's outrage. Archaeological digs were controlled spaces with a strong emphasis on order and process. For the finds to have any decipherable meaning clear records needed to be kept. That someone was coming onto the dig at night, or when it was closed for the weekend, was bad enough, but worse, they were undertaking their own excavations, spoiling well-ordered trenches and jeopardising the integrity of the whole site. The persistence of the individual was worrying. Scavengers usually descended when there was news of a discovery on site, sometimes treasure, occasionally bones for the more macabre collector. Nothing, however, had been identified yet, leading to confusion as to what the intruder was looking for.

'Are we any nearer,' asked Carla, 'in identifying who might be responsible? It strikes me that trying to secure the site is proving impossible, so the only way to stop the intruder is to discover their identity.'

Jeanette gave a snort. 'The police couldn't give a damn. I've been dealing with Charlie Baros and he's made it perfectly clear it's nothing to do with him. You know, he had the gall to suggest it was one of our archaeology students who was doing a bit of moonlighting to up their grades. I told him that a student straight out of junior high would have a better idea how to dig a trench than whoever has been messing around. This is the work of someone who has no idea what they're doing.'

Carla wasn't so sure about that. The site being excavated was at the Wilmington farmstead, a one hundred and fifty-acre farm that had fallen into disuse. On the farm, a traditional New England structure had once been thought to be a barn for cattle, but an enterprising doctoral student, Ashley Jones, had studied old maps of the area and discovered it had been a trading place for early settlers around 1710, and she and Jeanette were leading the dig. The Wilmington family had already owned the land and had built a structure to allow other settler families to barter their animals, craft ware and anything else with a monetary value. It could prove rich pickings for a dig – wherever there was trade, there was the potential for the discovery of money, metal objects and organic evidence in the soil. It was early days, however, and the trenches at this stage were largely exploratory.

Sabine sighed and ran her hands through her hair. 'As I've mentioned before, departmental budgets preclude the purchase of CCTV or hiring any security personnel to guard the site when we're not there. I'm sure we all have our own stories of metal detectorists trying to race us for pickings. Are we sure that isn't what's going on here?'

'I don't think so,' said Jack. 'Nighthawkers are like crows looking for worms on newly tilled soil. They want access to substrates so they can find buried artefacts before us and remove them without the care we show. What's happening here is trench digging which is far more unusual. It's hard work, for a start, without recourse to the machinery we use. The neighbour who lives in the hill above the Wilmington farm is adamant that there has been no mechanical noise.'

'Then, if not detectorists, who?' said Jeannette.

'We don't know,' said Sabine. Her frustration was palpable and Carla could see she was keen to move on to other matters. 'Does anyone have any other suggestions on how we might tackle the issue?'

'Mount a watch,' said Simon Drake, a military historian Carla had spoken to only once. He kept himself to himself and had been a friend of Max Hazen. Carla was treating him with caution but the resolute way in which he put forward his proposal made her smile.

'I'm up for it,' she said. 'We could catch them red-handed.'

'Me too,' Jeanette leant forward in excitement. 'We'd need to be in pairs in case there's more than one to contend with. Detectorists usually like a pal.'

Sabine looked pained, the meeting clearly not going as she'd planned. 'What do others think? I don't want anyone putting themselves in danger. We don't really know what we're dealing with at the moment.'

'I'm in,' said Jack. Others around the table nodded their heads.

Sabine sighted. 'OK, I'll get a rota sent round this afternoon. Check your emails. You go in pairs and we do it for two weekends starting this Friday evening. If nothing happens, we reassess. And remember, I want 911 on speed dial. No heroics. We're not confronting someone ourselves and, if we scare them off, that might be sufficient to stop this site tampering.'

Carla thought this unlikely as the culprit must be aware that their presence left evidence of their work. What the watchers needed to do was identify who was responsible even if they fell short of actually catching them. This meant strong torches and a night vision camera. It was time to raid the supply room in the environmental sciences department and put a stop to it.

—

Carla, who had a heavy teaching day on Friday, signed up for the Saturday night watch. She was the first name on the list and it wasn't until the Google Docs spreadsheet had been filled in with volunteers that she realised she'd be sharing her shift with Jack Caron. She was furious at his decision to put his name next to hers. Their near-romance before Christmas might be well in the past but there would be an intimacy in keeping watch through the night in the open air. She printed off the rota and stalked down the corridor, opening the door to Jack's room without knocking. Two startled faces turned towards her and Carla could see she'd interrupted an argument. Jack was sitting back in his chair as a man leant over his desk, his manner threatening.

'Sorry... I didn't realise you had someone—'

'I'm just going.'

Jack threw the dregs of his hot drink into a nearby plant pot. 'Look, Rafe. Let me call you later about this.'

From the lanyard around Rafe's neck, it was clear he was a member of the college teaching staff but Carla was to get no introduction. He brushed past her without giving her a second glance. She was partly relieved. It had been a long teaching day and she was aware her hair stuck up in spikes at the crown of her head. Nevertheless, his casual dismissal of her rankled.

'Charming man,' she said to Jack, shutting the door behind her. 'Who is he?'

'His name is Rafe Westphal, one of our eminent law tutors.'

'Is he always that rude?' asked Carla, taking the seat opposite Jack.

'Well, you did barge in on us. Ever hear of knocking?'

'I wasn't thinking, to be honest.' Carla lay down the printed rota in front of Jack. 'So, what's the idea? I put my name down for Saturday evening and you take the second slot?'

Jack shrugged, not looking her in the eye. 'I actually don't think a stake-out is a brilliant idea now I've had time to think it. We've all been watching too many of these cop shows. If it is a pair of metal detectorists, I've heard they can be vicious and I think we should either have more than two of us watching or make sure the genders are mixed up.'

'Right. But next Saturday is waiting to be allocated. Why not choose that one?'

'Because,' said Jack, 'I think whoever is responsible is going to show up this weekend. Next Saturday will be too late and I want to be around to see who is messing with the site.'

No mention of wanting to spend time with her. Carla wasn't sure whether to be relieved or disappointed.

'Fine. Well let's hope our intruder appears tonight so it'll save us a cold watch in the open air.'

'Sure.' He was dismissing her, his mind clearly on something else. The room buzzed with the crackle of tension and Carla wondered again what the two men had been arguing about.

Chapter 6

Saturday morning was a glorious spring day but Carla was full of pent-up tension for the night ahead. She messaged Erin about brunch but her friend had been called in to oversee the autopsy of victims of a road traffic accident during the night. Instead, Carla paid a visit to her old landlady Patricia; as she stepped over the threshold, she was assailed by the familiar aroma of cookie dough and cinnamon. So much had happened to Carla while she'd stayed under the roof of that solid townhouse, and although she much preferred having her own space, she missed the chats with Patricia. The day was warm enough for them to sit under the canopy of an ancient sunlounger, its rusty frame groaning as Carla sank into its depths. Patricia switched on an equally ancient gas heater and this combined with the sun's rays made Carla feel sleepy as she sipped Patricia's iced tea and listened to Jericho gossip. It was Patricia who had first alerted Carla to the underbelly of the college town and she wanted to ask her if she thought that dark side was still there, but she found it difficult to broach the subject. Carla shut her eyes, at risk of falling asleep completely when she realised with a jolt that Patricia was talking about Lucie Tandy.

'What did you have to say about Lucie?' Carla struggled upright, pushing her hair out of her eyes. 'Have you seen the posters?'

Patricia, who had been sewing a little patchwork blanket for her new grandson, paused, needle suspended in the air. 'Of course I've seen them. They're all over Jericho, as much good as that'll do. There's been no hide nor hair of that girl since she disappeared which means she's left town.'

'Is that what everyone's saying after everything that happened with Max Hazen? That she's long gone?' Carla thought of the woman she'd met by the tree who'd said the same thing. 'It's not so long ago that we had a serial killer in our midst.'

'But she told her friend she needed to take time out. It's all about self-choice these days, isn't it?'

'I suppose.' Carla suddenly wondered if anyone had checked to see if Lucie had used her bank cards or mobile phone. Surely Baros, disinterested but not incompetent, would have run those most basic of checks. 'You've not heard anything about where she might be?'

Patricia peered into the seam she was sewing. 'No one has anything useful to add to the conversation but the thinking is that she's bailed out of Jericho.'

'Hmm.' Another vote for Lucie having voluntarily disappeared, and Patricia was no fool. 'I saw posters tacked to trees the other day. Do you know who put them there?'

'There's a brother in town who's trying to keep interest alive. She was originally from the Seattle area and her parents are quite elderly I believe. The brother, Dominic, has taken leave from his job running a health food store. He's sufficiently worried about her to have shut the shop for a month while he does some digging around.'

'You know a lot about it all. Your quilting group?' Carla knew that Patricia's various crafting circles were a hotbed of gossip. Patricia picked up on Carla's tone and gave her a wink. 'Church,' she said. 'Dominic came to the meeting on Sunday and spoke about Lucie.'

Carla had soon realised that religion in Jericho had an important place in the town's social activities. Carla had told Patricia upfront that she had no intention of going to church and there had been little discussion about anything to do with religion since.

'I guess it's all about getting the message out, isn't it?'

Patricia frowned. 'You know, I'd like to do something for that young man. He's staying at the Ranch Hotel up by Suncook but I know it's expensive there. Do you think I should offer him the room you stayed in?'

'I guess so,' said Carla. 'Do you know anything about him?'

'The pastor says he could call the church in Seattle for a reference but he does seem like a nice young man.'

'So did Ted Bundy,' said Carla grimly.

'Carla!' Patricia put down her quilt and stared across at her. 'What's the matter?'

'Oh, I don't know.'

'Yes you do. Tell me.'

Carla grimaced. 'There's a couple of weird things going on at the moment and that comment you made about the dark side of Jericho my first night in town has stuck with me.'

'Maybe I'd just picked up on the deaths of those poor women and that Max Hazen was still loose amongst us.'

Carla kept her eyes on Patricia, her head bent over her sewing. 'So has your opinion of Jericho changed?'

Her silence spoke volumes. Carla looked around the garden with its staked sweetpeas not yet flowering and the large hydrangeas blowing their blue blooms gently in the breeze. The darkness certainly wasn't here, so where?

'Has anything happened?' asked Patricia, finally looking up.

'Erin asked me to look at the baby found in Shining Cliff Wood. She wanted my professional opinion on something and I think it's got to me a little.'

'Oh my word, the poor mite. It was a girl, wasn't it?'

'It was.' Carla was desperate to tell Patricia about the swan's wing but Erin hadn't given her permission to do so. She cast around for a way to explain to Patricia the disparity between how the baby had been discovered compared to the care taken to swaddle the child.

'I'm trying to put all my professional knowledge into helping out, but I feel a bit at sea. The baby was found against a dumpster which for me is suggesting lack of care, fear, an unwanted pregnancy. But the baby was wrapped in something organic – I really can't say what it was, Patricia – and that's bringing to mind something completely different. An act of reverence or love, maybe.'

'Reverence?' Patricia frowned. 'So something more than a blanket.'

'Yes.'

Patricia leant forward to refill their glasses. 'Childbirth is a difficult process that brings forth a complex set of emotions. You can be both frightened of something and find the act almost spiritual.'

'Is that how you found it with your children?'

'Not really.' Patricia smiled. 'I just remember being tired all the time, which reminds me that you've spent the whole morning yawning.'

'Oh, God, I'm sorry. I've not been sleeping well and I've a long night ahead of me.'

She told Patricia about the plans for a stake-out at the Wilmington farm.

'I know the Wilmington place and I remember Mary Wilmington from when I was a child. She was the last of the family to live full-time at the house and died some years back. It's been sitting empty for years, although the family used to come back and camp each summer, decades ago now.'

'I'm looking forward to seeing the site from a professional point of view. Long before Jericho was known for its college, it's thought a barn on the property was a well-known trading post.'

'The Wilmingtons were always respectable folk, but the land got too much for them to manage. Maybe the place will have a new life as a tourist attraction, but I'm not sure I like the idea of you acting as a security guard. Things might turn nasty, especially if it's treasure hunters involved. Are you sure you'll be safe?'

'Jack Caron will keep me company.'

Patricia pursed her lips. 'I believe that young man is back with his wife.'

'Patr— how do you know these things? Don't tell me – church. He's a colleague, and it's better it's not just me and another woman, isn't it? There's mobile reception out there – at least that's what I assume – and if there's trouble, we'll call the police. What's more likely to happen is that we spend an evening in the cold.'

Patricia looked into the distance. 'I always wondered why the Wilmingtons stopped coming for their summer camps. It really would be good to have that place buzzing again.'

Chapter 7

It was a night made for romance which was a bloody shame as Carla was standing as far away from Jack as she could manage. The air hung heavy with fragrance – earthy compost from where the digger had pulled away the subsoil to make a new trench, combined with the fragrance of flowers from nearby clumps of rhododendrons. Native to New England, the bushes had also been planted around homesteads for their perfume and vibrant flowers. However, these bushes were positioned relatively far from the farmhouse and Ashley Jones, the doctoral student, had spotted the shrubs now taken over by woodland and suggested they might have been planted next to the original trading barn. The map where she'd spotted the presence of the edifice was more artistic than accurate.

Jack had briefly kissed her the French way when they'd met on the roadside, one chaste peck on each cheek and a third for luck. As his face met hers, Carla was sure she'd smelt brandy on his breath or some other dark liquor. Maybe, then, his insouciance about their task for the night was only skin deep – she couldn't imagine brandy being a regular drink on a pleasant spring afternoon so he had clearly felt the need to fortify himself.

They stood with their eyes fixed on the trench that had been disturbed the previous week. Someone poking around possibly, but to Carla's eyes, the sabotage looked too deliberate – as if the culprit didn't care that they were leaving traces indicating that the site had been disturbed. It suggested whatever they were looking for was more important than any attempts to conceal their presence. An email that afternoon had confirmed that the department was making efforts to contact the family member who had given permission for the site dig. It was now thought that as late as the 1970s, members of the Wilmington family had used the place as a summer camp, pitching their tents and using the nearby stream for their washing needs. It had been what Carla called wild camping but she had already learnt that what she considered wild in Britain was not the same in this vast landscape. The farm's nearest neighbour, a brick house on the hill occupied by an elderly woman known as Gracie, remembered with fondness the group descending on the site each summer as she watched Mary Wilmington's children and grandchildren grow up.

'Think this is a wasted trip?' asked Jack, crouching on the ground as he tried to make himself comfortable. The light was fading fast and the encroaching darkness cast shadows across the landscape. They'd left their cars on a track leading away from the site, tucked into the trees. It had been a half mile walk to the Wilmington farmstead and Carla had welcomed the exercise to clear her head. She'd noted that it was possible to get much closer to the site in an ordinary vehicle, right up to the chained gate leading to the field where the dig was taking place. With any luck, even if they didn't catch the culprit, they'd get a licence plate for authorities to trace.

'I don't think the plan to keep a watch is wasted, I'm just not convinced we'll get lucky tonight. I'm pretty sure we'll eventually spot the perpetrator but I'm just wondering how many broken nights' sleep it will take.

The odd thing is that whoever it is appears to be coming at night. The site is isolated enough that you could come out on a weekend during daylight and I don't think anyone would notice you poking around the work.'

'Never underestimate the power of a nosy neighbour. Gracie, the neighbour at the top farm, was outside all day, unseen by any intruders, and she assured us she saw nothing untoward on the site.'

Carla sat on the remains of an old millstone, its surface smoothed away by years of work. 'When I was a student, we were excavating a field in Suffolk when we discovered a hoard of coins at four o'clock on a Friday before a bank holiday weekend. Before we knew it, the treasure hunters were out on the brow of the hill watching us. We worked through the night to get everything out of the ground using torches, car headlights, even the light from our phones. Anything so we didn't leave the site for the scavengers over the weekend.'

'They're a nifty lot, the detectorists, but I've got Baros on speed dial. If it all kicks off then he says he can get down here in thirty-five minutes.'

Carla rolled her eyes. Detective Baros had proved a royal pain in the arse the previous term, although he had eventually admitted that Carla's assessment that there was a serial killer in their midst had been correct. If he was working tonight and had been forewarned that was some comfort, but God knows what he thought of their private enterprise.

Jack didn't appear to share her animosity towards the belligerent detective. 'You know, if something's gonna happen it'll be sooner rather than later. This place is pretty isolated with the exception of Gracie's place and, according to her, she turns in at ten p.m. every evening.

She says, though, that she got up to go to the bathroom one night and saw a light about midnight.'

It was a good time to visit the site. It suggested the intruder liked the cover of darkness and once that was in place, there would be no reason to delay. Furthermore, a car on the road would attract less attention at midnight than in the early hours. The problem was if they were a no-show tonight, she and Jack would still be obliged to wait until dawn as Sabine would never forgive them if the person turned up after they'd left. That was the agreement. A watch dusk until dawn, and that was what she and Jack had signed up to.

The night cooled and Carla pulled up the hood over her old dig jacket, still comfortable after all these years and a kind of therapy blanket. It soothed her to know that Dan, her dead husband, had known her wearing it, a tangible link to a past life that now seemed decades away. Carla was trying to estimate how many digs the coat had seen when she felt Jack stiffen next to her.

'What is it?' she whispered.

He moved towards her, his mouth next to her ear. 'There's a flashlight over in the distance. Just one but it's coming this way. No more talking.'

'What time is it?'

'Coming up to twelve thirty. About on time. When they start digging, I go first, all right?'

'Shouldn't we call Baros now if it's going to take him over half an hour to get here?' That had been the agreement and Carla wasn't going to be part of any heroics on Jack's part.

'Call him because of a flashlight?'

'What other reason might someone come down here?'

'Maybe one of the students has decided to take matters into their own hands,' hissed Jack. 'Ashley must be feeling kinda territorial towards her dig. Jeanette must have told her about us all mounting a watch. I don't want to call the cops on one of our students.'

Carla wasn't convinced given Ashley, aware of the watch, could come and go as she pleased since she was in charge of the site. There was no reason whatsoever for her to come down at night and put herself in the position of suspect. 'Look, why don't you give Baros the choice whether to come or not. If it's a quiet night, he might want the opportunity to come down here. If he's busy he can ignore you.'

'Right. I'll text him. After that, the phone goes away until we've caught whoever it is.'

Shielding the phone with his jacket to hide the glare of the screen, Jack typed in a message. A reply came immediately. 'He's on his way,' said Jack. 'Let's hope it's not Gracie bringing us a milk and cookies.'

'It's not. I saw the lights go off on her property at ten prompt.'

Carla could feel her heart thumping in her chest as the light in the distance got closer. Sometimes, they lost sight of the beam which was more terrifying for her as she wanted to know where the incomer was at all times. Once, she wondered if they had an accomplice, perhaps approaching the site from a different direction, but around her was only blackness and silence. All of a sudden, the beam was upon them, its yellow light focused not on them but on the dig.

Carla listened as they heard the unmistakeable sound of metal on earth. The intruder to their site was digging by hand, a back breaking task but they couldn't afford the sound made by anything mechanical. In the darkness, Carla tried to estimate where on site they were. She reckoned they weren't near any existing trench but towards the north-east of the enclosure. Had they given up on plundering the work of the day team? If so, it would be slow going. What a digger could unearth in minutes might take hours with just a spade.

Carla felt Jack turn his head towards her, probably going through the same thought processes. He lay a hand on her arm, telling her to wait. It was a sensible decision; while trespassing on a site was... well, trespass... a prosecution case would be greatly improved if they were found in possession of something that could be realistically termed an artefact. Then they could add theft into the mix which would hopefully go some way to appeasing Jeanette's outrage at the tampering of the site.

They continued to listen in silence and Carla began to identify a pattern of sorts. The digger went through a period of intense activity and then stopped for a moment to catch their breath. They'd then continue and – she could swear this – would move on and start afresh. They weren't concentrating on a single spot but were looking for something specific.

After half an hour or so, they heard the spade holder sit down and the unmistakeable sound of a bottle being unscrewed. A quick nip of something like Jack had imbibed? It was possible. Whatever, the action revived the digger and they started once more.

Carla moved in as close to Jack as she could. 'They're looking for something. There's intent in the digging, not just randomly skimming the surface to see what's been unearthed.'

'Agreed,' murmured Jack. 'The fact they're coming back suggests it's not easy to find. Shall we go get them?'

'Shouldn't we wait for Baros? He'll be here any moment.'

'Shhh.' They were aware that the digging had stopped. A break in the pattern as they'd only been going for a minute or so from the previous break. They heard a rustle, the sound of a sack or other material being moved.

'Go,' said Jack and was off, taking Carla by surprise who shot after him, trying to keep up with her colleague. She heard a scream – not Jack – but shortly followed by a stream of invective in French.

'The bastard.'

'Are you OK?' Carla switched on her torch, spotting Jack on his knees.

'He hit me with that bloody spade but only clipped my arm. Don't go after him.'

A couple of flashlight beams hurried towards them from the top of the hill and for a heart stopping moment, Carla thought the digger had reinforcements until she heard Baros's unmistakeable drawl. 'Looks like I'm too late. Which way have they gone?'

'Towards the stream,' said Jack.

'We're after him.'

Carla saw that Baros was accompanied by Amy Perez, his more amenable partner, and together they set off after Jack's assailant. Carla rushed up to her colleague and saw him nursing the top of his arm. 'You OK?'

'Yes, thank God. He was aiming for my head.'

'He?'

'Definitely a he and fast, I'll give him that. Baros and Perez don't stand a chance.'

'I'm not so sure about that. They're professionals as opposed to us rank amateurs. At least he'll know we're onto him. We might not have caught him but at least he'll think twice about returning.'

'What made him stop though?' asked Jack, climbing to his feet with Carla's assistance. 'He definitely paused his digging to look at and possibly retrieve something. Maybe he's had to leave behind whatever he found.'

They shone their torches on the ground, Carla's blood boiling at the series of rough holes the intruder had dug.

'It's a bloody mess,' Jack said. 'There's no pattern here at all.'

'Even if it's random, it still tells us something. He thinks this might be a significant area and is doing some exploratory digging. Can we work out where he began this evening?'

'I'm not sure. When I launched at him, I'd say he was a little nearer to our stake-out spot than when he first started.'

Carla crouched down and shone her torch nearest to the spots where she and Jack had been hiding. All she could see were mounds of earth piled next to roughly dug holes. Then, her beam caught the shine of something that wasn't soil. She moved in closer.

'Jack,' she said. 'Take a look at this.'

They moved in closer and stared at the object in her beam.

'Christ,' said Jack. 'What the actual fuck.'

Chapter 8

Erin arrived on the site at five a.m. Her assistant Scott had messaged her an hour earlier as the on-call pathologist. She'd been half inclined to let him go ahead and check out the situation first, standard practice in cases she wasn't sure whether they were a priority or not. However, when she realised Carla was at the scene, she decided to head down there herself, a little intrigued as to how her former mentee had got herself involved in a scrape in the middle of the night. The night air was cool as she drove to the site with her window down, enjoying the silence punctuated only by an owl hooting in the distance.

Carla, to Erin's surprise, was standing next to Jack Caron. Scott had told her it was an archaeological site, although Erin would probably have guessed it from the three long trenches, one at the far site near the remains of a stone building, another near the centre of the semicircular space and a final one towards the gatepost. A group, however, was congregated towards a patch of land near a small area of woodland. Erin headed towards them and the figures parted at her arrival, Carla and Jack pushing themselves forward, clearly wanting to be a part of the discussion. She noticed detectives Baros and Perez standing to one side, unusually passive while a tall blonde woman talked to them with an urgent expression on her face.

Erin leant over the earth as she felt Carla and Jack crouch down beside her. 'Three distal phalanges,' she murmured. 'Probably the middle three fingers of the hand.'

'That's our conclusion too,' said Jack. 'We haven't touched the remains but we're both of the opinion that the fingertips—'

'Are attached to more bones.' Carla finished the sentence for him.

Erin nodded. That the three fingers were still together was unusual as the body's extremities were usually the first to be scavenged by animals. The fact that this hadn't happened suggested a decently deep burial. She stood, looking around.

'What is this place?'

Carla stood and gestured at the dig. 'We think it's an early settler homestead where the original barn was an important trading post with a newer property built along the stream. The family sold most of the land to Mrs Gracie Oldcastle who lives in the farm above. However, they held onto the old farmhouse and surrounding field probably for sentimental reasons. We got permission to dig from a resident by the name of Step Wilmington who said it was owned by all the family. He signed a disclaimer and off we went.'

It didn't, thought Erin, explain what they were all doing here in the middle of the night though – she supposed that would come later.

'You don't think,' she said slowly, 'that the family kept hold of this field because it was used as a burial plot. It's not that unusual to inter your loved ones close to the home in rural settlements.'

'It's possible,' said Carla. 'But I don't think this is a typical inhumation. For a start, it's too close to the surface. The body's deep enough to deter predators although if the soil was loose when it was first dug, a coyote or other scavenger would have made quick work of the scavenging. However, burials – including here in New England – are usually placed at four to six feet. This is way too shallow.'

Jack nodded. 'Once excavation gets underway, we can look for evidence of any burial material or shroud or perhaps wood that might give us a clue of a rotted coffin.'

'If it's an early settler,' said Erin, 'they might have been buried in a shroud that's rotted into the earth.'

'Possibly.' Carla looked unconvinced. 'We're not going to know until we start digging to uncover the remains of the rest of the skeleton.'

'Well you have my permission for that.' Erin looked over towards Detective Baros who had been waiting for his cue. 'I'm not going to be able to find out the cause of death or date the bones until we see the whole skeleton. You need to start excavating it as soon as possible as I'm worried about the exposure to the elements.'

'You don't think it's just some old settler burial?' Baros looked hopeful as it would make his paperwork a damn sight easier.

'Can't tell,' she told him crisply. Saw three uniformed officers standing behind him with a variety of tools designed to break and loosen the earth. 'You've got both the brawn and experts already on site. I suggest everyone gets digging.'

–

Gracie, an early riser, had seen the people congregating in the field and brought a trayful of coffee to hand around.

As Jack conferred with the blonde woman, now identified to Erin as Sabine Bauer, the head of department, Carla brought her up to speed on the night watch where they'd hoped to catch the intruder red-handed.

'Shit.' Erin drained her coffee and set the mug on the grass. 'That puts paid to the theory of the settler burial.'

'I guess so, although we can't rule it out completely. I mean, admittedly nighthawkers and others who disturb archaeological sites are usually after treasure – metalwork, jewellery and so on – but there are some of the morbid variety who'd be interested in old bones.'

'But how'd they know there was a body buried there?'

Carla shrugged. 'I don't know. Maybe they were looking for something else and found the bones. There was a pause as if the digger was contemplating what they'd discovered. What I'm saying is we can't rule anything out yet.'

Erin looked around. At least the weather was holding out as excavating in the rain would be a nightmare even inside a tent. Mud had a habit of contaminating everything. Extracting the bones would be a laborious process and she didn't have time to monitor each step. She'd rely on the police photographer to record each stage of the excavation so she could take a good look at them back in the facility. In the meantime, she had plenty of more recent dead to keep her occupied until this poor soul rose from the earth.

'So you were keeping watch with Jack Caron, huh?'

She saw Carla redden. 'I put my name on the list first,' she said with gritted teeth, 'and he added his name next to mine.'

'Did you ask him why he did that?' asked Erin. 'He and Anna looked pretty cosy when we saw them at Morrell's the other night.'

Carla shook her head and stood up, brushing herself down. 'I'd like to be involved with the extraction of the remains. Can we catch up later? By the way, I've sent you more info on the Vedbaek burial. I logged into some online journals last night and found some specifics about the location of the grave. Give them a read when you get a chance.'

'Christ knows when that will be.'

—

Back at the facility, Erin began the autopsies scheduled for the day. She split her time between pathology work at the centre and teaching work at Jericho College. However, it was coming up to the exam period and her teaching had tailed off giving her more time to spend with the town's dead. The first autopsy was of a young child who'd died after being left unsupervised in the bath while his mother answered a call. She claimed he was out of her sight for only two minutes and Erin could well believe it. Drowning took as little as twenty seconds to kill and despite best efforts of paramedics, the child had died.

As she began her autopsy, Erin briefly thought of Fionnuala, whose unclaimed body was now resting in the storage facility. Little progress had been made in identifying the mother, even once a rudimentary DNA profile had been obtained. Not much use, of course, without anyone to match it to unless either parent had a criminal profile. The issue was that they were unable to feed the information into any of the popular family history sites.

They guarded their data and although GEDmatch had been used to catch the Golden State Killer, it had principally been down to the hard work of forensic genetic genealogists. Erin thought the chances of getting anyone interested in Fionnuala's case was non-existent.

After the autopsy, Erin took a shower and read her emails as she towel-dried her hair. Carla's message on the Vedbaek burial contained three attachments, each with different focus on the bodies in Grave 8. Carla had chosen well, Erin enjoying the precise prose of the academic writers rather than the lurid speculation of the Reddit article she'd first come across. The problem, it appeared, was that there were so few Mesolithic burials it was hard to draw any definite conclusions about the presence of the swan's wing. Did the answer lie in the archaeology department? Erin wasn't sure but she'd give anything to discover the whereabouts of the child's mother at this moment.

Chapter 9

Carla and Jack watched in silence as the team began the careful uncovering of the bones unearthed in the night. Although Erin had asserted their right to be there, the forensic lead, a woman named Kathy with iron grey hair clipped close to her head, supervised the excavation. As an archaeologist, Carla was appalled at the lack of awareness of stratigraphy – how layers in the ground related to each other – but she felt she had little authority at this scene. They watched as fingers became a hand, a wrist and then an arm. Carla felt Jack stiffen as they regarded the bones and saw the placement of the arm.

'The palm would have been facing the earth,' murmured Jack, moving forward a little. 'It's a prone burial.'

Kathy glanced across at them but said nothing. The position of the body would be a small part of the wider crime scene picture, but for archaeologists, the discovery of skeletons lying face forward came with a raft of connotations. For most of history, bodies that had been buried in the ground had been done so on their backs. These supine inhumations suggested reverence and ritual. That wasn't to say it was missing with prone burials but the face down placing of a body in a grave was not traditionally associated with New England burial practices. A body lying on its front was not a good sign.

'Can you even guess how long these bones have been in the ground?' Kathy shouted over to them. 'It's not a recent burial, I don't think.'

Jack answered before Carla had a chance to speak. 'The most accurate tests will be with radiocarbon dating but if the bones are very old, there are other histological tests that a specialist lab could carry out.'

Carla personally thought it wouldn't come to that. The skeleton was intact and someone had knowledge of its existence which suggested to her that the deceased was less than fifty years old and probably a damn sight more recent than that. Carla remembered Patricia's comment about the Wilmington summer camps and wondered if this body could be dated back to those days. If so, this old New England family was going to get a horrible shock in the coming days.

The morning became warmer and the diggers pushed on, carefully revealing the skull, ribs and pelvis. Carla and Jack moved closer, their tacit agreement to let the team get on with the work, and began to speculate on the sex of the skeleton.

'Female,' murmured Jack into her ear.

'Maybe,' said Carla. The wider subpubic triangle suggested the body was that of a woman but there was a range of variables and only after a close examination of the complete skeleton could a more probable, but not definitive, conclusion be drawn.

When the body was completely uncovered, Kathy motioned them forward. From the rear, Carla could see the pelvis was wide and shallow and the skull, its face turned towards Carla as if in a greeting, had small brow ridges and smooth contours.

'I'm thinking female,' said Kathy. 'Any idea of age?'

Carla's eyes swept over the bones. 'Can I get in closer?'

'Of course.'

Kathy's relaxed demeanour suggested they weren't treating it as a crime scene which might be a mistake. Carla looked across to Baros who was standing watching with an unusual intensity. Perez standing close to him, her gaze also focused on the body. Carla frowned, trying to decipher the tension between them, as she knelt down to handle the left femur.

'There's no immediate sign of osteoarthritis so possibly twenty to forty-five but that's just a guess. I might narrow the age range on closer inspection but not by much. Erin will need to examine everything in the post-mortem – the teeth are intact which is a good thing as isotope testing will help.'

Baros came forward, his eyes never leaving the bones. 'Any obvious cause of death?'

Carla moved closer to the skull, desperate to lift it out of the ground, but the removal would need to be in a methodical manner. The cranium was smooth and although the jawbone had detached itself from the skull there was also no sign of damage. Carla's eyes swept down the rest of the bones. The ribs had collapsed onto each other. It was a common preconception that skeletons hung together like those in cartoons but in the absence of sinews and ligaments there was nothing to keep bones together.

'It's impossible for me to tell. I can't see any immediate damage – there's nothing obvious – but even a blade mark on a rib might give clues to how the person died. It's a job to be done in a lab.'

Baros grunted. 'Female below the age of forty. Any idea of how long those bones have been in the ground?'

He was almost pleading with her. Carla stood and looked at Perez for help but she averted her eyes.

'I don't think we're talking about hundreds of years. I've only had a brief glance but I can see evidence of modern dental work.' Carla saw that she'd failed to reassure him.

'So what do we do with the rest of the ground?' asked Kathy. 'This is your site. Reckon there's more to unearth? We can keep digging.'

Carla thought of Ashley, the doctoral student whose thesis was bound up in this site. 'Perhaps we can find a way that we take the lead on further excavations and we call you in if any further bodies are discovered.'

Kathy glanced at Baros who shrugged. 'Sure.'

As the bones were carefully removed from the ground, Jack left saying he had to catch up with some sleep as he had a dinner engagement. All right for some, thought Carla sourly. She was still perplexed by the presence of Baros and Perez who were lingering at the site.

'Quiet day?' asked Carla.

Perez shrugged. 'Been a quiet one since all those bodies you found last year. Bit more like the old days when I was first starting out.'

'Don't tell me you miss all those killings,' Carla said.

'Nope,' said Baros, 'but I want to be around for this one. Sure you can't help with the description of the man you saw?'

Carla shrugged. '"Saw" is a little ambitious. A flashlight and the sounds of someone digging. It's not going to help you find the suspect.'

Baros made a face. 'What about the bones, then. Want to share with us what you think?'

Carla felt like dropping to the floor with exhaustion. She might not have a dinner engagement that evening but losing a night's sleep would likely put her off-kilter for the rest of the week. Thank goodness the students were about to start exams so that her teaching duties were lighter.

'Shall we grab a seat somewhere?' Carla looked around and saw through the fields a clump of rough-hewn wood, perhaps a makeshift camp from back when the space was used for summer holidays. They sat in a triangle, Baros chewing some gum while Perez got out her notebook. Carla hoped that they weren't going to press her any more in relation to the dating of the bones. Science was going to help them more than a tired archaeologist and Baros, never the most intuitive of cops, nevertheless seemed to sense this and began gently.

'Let's start with the Wilmingtons who own this site. I hear you were given permission to excavate that site by Step Wilmington but I believe he's not the only owner.'

'You need to talk to my boss Sabine to get the exact details. I've followed this site from its inception as a dig, but it's mainly been through discussions at team meetings.'

'Well, I've already called the Prof. who's filled us in as much as she could. She's out of town, otherwise she'd have come down this afternoon. No one can find any papers in relation to land ownership – it seems the initial grad student was poking around on what she thought was abandoned land. Then, when the dig was planned, your department tried to find the landowner and it appeared the place was known as "Wilmington land" and that was as far as they could get. Step Wilmington, reasonably well known in Jericho as he runs the local body shop, gave permission on behalf of a family spread around the county. He's not very well, I believe, but was happy to act as family liaison.'

'These scenarios aren't that uncommon.' Carla thought of the paperwork behind these permissions – indemnities and disclaimers. Of course, the main preoccupation would have been health and safety considerations plus any potential claim on 'treasure' but there still would have been provision in there for the discovery of human remains.

'You mentioned to your colleague that it was a prone burial.' Perez frowned at her empty coffee mug, clearly looking for a refill. 'Do you think that's more likely to indicate a crime?'

Carla, put on the spot, prevaricated. 'In archaeology terms, not necessarily. Even some of the war dead have been found buried in a prone position. Sometimes the necessity of a quick burial, for example, might make laying a body on the ground important. But it can also represent lack of respect too. It's about context as much as anything.'

Perez stood, shaking her leg. 'What you're basically saying is that until we get the doc's conclusions we're not clear on what we're dealing with.'

They were interrupted by a shout and Carla followed Perez and Baros to the site. One of the police diggers was holding out a muddy lump that folded in the middle. 'Found this as we were removing the body.'

Perez snapped on a pair of gloves and examined the mass. It split in two, opening flat. She wiped her hand across it, smearing away earth. 'I think it's a small wallet.'

Baros, also gloved, took it off her and pulled out a card. It was a square of green, its edges nibbled away by a rodent of some kind. 'I can't read anything. Maybe a library card or something. Hold on there's a word here. I think it says Owl.'

'Owl?' asked Carla. 'It could be the Owl Club, the acting society.' Carla's thoughts turned to Lucie Tandy as Baros impatiently pulled out more cards. There had been no mention of Lucie's involvement in the society.

'I can't read anything else.'

Carla retrieved one of the discarded cards and looked at it more closely. 'This one's embossed. Has anyone a pencil or crayon?'

She found a pencil at the bottom of her rucksack and tore a page from her diary, rubbing her pencil over a long strip of numbers. It would give them something to go on. She remembered her mother's old credit cards where you used to put it into a device that slid the details onto paper. If it was a credit card, there must also surely be a name. She carried on rubbing.

'I'm getting a name. Fre… Frederika Brown,' she said triumphantly. She noticed the detectives had gone quiet. 'What's the matter?'

Chapter 10

Carla had known in her heart of hearts that the bones weren't that of missing Lucie Tandy. While the depth of burial had been too shallow to suggest anything other than a hastily arranged inhumation, even if Lucie had been killed when she went missing in April, decomposition in this loamy soil would not have left nothing but bones. The presence of a wallet seemingly belonging to a Frederika Brown was a far better indicator of the identity of the body, and from their reactions, both Baros and Perez were acting as if they knew who that person was. They just weren't readily giving her this information.

Carla stretched, conscious that her armpits were sweaty and her jeans uncomfortably tight after a day in the open air. She should really be getting back to her house for a clean-up. However, she needed to hear about Frederika Brown and why the detectives were so perturbed about the discovery of her purse.

'So, who is Frederika Brown?'

Baros moved away from her, his eyes on the credit card he was holding. Perez gave Carla a distracted glance.

'A girl from Jericho College, missing at least thirty years. I grew up on the story. "Where is Frederika Brown?" There used to be posters on the highways all over the state. That's all I can tell you right now – look it up.'

Perez wandered after her partner. Carla glanced around the farmstead now part archaeology site, part crime scene. The early settlers didn't have credit cards which meant really her role in this tragedy should be coming to an end. She wasn't sure if she'd be able to bring much more to the investigation now that the remains had been excavated and hoped that not too long in the future, archaeologists would once more be looking for evidence of that centuries-old trading post.

'Hey, Prof!'

Carla turned and realised that one of the police diggers was waving at her. 'Is there something wrong?'

'Come and take a look at this.'

Carla hurried over to the now empty grave, a wide and shallow scar on the landscape. The man, young with thinning blonde hair, was pointing at an object with a trowel. He lightly clinked the tip against it. 'I think it's ceramic. Maybe a pot. Do you think it's archaeological or related to this body?'

How the hell should I know until it's excavated, thought Carla. She took a deep breath.

'Look, let me.' She climbed down into the hole, noting that it would have lain less than fifty centimetres from the body. She began to slowly scrape away the dry, crumbly earth and saw a shape gradually emerge. It was definitely pottery with an embossed design reminding Carla of the Celtic goblets sold in Welsh shops. 'I think it's a vase or some kind of beaker.'

When the earth had been removed as far down as she could manage, she brushed away all the soil remaining.

'Is the photographer still here?' she asked.

'Just left,' someone shouted.

Carla looked at her phone, the battery long dead. 'We need to be careful removing it.' She gently prised the object out of the ground, the artefact heavy in her hand from the earth clinging to it. 'Does anyone have any water?' she shouted. 'There should be some buckets or water bowser here.'

'Over there.'

A man brought a small plastic bucket and Carla gently poured water over the object. It was a squat-looking beaker around four inches in diameter and six high. The pale blue ceramic had a series of score lines around its rim but the pattern was impossible to make out. It wasn't impossible that it had belonged to the Wilmington family and yet surely its placing suggested it belonged in the grave.

'I think this was deliberately put near the bones. It's too close to the site of the skeleton to be random. There's a practice from the early Bronze Age of burying people with their drinking vessels. It wouldn't be relevant to this site but it may be a modern recreation of the rite.

'I'm not sure of the significance of the find. I could ask the grad students, when they're allowed back on site to dig, to put a trench in here to check it's not part of some kind of hoard.'

'Sounds like a plan.' The man held out his hand for the cup and Carla hesitated.

'You will look after it, won't you? I'd like a closer look at it when it's been cleaned. Do you have a phone to take a picture for me?'

'Sure.' He took out his mobile and took a snap from different angles. 'What's your email?' She watched him type it into his phone to be retrieved later. He placed the cup into a clear evidence bag, his face furrowed. The dedicated type, she decided. She'd have loved to know what was carved into the clay but the inscription was too delicate to decipher in the bright sunlight. Carla didn't think she'd be allowed to do her pencil and paper rubbing trick again. She wanted to ask for the cup back to take a closer look but something in the cop's demeanour held her back.

Dragging herself up the hill towards her car, she slung her rucksack onto the passenger seat and set off. As she passed the house at the brow of the hill, she saw Gracie standing in her garden, her eyes on the people clearing away the field. Carla slowed and shouted across.

'Thanks for the coffee. Is everything all right?'

Gracie shook her head and turned without looking at Carla and went back into her house.

—

In her flat, Carla took a shower and changed into a pair of linen shorts and a T-shirt, glad to shake off the earth of the Wilmington place. Feeling restless, she opened up her laptop but there was precious little on the internet about a Frederika Brown except that she had disappeared on 26 September 1999, twenty-five not thirty years ago, as Perez had told her. Yet Perez had given the impression that her disappearance had been state-wide news at the time. Perhaps the lack of information was because her disappearance had taken place in the early days of the internet, but there was a whole generation of online sleuths who loved cold cases. It appeared that the disappearance of Frederika Brown had disappeared from view, failing to catch the interest of armchair detectives.

Shutting her laptop, Carla looked at her watch. Although it was a Sunday, the college library stayed open through the weekends and overnight during the exam period. She packed up a fresh bag, happy to leave cleaning her manky-looking rucksack for another day and resolved to conduct some research into the enigmatic Frederika Brown. She'd be looking for facts about Frederika but also engaging her archaeologist's brain about the position of the body and any clues the grave offered. Remembering the beaker, Carla checked her newly charged phone for the email from the police officer but found nothing. Damn – he'd assured her he'd sent her the image of the drinking vessel. She'd have to put in a request to see the photo through Perez or Baros, the former likely to be more amenable.

A new library had been recently commissioned, its glass and steel frame in contrast to the red brick of the other buildings. As you walked through the sliding doors, a huge wall enumerated all of the patrons who had contributed to the building's construction and the name James Franklin was in a prominent position. Although educated out of town, Franklin came from a long line of Jericho students and was one of the richest men in the state. As Carla had discovered last year, his influence over Jericho was immense. Carla had forgotten about the coolness of the library and she shivered, glad she'd put a light woollen jumper into her bag. She naturally gravitated towards the archaeology section, even if the answers to her questions would not be found there. Leaving her things on her chair, despite a sign asking users not to reserve seats, Carla went over to the reception desk where a man was frowning over a book.

'I'm looking for some local newspapers from the Nineties. I assume they're all on fiche.'

The man lifted his pencil and pointed to a series of small drawers. 'They're all in there. The *Jericho Tribune* from 1964 to present day. You know how to work the machines?'

'I do.' Microfiche was still used extensively in archives despite the heralding of the digital age. Many libraries were too impoverished to upgrade their technology, surely not the case here, but perhaps local newspapers didn't warrant such investment.

Carla found the case easily enough. It had been front page news between late September and early December 1999. Frederika Brown had been a grad student at the department of archaeology who had gone missing after a party in one of the college residences. An evening of drinking and music had quietened to a poker game which she'd declined to join in and had left the party to return to her room across the river. She was never seen again. The first newspaper report was in Carla's opinion what she'd expect from such a mystery in the present day: shock, bewilderment, anxiety. All these emotions were present on the page and there was the worry about a possible sinister presence on campus. Carla sat back in her chair and considered the similar disappearance of Lucie Tandy which had not made it into the papers. In an age of social media, Lucie's casual text that she was taking time out had immediately changed a possible missing persons situation to a voluntary, if unauthorised, absence. It was something to consider – a possible link between the discovery of Frederika's body and Lucie's disappearance.

Carla turned back to the screen. The article in the following week's edition was written in a similar tone but its emotions more muted. *What had happened to Frederika Brown?* The only update the newspaper was able to give its readers was that a sniffer dog had picked up Frederika's scent from the location of the party to the river where she'd have had to cross the nineteenth-century stone bridge. The belief was that if a drunken Frederika had accidentally stumbled into the river, then her body would surface downstream in due course. Carla moved the lever to find the following week's paper and frowned. Just two weeks after her disappearance, Frederika had been bounced off the front page by a road traffic accident involving three senior citizens. Carla found an update on Frederika's disappearance on page four. The river had not given up a body as expected and family was losing hope that the student would ever be located.

Not much of an update, thought Carla. She had to put in a new fiche to look for the following week and, to her amazement, she saw nothing. No mention of the missing girl whatsoever. Her disappearance had faded from Jericho news, hardly awash with any competing sinister cases. Even more perplexing was the reaction of Baros and Perez. They'd stalked off as if they'd discovered the body of the state's most high-profile crime and yet here was proof that Frederika had been almost forgotten a month after her disappearance.

Carla put the film away and looked down at the page of her notebook filled with only half a page of notes on the case and wondered where to go next. An archaeology student turning up dead on a dig was almost gothic in its horror but she doubted any of her colleagues had even been in the department at the time. At the desk, the librarian was now using his pencil to doodle, a series of circles with intersecting lines.

'Why are you drawing those?' she asked him, her sharp tone causing a student to lift his head and glance over at them.

The man looked surprised. 'No reason. They're just doodles.'

'They're daisy wheels.' She looked at him but the name meant nothing she could see.

—

Carla needed to see her former landlady again. Patricia was the fount of all local knowledge but her phone rang out unanswered. She was probably having Sunday lunch with her son and his family and Carla wouldn't disturb that. Hungry and loath to eat yet another solitary meal in her flat, Carla slid into a booth at Morrell's and ordered a hamburger, asking the server not to stack the bun too high. As she sipped her Pepsi, she looked around the room which was doing a pretty decent trade given they had no outside tables. Not everyone, it seemed, was a sun worshipper. Carla had assumed she would be the only solo diner, but another woman was sitting in the third booth away from her. Carla realised with a jolt it was her neighbour.

Their eyes met and the woman smiled and raised a glass. It looked like the woman was drinking cocktails, nothing in that Carla supposed, although it was only midday. To her surprise, the woman moved across her seat and came across to Carla's table and held out her hand.

'I'm Nicole. I often see you in the mornings but we're both in a rush to leave.'

'Do you want to join me?' Carla looked dubiously at the drink in Nicole's hand.

'It's a mocktail. I'm a teetotaller but I like to pretend.'

Nicole took a seat opposite and motioned to the waitress that she'd moved her seat. 'I'm having the burger too. I heard you order one and it's definitely the best choice.'

Nicole might not have been tipsy but she had a garrulous manner that Carla hadn't expected given her polished appearance. Even now, she was wearing an expensive-looking linen dress, belted at the waist, matched with red pumps. Carla yawned which Nicole pounced on.

'I feel the same. Saturdays I'm usually OK – I think I'm running on adrenaline but I'm exhausted on a Sunday. It's the day when the week catches up on you.'

'It's not just that.' Carla found herself talking about her night watch and the discovery of the bones. She hadn't been explicitly told to keep the discovery quiet; most likely it would all soon be in the public domain anyway as police talked and it was also probably all round the archaeology department too. She left out of her account the discovery of the purse and the possible identity of the victim.

Nicole's eyes widened. 'What an adventure. Didn't you feel like Nancy Drew?'

Carla shrugged. 'I'm not sure. It was all over in an instant. Now it's a case of identifying the bones and the circumstances by which they came to be in the ground.'

'Hey, you don't think it's that missing girl do you? You know the one with the posters all over town?'

'Lucie Tandy?' Carla shook her head. 'I don't think so – these bones looked older than that.'

'Not Lucie. Hey, what about that other missing student? God, it was years ago. What the hell was her name?' Carla held her breath as Nicole's brow furrowed. 'I just don't remember. I think it began with "R".'

Carla grimaced. She'd probably been more indiscreet than she intended and there was no way she was going to feed her neighbour Frederika's name. Nicole, however, was reminiscing about the tragedy.

'They think she went into the river which never made sense to me. It's not exactly the Hudson here. Any suicides usually end up a mile or so downriver and they never found this girl. *What* was her name?'

'Maybe she never made it into the river. There must be a range of accuracy for sniffer dogs if they were used. Perhaps they simply lost the trail there.'

'Maybe. From memory she was an archaeology student, but maybe I'm making that up after what you told me this morning. It was the early weeks of term and I definitely remember that. I was sure she was a victim of some horrible sorority prank that went wrong. Those early weeks can be quite brutal.'

'A prank? What makes you say that?' Carla thought of the card inside Frederika's wallet referencing the Owl Club.

'I'm not sure. I mean, I'm from Jericho but went to Boston for college so I'm not an expert on what goes on here. I joined a sorority but the whole "commitment for life" wasn't really my thing. I tried to leave and things turned nasty and ever since I've given groups a swerve.'

'Nasty in what way?'

Nicole raised her glass to shield her expression. 'I was forced to sleep with a frat boy of their choosing.'

'What?'

'They said that was the only way they were going to let me leave. I was so desperate to get the fuck out of there,

I slept with the guy which was no great shakes. As I said, nasty.'

'Christ. And what makes you think something similar might have happened with the student?'

'I was just musing out loud I suppose. First couple of weeks of term, as I said. That's when the initiation rites take place and I've heard some terrible shit. All hearsay, of course, and I'd not go on record about any of it, but that's what happened to— I remember!'

'Remember?'

'I remember her name. Rika Brown!'

Chapter 11

Erin made dinner for her son Ethan who shovelled the pie into his mouth with his usual distracted air. It was gone eight by the time she got home as she'd wanted to make a preliminary examination of the bones found at the Wilmington farmstead. The skeleton had been reconstructed, bone by bone, with the assistance of her co-worker Jenny while they had looked for any obvious indicators of violence. The body had been buried deep enough to ward off scavengers and the only fracture on the right fibula looked an old one that had healed before death. When they were happy with the arrangements of the relics, they'd started the examination again, Erin sure that while the initial visual assessment was absolutely essential, it was only once the bones were off to the lab that the woman's story would begin to open up to them. As it was, she made a very preliminary conclusion that they were looking at a female, height five three to four and below the age of forty, most likely much younger.

Unusually, they had been interrupted by Perez stopping by the facility to update her on the discovery of the purse, her cheeks flushed with suppressed emotion. Erin briefly wondered why Perez had wanted to inform them in person; the name Frederika Brown meant nothing to her, but Erin now had a name to attempt a match both through the confirmation of the fracture in her medical records and also comparison of dental profiles. In the morning, a selection of bones would be sent for radiocarbon dating and isotope analysis of the teeth. There was always the possibility that the body wasn't that of Frederika.

As they were finishing dinner, Erin jumped at a knock on the front door. Ethan shrugged, as if to indicate it wasn't for him and Erin opened the porch door to see her assistant Jenny standing in the mellow sunlight.

'Is everything all right?' They'd said goodbye to each other only an hour earlier and Jenny wasn't the type to stop by unannounced.

'Can I come and see you for a moment?'

'Of course. We're finishing dinner and there's plenty left. Would you like some?' Ethan, with his enormous appetite, looked up, hurt at the thought of a second helping disappearing.

Jenny, tiny as her wren namesake, shook her head.

'Then come into the living room,' said Erin. 'We'll have more privacy there.'

She saw that her assistant wasn't nervous but keen to get something off her chest. She was wearing the same outfit as when Erin had last seen her – dark blue jeans and a black T-shirt with a crow and a distorted man's head. Looking closer, as she shut the door, Erin saw that it was Edgar Allan Poe.

'So what's the matter, Jenny?'

'I wanted to talk to you today about this but events overtook us with the discovery of the body at Wilmington. I know it's outside working hours but I'll be kicking myself if I don't at least tell you what's on my mind. I've been thinking about that little girl found in the swan's wing.'

Erin frowned. 'Baby F? Do you have an idea who the mother could be?'

Jenny played with the piercing in her eyebrow. 'No idea at all, but I haven't been able to stop thinking about her. I mean, it's the swan's wing that's the most interesting thing, isn't it? Babies get discarded all the time.'

Erin winced. You developed a sense of dislocation working in a pathology unit which was only natural, but she sometimes wondered if Jenny pushed this too far. 'We don't get many abandoned babies in Jericho and this is only the second fatality under those circumstances in my career.'

The first had been over ten years earlier when the baby had been left in one of the Safe Haven drops already deceased although the mother had never been traced. DNA had nevertheless been extracted in case the mother or father turned up on a database, and the baby had been buried in a small grave at Lawrence Hill cemetery. Erin thought that Fionnuala would most likely end up in a similar resting place.

'The thing is, I was chatting about swans with my pals.' Jenny caught sight of Erin's face and grimaced. 'I promise you I mentioned nothing about the baby. I'd never do that.'

'OK.'

'We were just talking about swans generally. I mean, getting hold of a swan's wing isn't that easy. You'd surely find a mutilated bird unless it was procured after some kind of accident. I was talking to friends about where you find swans in Jericho and there are two main places: under the bridge near the town and further upstream around the curve in the river where you can swim.'

'I know it,' said Erin, getting impatient. 'Has anyone heard of something happening to a swan there?'

'Nah.' Jenny, still standing, scratched her arm, leaving red wheals on her pale skin. 'What my friend did tell me though is that there's a woman in Jericho who's obsessed with swans.'

Erin stilled, listening to the muted sounds of her son clearing up his dishes and putting them in the machine, an unusual act probably put on for Jenny's benefit.

'A woman? How old is she?'

'Well this is the thing. I get the impression she's in her early sixties so she's not going to be the baby's mother. I have her name, it's Maureen Campion and she lives on the road east out of Jericho.'

'The one that passes Shining Cliff Wood.'

'Yes exactly.' The two women looked at each other. The baby had been found next to a dumpster at the entrance to the woodland. Of course, it didn't necessarily mean anything – the child might have been brought to its resting place by car, but still, it was one heck of a coincidence.

'It's nowhere near the river,' said Erin. 'Isn't that an unusual place to live if you love swans?'

'She lives in the trailer park off the highway called Deerbrook Terrace. I don't think she has much of a choice where she gets to live.'

'And when you say obsessed with swans – what do you mean?'

'Apparently her trailer is filled with soft toys, photos, paintings, that sort of thing. My friend Kat goes there to visit a relative and you can see all these mobiles hanging in the window.'

Erin's hopes sank. Some women filled their homes with stuffed owls, others particular breeds of dogs. She wasn't sure what that had to do with a baby left by a dumpster, although the location was an interesting connection.

'I think she's worth a visit. Do you want to come with me?'

Jenny shook her head. 'She doesn't like my type apparently. You know, piercings, tatts. Apparently she's suspicious of anyone she doesn't know and also of cops in case you were thinking of giving Baros a call.'

'They're going to be busy with the victim found earlier today, I'm sure. You think I might have more luck?'

Jenny shrugged. 'Maybe. Kat had heard the woman might be British or maybe Australian. You might want to ask your friend along.'

'Carla?' Erin looked at her watch. 'I have a feeling she might want an early night but I'll give her a call. Maybe we can head out there tomorrow.'

Jenny looked relieved now she'd said her piece. 'You don't think I'm worrying over nothing?'

'I think it's worth pursuing and I'm not sure law enforcement is sufficiently engaged to send someone round. Leave it with me.'

After Jenny had left, Erin tried Carla's phone but it was switched off. They'd been playing call ping-pong all day, each missing the other's attempts to contact each other. Carla had looked tired when Jenny had seen her at the Wilmington place. It could wait.

'Hey, map-meister,' Erin called to her son.

'Me?' Ethan was eating a Hershey's and had chocolate on his mouth reminding Erin of the little boy he'd once been.

'Can you call up Deerbrook Terrace on your tablet and show me it in relation to Shining Cliff Wood?'

Ethan snorted. 'You can do that yourself, Ma. It's not that difficult.'

'It'll take me twice the time of you,' said Erin handing him a facecloth. 'Wipe your mouth first.'

Grinning, Ethan took the towel and with one hand wiped his face while searching on his phone with the other. Once the map was open, he handed it to Erin who saw the trailer park fanning out from the road, its meagre entrance belying the scale of the development. A steep climb up the hill would take you directly to the entrance of Shining Cliff Wood, the location where Fionnuala's body was found. Maureen Campion was definitely a person of interest.

Chapter 12

The department was buzzing with news of the body found at the Wilmington site. Sabine had decided to call an unscheduled team meeting and set her secretary the near impossible task of trying to coordinate everyone's diaries at short notice. Exams were taking place in the morning and Carla hung around her office to give advice and reassurance to two anxious students, one of whom looked like she was about to be sick. In class the pair had been confident and relaxed – it showed once again the intolerable stresses exams placed on some students. When they had left, Sabine knocked on her door, smiling hesitantly. Carla was reminded of her previous boss, Albert Kantz, and his uncertain manner. How did these people rise to the top? Not a result of their confident people skills certainly.

'Is everything all right?' asked Carla.

'I suppose I should be asking you that,' said Sabine, finally entering the office and taking a seat. 'It can't have been much fun having a near miss with a possible killer.'

Carla shrugged. The person they'd encountered had certainly known there was a body in the ground but calling them a killer was a big leap. Baros and Perez hadn't yet asked for a description from her of the man they had disturbed, although, given that she was unharmed, perhaps they'd interviewed Jack instead who'd seen the person up close.

'I'm fine. I caught up on some sleep yesterday, there's no need to worry about me.'

'Actually, I wasn't.' Carla choked on her tea and caught Sabine's good-humoured expression. 'What I am worried about is our doctoral student Ashley Jones who is due to be questioned later today by a detective, Charlie Baros. She spent the weekend at her parents' house and is driving back up here today but won't make it until around five. The police are naturally keen to speak to her about the site.'

'Of course,' said Carla. 'Do you want me to go along to the interview with her?'

'Would you?' Sabine's voice came out in a rush, revealing her anxiety. 'I did suggest one of her parents come back with her even for just moral support but she says they're away on a cruise and she was up there doing a house check as promised.'

'How old is she?' asked Carla.

'Around twenty-four, I think, but Jericho does like to make sure it's giving support to its students.'

Sabine turned her face away and Carla was struck by how little she knew of her boss.

'I'll go at five. I've got a free-ish afternoon apart from a single tutorial so I'll hang around here.'

'The detectives, I believe, want to speak to Ashley out at the site. I suppose it makes sense. They'll want to get a feel of what drew her to the place and who she's seen hanging around during our digs. I've answered Detective Baros's questions to the best of my ability – he was particularly keen to know the background to the site being disturbed – but these detectives aren't used to the thought processes that we go through when assessing a site for archaeology work. Some of what Ashley says might not make sense to them and I'd like her protected.'

Protected? Carla thought that a little beyond her abilities, especially if Baros was doing the questioning, but she could certainly be a reassuring presence.

—

Carla was buried in a pile of exam marking when her mobile rang. Her eyes were gritty from concentrating too long at the screen, finding it difficult to keep her mind on Bronze Age settlements.

'We've been missing each other,' said Erin down the phone, her usually strong voice hushed. 'I've been dying to catch up on your escapades yesterday. Want to talk about it?'

Carla sighed and pushed her chair away from the desk. 'I'd love to but not now. I'm bogged down and I need to get back to the Wilmington place for five p.m. to support a student who's going to be questioned by Detective Baros. Perhaps after that I could swing by your house if you're back by then?'

'Five? Well, OK. Look I've got a lead on the baby we found in the swan's wing. I was hoping to get you to come along but maybe it can wait until later.'

'Fionnuala.'

'You remembered?' Erin sounded pleased. Carla listened as Erin updated her on Jenny's visit and news of the woman in the trailer park. Her eyes strayed to the clock. Shining Cliff Wood was around a twenty-minute drive so there should be plenty of time for her to get up to the Wilmington place afterwards. She could catch up on the marking later that evening.

'How about I meet you there,' she said to Erin, gratefully pushing the papers to one side.

The drive out took her east, past Silent Brook where she'd been called to the site of a woman's burnt body the previous year. The place hadn't improved despite promises from the town's mayor to plough public money into improving the space. Carla thought there was little they could do with the place, too near the main highway and its reputation of the haunt of lost souls – it had once been the preferred spot of those deciding to die by their own hand. She crossed the river and headed away from town as the buildings thinned out until all she could see were gaps in hedges with freestanding mailboxes and gravel tracks leading to distant properties. Finally, she approached a large sign, well maintained, if a little old, which heralded their arrival at Deerbrook Terrace. Carla wondered who the hell came up with the names. Always alert to the landscape, she could see no evidence of deer, a brook or a terrace.

Erin was already there, eating an ice cream she'd bought from a booth that consisted of little more than a giant freezer. Erin waved and walked towards the car as Carla stepped out into the sunshine.

'Want one?'

Carla, still queasy from the lack of sleep despite an early bedtime, shook her head. 'I've some water in my bag.' She looked in dismay at the rows of trailers rising up the slight incline. Here, at least, was the terrace. There must be at least five hundred buildings, maybe more past the brow of the hill. She had no enthusiasm for knocking on doors to find the swan woman.

'Huge, isn't it?' said Erin cheerfully. 'The good thing about buying an ice is that you get chatting to the staff.

Maureen Campion is pretty well known around here and I've directions to her trailer. She likes to be known as Leda but people prefer to use her real name.'

Carla groaned. 'Leda? Really? I think I prefer Maureen.'

Erin gave her a side glance. 'I looked up the reference on my phone while I was waiting for you. Leda, a spartan queen, is raped by Zeus in the form of a swan. It's suggesting a disturbed mind to me, trying to adopt that kind of name. Sure you still want to come? She's English though so she might open up to you rather than me.'

'I'm hardly going to let you go on your own.'

They set off up the main asphalt drive, Carla amazed by the lack of curiosity of the people they passed. In her long skirt and linen jacket, she felt she stuck out like a character from *Four Weddings and a Funeral* but no one commented on their presence. Only one man, putting out his trash, gave them a salute with two fingers against his forehead.

'Seems quite a nice neighbourhood,' said Erin. 'Trailer parks over here don't always have a good reputation. Is it like that in England?'

Carla shrugged. 'I guess so but I don't think we have anything like this size. It's interesting how each home is similar in design but people have personalised them.'

Erin snorted. 'Wait till we get to Maureen's trailer. It's quite a sight apparently.'

They spotted the trailer as they turned into a row marked Terrace J. Clearly the evocative naming stopped when it came to street monikers. About halfway along the road to the right was a fern green trailer with the sound of chimes tinkling in the wind. From the distance, a couple of inflatable balloons bobbed up and down. Carla squinted her eyes, trying to make out the shapes.

'Think they're swans?' she asked.

Erin nodded. 'That'd be my guess. It looks like it belongs in a fairground and I need to buy some cotton candy. God knows what it's like inside.'

As they approached, Carla saw a row of lights had been set around the door and were beating a regular pulse in the sunshine. She wondered what the neighbours thought of the constant light in the winter which would drive her insane. Erin rapped on the door and turned to look at Carla as they heard a sound of feet shuffling towards the door.

'Who is it?' A voice unmistakeably British seeped through metal. Erin stepped back, motioning Carla to reply.

'Um, hello. I'm Carla, a professor from the college. I wanted some information about swans and someone told me you would be the person to speak to.'

'What?'

Carla and Erin shared a glance and Carla saw her friend was trying not to laugh.

'I want to talk to you about swans,' Carla hollered. 'Swans!'

There was silence. 'Hold on.'

They listened to the sound of a bolt being drawn and the door swung outwards, clipping Carla's shoulder.

A woman stood in the doorway, grossly overweight, wearing a floral dress that hung off her like a tent. Her badly dyed ginger hair looked like it had been subject to a home perm and a faint smell of sweat and talc drafted across in the spring air.

'I'm sorry to disturb you. I'm Professor Carla James from Jericho College and this is Doctor Erin Collins. We wanted to talk to you about swans.'

'Then you've come to the right person.'

She walked back into the trailer, leaving the door open to allow Carla and Erin to follow. The woman was surprisingly agile on her feet and had already settled into the armchair in the main room which was roasting hot. A fan sat on the side table but wasn't switched on, the woman happy in the heat. Carla had expected chaos given Maureen's physical appearance, but the room was spotless with the scent of lemon cleaning fluid in the air. It must take her hours to dust the place as it was filled with ornaments, paintings, snow globes, cushions and plates all depicting the same subject: swans. It should have been the height of kitsch but instead, because the fact each piece had been lovingly cared for, the place was more like a museum.

'Is it Maureen or Leda?' asked Erin.

'I prefer Leda, if you don't mind. The people round here haven't taken to it but I'm trying.'

Carla and Erin took a seat on a small unsteady wicker sofa that surely Leda must never use. Carla could see that the room wasn't having the same effect on Erin who was trying to hide her distaste. Maybe it was because, in its clutter, the place reminded Carla of her mother's own sitting room.

'Can I ask why you chose the name Leda?' asked Carla. 'I understand the Leda myth is related to swans but it's a violent association.'

'Leda was a victim like me. Let's just say I'm a sucker for bad relationships.'

'What part of England are you from?' asked Carla.

'Lancaster,' replied Leda with reluctance, 'but I never think about it as home. My father was American so I had a US passport and I finally came out here to live thirty years ago once my mother had died.'

Hardly the American dream, thought Carla glancing around the trailer and yet who was she to say what constituted home? 'The reason we're calling is that you might have heard about the baby who was found dead up at Shining Cliff Wood.'

Leda frowned. 'I heard, though it's nothing to do with me. I can tell you that ship sailed long ago for me, not that I fancied children anyway.'

Carla looked to Erin who took over. 'I'm not just a doctor, I'm one of the state's pathologists. It was me who carried out the autopsy on the child known as Baby F.'

'Baby F? Couldn't you think of something better than that?'

'I call her Fionnuala,' said Erin and Carla was surprised to see the woman's face light up.

'The Children of Lir.'

Erin nodded. 'Exactly. Look, there's a search on for the child's mother and we're keen to help find someone who may be in distress.'

'I don't know who the mother is.'

'That's fine,' said Erin, 'but if I tell you something in confidence, would you keep it to yourself?'

'Who would I tell? Barb next door is my only friend round here and she's visiting her son in Maine.'

'Well, the thing is,' said Carla, 'when Barb comes back we'd still like you to keep it quiet. It's an important piece of evidence in helping us find the mother.'

'And it's to do with swans?' asked Leda.

'It is.' Erin paused. 'When the baby was found, it was wrapped in organic matter. Feathers, bones and leaves.

Analysis of the bones leads us to believe it was a swan's wing.'

'Like the baby of Vedbaek?' said Leda, immediately getting the reference. 'You know I love that story of how the mother was found wrapped around the child who'd been laid to rest in a swan's wing. Swans have always been an animal to be revered. I think it's beautiful.'

'It's possible whoever put the baby in the woods knew of the story,' said Carla. 'Someone like yourself.'

'But the Vedbaek baby was a boy,' said Leda. 'The newspaper said it was a baby girl.'

Carla frowned trying to understand the point the woman was making. 'Does it matter?'

Leda shrugged, inspecting a bite on her arm. 'Just saying it's not the same thing. If you're going to recreate a burial, you need to do it exactly.'

Do you? wondered Carla. She wasn't so sure.

'I suppose not. Where would someone get hold of a swan's wing from, Leda? We know there are swans in Jericho but they're throughout New England aren't they?'

'Trumpeter and tundra swans are native to here. Mute swans are the most common but brought in by settlers. What kind of swan was it?'

Erin, to Carla's relief, knew the answer. 'A mute. Do you think it makes a difference?'

'They're the ones you'll find on the Alford River so it was probably local. Swans go missing occasionally so someone may have taken it alive or dead.'

'Have you any idea who that might be?' asked Carla.

Leda shrugged. 'Hunters, or students for a lark.'

'Students?' asked Carla. 'Are you serious?'

' 'Fraid so. Things get a bit excitable when term starts and swans have been targeted before now. One frat society thought it might be a laugh to roast a swan for its start of term dinner.'

'Christ,' said Carla. 'Which society was that?'

'The Norsemen, I heard. They're a group who think they're beyond the reaches of the law but really it could have been any of those societies. Bunch of idiots.' Leda wrinkled her nose. 'If you catch a swan intending to eat it, there would be feathers, bones, a wing to discard. Might be worth checking if they've had a dinner recently.'

'I'm wondering,' said Erin, 'whether it wasn't in fact the mother who wrapped the baby in the swan's wing. It could have been someone else: partner, parent, friend. Have you heard anything about someone asking about a Vedbaek burial, or discussion of a dead swan, for example. Anything?'

A tear of sweat trickled down Leda's face, smearing her thick foundation. 'I've heard nothing and as far as I'm concerned there have been no swan casualties recently. I can understand why you came to me but I promise you I don't know how that poor child came to die.'

Carla caught Erin's eye and shrugged. Leda might be eccentric but her manner was direct.

'Do you ever go up to Shining Cliff Wood?' asked Carla, trying to make the question sound casual.

'Sometimes. I can get the bus from the bottom of the hill to the public footpath but it takes me time.' Leda pointed at a walking stick. 'My feet aren't what they should be.'

On the way out, she dipped one of her enormous hands into what looked like a ball of glass and handed a soft pointed object to each of them. On closer inspection, Carla saw it was an origami swan in rainbow colours.

'It's beautiful,' she said to Leda.

'I hope this swan provides you with some comfort as I'm sure the wing did to that child. I've something extra for you, Prof.' She pulled open a drawer and looked at its contents, chewing her lip as she considered. Finally, she handed Carla a wide flat pebble onto which a swan had been drawn. Although amateurish, there was a gracefulness to the swan's pose with its wings high above its head that touched Carla.

'Did you paint this?'

Leda nodded. 'Have it as a keepsake. I remember you now from the newspapers, how you solved the deaths of those poor girls. I want you to have this to prove stones in your pockets can bring you luck too.'

Chapter 13

Ashley Jones was a long-limbed brunette with locks flowing down her back. Only her hands hinted at the time she spent on digs, the pale skin overlaid with a rawness from frequent scrubbing. The girl was happy to get her hands dirty, there was no way to prevent it really, most archaeologists not wearing gloves in the field while artefacts were yet uncleaned. She looked round the Wilmington farmstead as if she could hardly believe what had been found here. Any suspicions that Ashley herself might have been involved in the attempts to discover the body – after all it was she who had successfully applied for funding for the month's dig – were wiped away for Carla. The girl was astounded at news of the body's discovery, her eyes straying to the excavated grave at the far side of the site.

Baros was taking charge. No change there, even though both he and his partner Perez were the same rank. Carla noticed how his eyes lingered on Ashley's brown legs encased in khaki shorts as the four of them walked towards the large pit from which the body had emerged. Overnight, the strategy had changed, law enforcement now concerned that the place might be a makeshift graveyard for other possible victims of crime, and a series of other trenches were being dug. At least they hadn't just brought in a digger – Carla wondered what damage to the site the work might do. On a professional level, Carla felt sorry for Ashley. The discovery of an earlier dwelling on the Wilmington farmstead had been a coup for the grad student and responsibility for the site had now been pulled away from her. Any findings might be contaminated by police work and she must now be assessing her options for her doctoral thesis.

As the four regarded the grave, Ashley wiped away sweat that was forming on her brow.

'We never even made it this far. Finding human remains is sometimes the ultimate goal of a dig and it's certainly what generates plenty of excitement. The funny thing is, it's not what I'm interested in. I love places, the layering of present and past to create a palimpsest of histories. It's what led me here.'

'OK.' Perez looked around. 'You need to be more specific about the process that brought you here because it's no coincidence that you start digging and someone is on your tail.'

Ashley took a breath. 'OK, so my period, the time I'm particularly interested in, is early settler home life. It's obviously known that in the mid-seventeenth century, the Puritan pilgrims arrived and engaged in farming, lumbering and fishing on the land. However, the area had also been visited by French and Dutch traders where metal and glass were exchanged for local fur products.'

'Who were they trading with?' asked Perez. 'The indigenous population?'

'Yes, exactly. The thing is, I looked at a map from the early seventeenth century. It had been languishing in the Franklin library and no one had ever properly examined this farmstead. I was looking for somewhere to dig that might give me insight into how the early settlers lived and I spotted something I hadn't expected. On the map, it said "stone barn trading post". Of course, it's not as accurate as we'd expect maps to be today, but it did tell me it was here just above the bend in the river.'

'So you decided it was worth a look,' said Baros. 'Did you tell anyone else about your idea?'

'Well, not at that point, although I did tell my supervisor, Doctor Jeanette Lavigne, that I was checking out the place.'

'And what did she say?' asked Perez.

'She seemed pleased. We actually visited the site together and saw immediately that the present house – I mean the disused one – was probably mid-nineteenth century, so we'd need to survey the site to look for the location of the original barn.'

'So when it was agreed you'd dig the site, was it common knowledge that this was the plan?'

Baros's dark eyes were fixed on Ashley. Carla realised with a jolt that his attraction wasn't sexual but driven by something else. There was an intensity that wasn't to do with the girl's physicality but by the story she was telling. Perez, too, was acting out of character. She fidgeted as Ashley spoke, her eyes returning to Baros's with a faint air of anxiety.

'Of course,' said Ashley. 'I had to ask for student volunteers to help me with the dig. I was supervising the site and I recruited a team of six through notices around the department and via email.'

'So, in effect, anyone could have seen the news about your decision to dig the site.'

'Yes…' Ashley frowned. 'But you'd need to be at the college. I mean, the posters never went up round town.'

'What about getting permission from the Wilmington family?' asked Perez.

'We found a spokesperson called Step Wilmington who was able to prove part ownership of the site. He said he'd consult with family and about three weeks later, he gave us the go-ahead.'

'Any idea how many family Step consulted?'

Ashley shrugged. 'No, you'd need to ask him, but given the site was used as a summer camp for over twenty years, I get the impression there was quite a large group. It's been pretty straightforward from an archaeology point of view to distinguish what detritus is left over from those times. Modern soda cans and glass bottles from the 1970s near the surface.'

'How did you decide where to dig?' Baros asked impatiently, uninterested in archaeology. 'Can you show me the order of the holes?'

'Trenches,' said Carla which earnt her a contemptuous look from him.

'Our main aim was to discover the footprint of the building that I was sure once existed. Given that the usual trading barn could vary considerably in size, my first objective was to find evidence of one of the outer walls of the building. The first trench over there that we dug revealed nothing, we moved along, looking at the results of geophysical surveys.'

'They're images taken of disturbances in the ground,' said Carla. 'They show natural and non-natural changes and the key is working out which is which.'

'The second trench was this one.' Ashley walked over to a rectangular cut in the earth. 'The darker circles of soil indicate posts which were put in the ground to support what we now know was the east wall.'

'And this was the first trench that was disturbed, wasn't it?' asked Carla.

'Exactly.'

'Tell me about that,' demanded Baros. 'How did you know someone had been there?'

'It was Monday morning.' Ashley glanced at Carla. 'We tend not to dig weekends so we secured the site on the Friday as usual, which largely means looking after the equipment. Most tampering on archaeological digs is either looting of machinery or treasure hunters looking for artefacts. This isn't the Klondike – all we were hoping for that might be of interest to a detectorist were broken clay bowls, iron agricultural implements and old glass bottles. Archaeology has become much more lab focused so we wanted to take soil samples to look at pollen, seeds and other organic matter to give a clue as to what type of crops might have been grown here. Our focus was on securing the machinery.'

'Got that.' Baros was impatient to move on. 'What did you see when you arrived on that Monday?'

Perez looked across at Carla, her expression difficult to read.

'You can see how our trenches look.' Ashley pointed to the second rectangular cut in the ground. 'The edges are neat. We work methodically scouring for information, taking note of layers of changes in soil composition and evidence of human activity. When we arrived on Monday it was clear someone with no archaeological training had been digging in the trench. See here.' Ashley pointed at a cut out about a metre or so from the end of the trench. 'We're the ones who have squared it off. What we found were a series of spade marks and turned earth but no attempt at order.'

'What were your first thoughts when you saw it?' asked Perez.

'My guess was that someone *had* been treasure hunting. The nighthawkers are a pest and you never know, they might strike lucky with old coins.'

'But didn't you say they were always digging around your existing trenches?' asked Baros.

'Yes.'

'So why did they suddenly decide to dig ten metres away from where you're revealing the foundations of the original settler house.'

'I don't know.' Ashley looked close to tears. 'I can't think. We never had any intention of putting a trench in there. It's too far away from the existing house and my theory was that the new building was constructed opposite the old.'

Baros crossed his arms. 'OK. Are you back now for good? You were away at the weekend, I believe.'

'Visiting my parents' house, yes. They're away on a three-month cruise and I've promised to check the house occasionally. It's also a chance to get away from student rooms I have at Exeter House and have a bit of luxury. I came back as soon as I heard.'

So Sabine hadn't informed the student team what was taking place. It was a good strategy because not all artefact thefts came from external sources – there had been cases of light-fingered archaeologists too.

'Weren't you worried,' asked Perez, 'that the site would be disturbed while you were away?'

'Yes, but I can't live onsite permanently and, in any case, I'd agreed to Facetime my father Saturday evening to discuss my plans for the summer. I need to support myself while I continue my studies and I wanted to check he was happy I stayed in Jericho while I pursued work on this site.'

Carla frowned. An odd note had crept into Ashley's tone and she was sure the girl was lying. Had she wanted money off her father for something else? Baros too had narrowed his eyes and was regarding Ashley but she held his gaze.

'OK. We'll be in touch if we have any more questions.'

They departed in separate cars, Baros and Perez in his vintage Mustang, Ashley in a burgundy mini and Carla in the small Yaris she'd bought cheaply when she first arrived in Jericho. It had been a strange day – first the visit to Leda surrounded by her swans and then a return to the site where the woman had been discovered. Carla hadn't liked to mention Frederika Brown's name while Baros was questioning Ashley and he'd not stayed around to chat in private. Once more, she wondered why Baros wasn't questioning her about the man at the site. All right, she hadn't got much of a look at the suspect but she'd expected to be interrogated beyond her official statement.

Back in her flat, Carla showered and contemplated opening a bottle of wine. Just after six, she supposed it would be OK as long she kept it to two glasses. She'd just poured out a glass of icy chardonnay when she saw two figures cross the road and head towards her front door. The woman leading the way was easily recognisable as Patricia although the man following in her wake was a stranger. He was tall, in his early thirties, with a shambling gait and pale sandy hair. Carla leant forward, confused. He reminded her of Ashley, something about the long limbs, but she hadn't mentioned a sibling in town. There was a rap on the door and Carla guiltily put her glass of wine in the fridge. It would save for later.

'Carla.' Patricia enveloped her in a hug. 'I saw your car on the street and knew you were in. I was giving Dominic here the lowdown on your history.'

'Really?' Patricia surely couldn't be playing matchmaker. She'd have given Carla time to put some foundation on her sunburnt cheeks or at least a brush through her hair.

Dominic put out his hand, an old-fashioned gesture, and gripped hers tightly. 'I hope you don't mind us dropping by unannounced. Patricia thought you might be able to help. I'm Dominic Tandy, the brother of Lucie whose posters you might have seen around town.'

'Dominic. Right.' Thank God she hadn't had that glass of wine. 'Why don't you take a seat and I'll make us some tea.'

'We'd prefer a glass of wine,' said Patricia firmly. 'It's been one of those afternoons. Don't tell me I have to go to the liquor store – I can usually rely on you, Carla, to have a bottle in the house.'

'Sure. Will white do? It's the weather for it.' Carla pulled the open bottle from the fridge and filled three new glasses.

Dominic took a huge gulp of his wine and set the glass back on the table. 'I suppose you're wondering what you can do to help me. I've been in town the last two weeks trying to drum up interest in Lucie's disappearance. The issue is that from the very beginning the police department hasn't been overly interested in the case. You'd think, given she was a young woman who lived a fairly straightforward life, that it would be a matter of concern, the fact she never came home but the fact is, they're convinced that she voluntarily has taken herself off somewhere because of the message she sent saying she was having some time out.'

'You think it's possible she sent the message under duress?' asked Carla.

Dominic shrugged. 'Maybe or perhaps a short voluntary break extended into something more sinister.'

'I heard Lucie had a history of occasionally disappearing. Is that true?'

'That was years ago when she was fifteen. There's been nothing since.'

'Which detectives have you been dealing with?'

'That's the problem. It's someone different each time. I don't think anyone has been assigned solely to Lucie's case and again it's due to the fact that they're convinced a crime hasn't been committed.'

'Other than her message to her friend saying she was taking a break and her past history, have detectives given you any indications of why else they might think Lucie's disappearance is voluntary?' Carla might at times have considered Baros a dismissive oaf but she hadn't pegged him and his colleagues down as incompetent.

Dominic hesitated, taking his time to answer. 'Lucie's private life, it seems, was a bit of a mystery. She was openly gay but recently she'd become secretive about her comings and goings. Her dormmates thought something was up but didn't know what.'

'You've spoken to them?'

'Previously, only by phone. I live in Seattle and it's a long way from Jericho. They invited me to drop by if I was in town and I saw them last week. They're nice girls and I genuinely don't think they know what's happened to Lucie.'

'You think she might have been in a relationship that put her at risk?' Carla's first thought went to the possibility of an affair between student and staff. These things were frowned upon and rightly so, the imbalance of power putting the student at the disadvantage. Dominic, it seemed, had been thinking the same thing.

'It's a possibility, isn't it? Maybe another student or even a professor. The problem is that I've no entry into the world at Jericho College. I went to grad school in LA and it was nothing like here, believe me. This place is like something out of *Brideshead Revisited*. I wouldn't be surprised to see a man in a cricket sweater carrying a teddy bear.'

Carla was surprised at the reference. Dominic might be playing down his education but he was clearly well read. 'You want me to help you?' Carla retrieved the bottle of wine and filled up his glass. If he carried on drinking like this she'd have to offer him the poured glass in the fridge. 'I think you should know that I'm coming to the end of my first year at the college so I'm not an expert on the dynamics of the place. It's been a steep learning curve for me.'

'I've told him that.' Patricia smiled across at Dominic. 'But I told him all about your stake-out the other night and what you found. Don't look surprised – the news is all over town – and he thinks your outsider status will help. You'll be able to see if anything looks odd. Could you ask your colleagues if they knew Lucie and who she might have been seeing?'

Carla made a face. 'Of course, although I have to tell you our department's priority at the present will be the site at Wilmington, plus ensuring that the discovery of the body doesn't affect any of the students especially given it's exam time. But, of course, we're all concerned about Lucie, so I'll be happy to ask the questions.'

Dominic put his head in his hands. 'My heart stopped when I heard a body had been discovered, but when I rang the station they told me it definitely wasn't Lucie.'

'I can't talk about it but from a professional point of view, but I don't think the burial is recent.'

'That's something anyway. Is there anything you need to know about Lucie that would help?'

Carla considered. She was pretty au fait with the details of the case but was struggling to remember Lucie as a person. Emotions were her forte and, if they wanted more from her than a way into Jericho academia, she'd need to understand the personality of Lucie.

'Could you describe her a bit more? I only know her from the class she briefly took with me.'

Dominic's eyes lit up. 'She was a dynamic person, spirited but caring at the same time. She's also very resourceful so if she's been taken by someone, I'm sure she'll do anything to survive. She has lots of inner resources.'

'You knew she was gay?' asked Carla.

'I didn't, but why should she tell me?' Dominic shrugged. 'It makes no difference to me although maybe my folks wouldn't be so pleased to hear that.'

'She never wrote to you of a relationship in her emails to you?'

'Nothing at all.' He paused. 'So you'll help me?'

Carla thought of Frederika's grave, the baby and the swan woman and felt like groaning. 'I'll try,' she said.

Chapter 14

Friday morning, Erin received the results of the radiocarbon dating of the tooth enamel from the skeleton found at the Wilmington farmstead. Adult teeth were considered to be the most accurate way of providing an age of bodies born from the mid-twentieth century onwards. Although the amount of radiocarbon in the atmosphere had remained flat over the centuries, an increase in above-ground nuclear testing between 1955 and 1963 had resulted in a huge increase in radiocarbon levels and tests had shown age could be predicted within one and a half years.

Erin sat down in her scrubs, put on in advance of the autopsy she was about to complete on a recent suicide, and studied the report. Tooth enamel from the skeleton showed that the deceased had been born around 1979. For comparison, she picked up the scant file Perez had dropped off on Frederika Brown whose wallet had been found in the grave. It was a miracle that the wallet and plastic inside it had survived as all other organic matter had returned to nature.

Frederika Brown was born in December 1979 in Nelson, a town ten miles outside Jericho. Her medical notes hadn't yet been located which was frustrating, but her dental records had. Frederika's dental profile matched that of the remains. For Erin, that would have been enough for identification purposes but she knew juries loved forensic evidence. Luckily, genomic DNA had been extracted from the enamel which was undergoing further tests in order to match it with Frederika Brown's nearest blood relative from the Baros–Brown family.

Erin paused, frowning. Baros was an unusual surname in these parts and the only person with that name she knew was Charlie Baros, one of the detectives working on the case. He'd been at the dig, she was sure of it, but she'd left before the discovery of the wallet so perhaps he'd been removed from the investigation if he was related to the victim. Erin tried to recall the conversation with Carla who she was sure had mentioned Baros questioning one of her students. She wasn't entirely sure about the professional ethics of this, if there was a connection. Erin's hand hovered over her phone as she considered her next move. She would need to feed back the results to the team but perhaps she should call Perez instead. But as she'd learnt to her disadvantage, police officers liked to stick together. She would call Baros and ask him direct.

He answered on the first ring, breathing heavily down the line. Erin's instincts were on high alert. Her number was programmed into his phone, she knew, and she was usually greeted by a laconic 'Yeah' whenever she called. This terse 'Baros' he uttered was out of character. 'I've got the early analysis of DNA found in the teeth of the remains found at Wilmington homestead.'

'And?'

She could feel his tension radiating down the line.

'I need to ask you first if you're a member of the Baros family identified in the report as Frederika's nearest relatives for DNA comparison.'

'What of it?' His tone was hard.

'For God's sake, how come I learn about this in a report? Does the chief of police know about your possible relationship with the deceased?'

'The chief doesn't give a shit about this case even though, if we can prove Rika was murdered, there's no statute of limitations on a prosecution. But for the record, yeah I told him. I was eight years old when Rika went missing and I'm not likely to be a suspect, am I? So, is it her?'

'Frederika Brown's dental records are a match with the victim.'

Baros exhaled heavily.

'I'm sorry, Baros. I really am but we now need to compare your DNA to that of the deceased. You'll need to provide a sample. Can you ask Perez to swab you and send the results to me which I'll then forward on to the testing facility?'

'Will do.' His tone was terse.

'Look, I know we don't always get on but if you're not getting any support from your superiors I might be able to help in some way. Will you tell me how you're related to Frederika?'

'Help? How?'

'When I know your story, and that of Frederika's, I might be able to place that in the context of what results come in from the various lab work I'm waiting for. It might help with the cause of death and how she ended up buried at Wilmington farmstead.'

There was a pause. 'OK. I'm not going to be able to get away until late. Can you meet me at, say, eight p.m?'

'Sure.'

To her surprise, Baros didn't suggest a bar or late-night cafe but asked her to meet at his house. It reinforced Erin's opinion that some of his investigations might be off the books which wasn't all right with her. She had no intention of being sucked into a quagmire of law enforcement politics.

—

Erin headed off that evening with a headful of questions. Baros had given her an address on Jefferson Drive, a street in an up-and-coming area where new homes built by the Franklin group had been marketed for busy professionals. Gardens were small with easily maintained shrubs but with parking for two, maybe three cars. Baros lived at the end of the street and Erin saw his Mustang sitting in the driveway next to a more modest Volkswagen. He must have been watching for her arrival, the front door opening as she parked on the roadside. He stepped back to let her in and Erin had another surprise. Given the sleekness of his usual car, she'd expected a black and grey masculine interior. Instead, muted slub brown walls were teamed with orange pops of colour. He must have had, Erin decided, brought an interior designer in to model the space.

Baros took her into the living room and sat down without offering her any drink. 'You're sure it's her? I provided a DNA sample this afternoon – I asked for you but you were busy with an autopsy.'

'It's been a busy day. Your sample will hopefully confirm what the tooth morphology has already told me.'

'You think it's Rika?'

Erin took a deep breath. 'I'm in a difficult situation – if I hadn't spotted the Baros name on the report, I'd never have known about the familial connection to you. I'd like to know your exact relationship with the deceased before I give you any more information. Was she your sister?'

'Cousin, but we were close enough to be siblings.' Baros, thought Erin, looked shattered. 'Rika's mother and mine were sisters and we lived close by. I had brothers and sisters but they were younger than me. Rika was ten years older and used to babysit for us. I idolised her.'

'Was Rika the name she was known by? It's got a Germanic feel to it.'

'The family originally hail from Saxony, something my mother was only too happy to ignore when she married my father who was visiting relatives from then Czechoslovakia. My aunt, however, liked to keep the German thing going though, hence the name she gave her daughter.'

'Are her parents still alive? The report mentions the Brown family, too.'

'Yes, but living in Berlin. She also had a brother, Christoph, but he's not been heard from in years. He was always on the wild side but Rika's disappearance sent him off the rails. Addiction issues, in short.'

'That's sad. You've no idea where he is?'

'Nope, which is why I'm probably one of the closest DNA relations you'll be able to test.'

It was a shame as Rika's parents and brother would be a closer genetic match, but Baros's sample would be enough to prove a familial link.

'So why are you working this case?' Erin sat down on a wooden framed couch and grabbed a bottle of water from her bag. Refreshments weren't forthcoming, more to do with Baros's state of tension than rudeness.

'The cold case team got disbanded earlier this year after the conviction of Max Hazen. The official reason was cuts, but Jericho took a hammering after the deaths of those girls. I think there was a decision higher up to sweep any unsolveds under the rug.'

'The absence of Viv Kantz can't be helping. Any idea if she'll ever be back?'

Baros shrugged. 'Viv was a good chief but we've been told to keep our distance. In the meantime, until someone tells me otherwise, I'm assisting in the investigation of the Wilmington remains. Perez is the official lead.'

'So why am I at your house? You know how things work – procedure needs to be watertight or the case will be thrown out of court.'

'I need to tell you about Rika because I think the heart of what happened to her doesn't lie with some external agency but at the heart of Jericho.'

Again, thought Erin wearily.

'She was at Jericho College when she disappeared, which was a huge deal in our family. She'd been smart from the get-go but she worked hard for her place there and got let in on a scholarship in the archaeology department.'

'Archaeology?' Although way before her time, Carla would be a good person to speak to, but she'd already dragged her into Fionnuala's tragedy. Baros was continuing to reminisce and Erin saw to her shock him light up a Camel Lite.

'I think she found it difficult to settle from the off. You know what the place is like, a world of privilege and, believe me, our family come from humble if aspirational backgrounds.'

'The American dream.'

Baros clenched his jaw. 'Not much of a dream for Rika. She wasn't happy there; even as a boy I could tell something was up, but according to her mother, she kept trying. Then four weeks after term had started, she was at a party – only a small gathering – and she bailed out of a proposed poker game. Losing money wasn't Rika's thing, and it was only a ten-minute walk back to her room.'

'She went home alone?'

'Jericho was considered safe then. Still is really, and as it was early in the term, lots of people were milling around. It's believed she reached the bridge, as a woman answering to her description was seen by a couple walking past. The theory was that she went into the river soon after.'

'And the people at the poker game?'

'They all alibied each other. There was a camera at the entrance to the dorm where the party was taking place. You clearly see Rika leave but no one else follows until two a.m. when the game broke up. By then, Rika was almost certainly gone.'

'The river? Did people think she'd fallen in as a result of some drunken accident?' There had been a drowning about eight years earlier, Erin recalled, not a student but a young mechanic who'd slipped into the murky depths.

'That was the working hypothesis. My family wasn't in a position to press for any greater resources. If I could find the file, I could share with you the cold way in which Rika's disappearance was treated.'

Erin frowned. 'The file's missing?'

'Not missing, no, but incomplete. I don't have the names of the couple who saw Rika by the bridge. Anything of significance is gone, so I think it's been tampered with, it might even have been at the request of Jericho College. She was a student there, after all.'

'The camera recording of Rika leaving?'

'Gone.'

'Statements of the party attendees.'

'Gone. I don't even have a list of names.'

'Shit.'

'So the thing is, Perez is leading on this one and she's straight. I've no complaints about my partner but she can only deal with the information she's got. She tells me there's no obvious cause for Rika, is that right?'

'No physical injuries except evidence of an old, healed fracture — but you know the score. Lab analysis of bone samples will tell us a lot more.'

'What agonises me is that Rika might have been taken from the bridge and kept somewhere and tortured. I find that unbearable. Are there any clues how long she'd been in the ground?'

'That's going to be harder to judge but Carla might be able to help on that. I've already got her assisting me on one case — Baby F found up at Shining Cliff Wood.'

'In the swan's wing? How can she help you with that?'

Erin told him briefly about the Vedbaek burial, but she could see his mind was already elsewhere.

'Do you think she'd take a look at Rika? I know I'm not her favourite person but she'd listen to you.'

So that was it. Baros had called her down not to pick her brains about the autopsy she'd undertaken on the remains. It was all in the file and Baros could dissect her findings as good as anyone. What he wanted was access to Carla and, in that, Erin couldn't blame him. She nodded.

'Of course. I'll ring Carla in the morning.'

Chapter 15

'Can I talk to you?'

Carla was in a rush, already late for the team meeting scheduled to start five minutes earlier. It was absolutely not a good time to chat to a man she'd once viewed as a potential lover but who was now preoccupied with his wife, schmoozing Albert and Viv Kantz, and in arguments with his colleague Rafe.

'I'd really like to hear any updates from Sabine, especially in relation to the dig at the Wilmington farmstead. Can we chat afterwards?'

Jack frowned, clearly not liking Carla's tone. 'You know what it's like after meetings, we've all got commitments even in exam season. This is urgent.'

Carla stopped in her tracks, aware that Sabine would give them five, possibly ten minutes grace for everyone to fetch coffees, chat about inconsequential matters and settle down.

'Go on then.'

Not the politest response but, if she was to be honest with herself, there was part of Carla that hoped Jack wanted to talk to her about his marital situation and explain why their budding romance had shifted to the distance of colleagues. It was clear that wasn't to be the case.

'Have any students come to you over the last year, concerned about the activities of any extra-curricular groups they belong to?'

Carla frowned as they turned and walked slowly towards the meeting room. 'You mean the frat and sorority societies?' These were a new phenomenon for Carla. Of course, societies existed in British universities, but the social organisations with their secret rules and initiations often referred to as Greek Life after the letters often used to name them were an American model that she didn't really understand.

'Well...' Jack was already backtracking. 'Not just them. I guess I'm also talking about any extra-curricular activities outside normal teaching or fieldwork. Not site digs for example, but even, I dunno, any student club where the rules might be upsetting to a student.'

'Like the Owl Club?'

'The Owl Club?' Carla could hear amusement in his voice. Clearly an acting society wasn't what was on his mind.

Carla shook her head, desperate to get to the meeting. 'I've heard no complaints from my students at all. Did you have anything specific in mind?'

'I... well... yes, actually I do. Do you have time for a drink later?'

'Not really.'

Jack looked surprised.

'I'll be in my office from four p.m. you can catch me there.'

They'd reached the panelled room where the meeting was taking place and Carla saw that Sabine was already talking. Damn, she'd started without them. Carla and Jack entered, taking the only free seats at opposite sides of the table to each other. Jack hadn't actually said whether he intended to come at four but she'd be there.

Sabine, Carla gathered, had been updating the team on what had been found at the Wilmington farmstead. It was factual and concise until she mentioned the name of Frederika Brown. The name raised a few heads which suggested that while the disappeared girl had been wiped from the front page of the *Jericho Tribune*, the memory lingered on at the college. She wondered if Sabine had been given permission to share the name with colleagues. Although Frederika had been a student of archaeology at Jericho College in the Nineties, no one had taught the student, but she had apparently taken classes run by Albert Kantz. Albert's name caused the meeting to fall silent and Carla wondered if anyone apart from Jack kept in touch with their former boss.

Of more interest was the decision to continue with the dig once the police operation was over. Excavation around the site of Frederika's remains had revealed no other bodies and it was expected that the site would be handed back to the college within two weeks. Ashley was going to come up with a proposal on how to integrate the discovery of the modern-day skeleton in her doctoral work, which Carla thought was a good idea. She could see journals and conferences snapping up a discussion on the site and how a modern burial had intruded on the farmstead's deeper past.

Sabine abruptly called the meeting to a close and everyone hurried off. Only Sabine seemed inclined to linger, toying with her disposable coffee cup, fragile after a new type of recyclable material was being used. Carla had already updated Sabine about the meeting between

Ashley and Baros by email and she'd received no response to her note.

Carla regarded her colleague, seizing the opportunity to talk. 'Um... have you heard from Ashley at all? The meeting with the police went as well as can be expected.'

'What?' Sabine was in a daze, as if the release after the effort of holding it all together for the meeting had drained her of all energy. 'Oh yes, of course. You know, don't you think it's odd that an archaeological student goes missing and is found at a dig? If we'd dug at a different place it could have been us who'd found Frederika.'

Carla winced. 'I think it's probably just coincidence, only I didn't really want to say in the meeting but it looks like Frederika was buried with a cup or beaker. One was found near the body.'

'A beaker burial?' Sabine got the reference straight away. Beaker-using communities were found across Europe from around 2000 BC. Their burials were characterised by a variety of grave goods and in particular sometimes ornately stamped drinking vessels. The placing of a beaker amongst grave goods suggested not just a belief in the afterlife, but the cup's role in the dead's journey to their destination. It added an interesting conundrum to the already confusing swirl of different clues as to how the body had ended up in the grave.

'Well it's obviously not a beaker burial as we know it but anyone with archaeological knowledge would know the history of placing a beaker next to a body. I wish the damn picture the officer took had come through to my email so I could show you. I'm sure it was some modern, well-made reproduction of an ancient drinking vessel. It's the placement that has significance, a reverence for the dead.'

'You think someone from the department might be responsible?'

'It's possible, isn't it, but there are few people here from the late 1990s as far as I can see.'

'But I'm going to have to give an explanation as to how it was our department who, in effect, found the body.'

'You surely don't think Ashley is holding anything back? She was born after Frederika disappeared.'

'No,' said Sabine slowly, 'I don't think that. But I think I might look at the approval process by which the site was approved for excavation. It was agreed before my arrival here, of course.'

'You're going to get in touch with Albert? You surely don't think he's involved?' God, Albert had enough on his plate with his wife suspended and he on an extended leave of absence. He wouldn't want to be dragged into this case.

'I think it would be better if I didn't speak to Albert but looked through the paperwork, meeting notes and so on. I just need to completely convince myself that there's nothing but coincidence that Frederika was found on our dig. How did you get on with Ashley?'

'Well, fine, I think.'

'Can you go through those early days again about her finding the map with details of the trading barn? I'm sure Ashley knows nothing about the body – she appears appalled by your account – but I want to see if anyone was guiding her to the Wilmington site. It's a remote place. I'd really like to satisfy myself that her story holds true.'

'Have you considered Jeanette's role in all this? She's Ashley's supervisor, after all.'

Sabine sighed. 'I haven't *considered* anyone yet, but given Jeanette's outrage at the incursions onto the site, I hardly think she's that good an actress as to have been using her anger to mask the fact it was she who was disturbing the dig.'

It was a good point, thought Carla, plus everyone in the department knew a watch was going to be kept on the place over the weekend.

'I'll talk to Ashley about discovering the map. While I have you here, I've been speaking to the brother of Lucie Tandy, the student who went missing in April.'

'God, is there any update on her? All I can get from the police department is that they're sure her disappearance is voluntary. She was a student of yours, wasn't she?'

'She took one of my modules at the beginning of term but decided it wasn't for her. I was surprised, to be honest, as she was clearly bright and I thought pretty engaged with the course. But she sent me a pleasant enough email and said she was switching to a literature module. Well, there's no competing with that.'

'True, but she's still officially a major in archaeology so still our problem even if police think her disappearance isn't suspect. What does her brother say?'

'He thinks she never settled in Jericho, but given he lives so far away, he doesn't really have any specific details. He's visited her three dormmates and believes their story that they're completely in the dark too. I thought I might pay them a visit but can you think of anyone else I could talk to?'

Sabine threw the paper cup she'd been playing with into the trash can. 'I've spoken to the police multiple times about Lucie's disappearance but not really got anywhere. The authorities here told me not to make any enquiries of my own but leave it to the student welfare office, but they've not been able to discover anything either.'

'I think Dominic would appreciate any lead, however small.'

'Has he spoken to Ashley's friend Anika who she was supposed to be meeting on the day she disappeared? They seemed pretty close and I saw them together around campus a lot.'

'You know Anika? I thought she was an accountancy student.'

'I gave a talk to SEEC on how we minimise damage to the environment on digs. It's an interest of mine and I chatted to Lucie and Anika afterwards.'

'You don't mind me asking this Anika if I can have a chat about Lucie?' Carla was, of course, free to speak to whoever she liked, but after her involvement in Albert Kantz's downfall, she got the impression that some of the department resented her.

Sabine shrugged. 'Makes no difference to me. Sure you've got time? I heard you were looking into that baby found in the swan's wing.'

'Oh… right. Out of interest, who told you that?'

'My secretary, but God knows where she heard that from. Let's just say on the Jericho grapevine.'

'I was just accompanying my former mentor Erin to see a woman who has a fascination with swans given the possible link with the Vedbaek burial. We thought she might have some ideas, if not to the identity of the baby, then why it was wrapped in a swan's wing.'

'And did she?' asked Sabine. 'Was she able to point you in the right direction?'

All of Carla's instincts were on high alert. Despite Sabine's diffident tone, her dark brown eyes were hard as glass as she waited for Carla's reply.

'She gave us nothing at all.' This wasn't strictly correct but it wasn't any of Sabine's business. 'Do you have any ideas?' asked Carla. 'The burial at Vedbaek is fairly well known in the archaeological world. It's why Erin asked me about it in the first place and whether it might be an act of love.'

Carla was astonished to see the effect her words had on Sabine. She jumped as if charged by electricity.

'Love,' she scoffed. 'I wouldn't be so sure about that.'

Chapter 16

Jack was early for the meeting, knocking on Carla's door and opening it without waiting for her reply. His face was pale and she saw he had a faint mark under one eye that she hadn't spotted while they'd been walking down the corridor together. His curly Byron-like hair was in need of a cut and she noticed a faint stain on his black short-sleeved shirt. Jack Caron didn't look like a man who was thriving to Carla, and she tried to shake off the pang of concern his presence provoked. He sat in the chair opposite her and folded his arms.

'Sure I can't persuade you to have a drink?'

'I really don't think so. I saw you with Anna in Morrell's the other night and I don't date married men.' Carla bit her lip. He'd only suggested a drink not a romantic liaison but perhaps it was better to get things out in the open.

'Ah.' Jack looked at his hands. 'I know this is going to sound like a cliché, but things aren't going that well between us.'

'You looked all right to me.' Despite herself, her curiosity was getting the better of her. 'How was Albert?'

Jack shrugged. 'Bored. In theory, he should be using his time away writing some papers, but he wants to be back in the department.'

'And Viv?'

'Viv's harder to read but I'd say she's missing the day job. Anyway, what did you think of the team meeting?'

Carla smiled. 'Executed with remarkable efficiency.'

'We didn't get that much information about the body at the Wilmington dig, did we? Given that we put our lives at risk camping out for the night, I think we might have had a little more information about how they think Frederika Brown ended up there.'

Carla curled her lip. 'Ended up? I think that's a little disingenuous. Someone buried her there, so that in itself is a criminal act.'

'How was Ashley when you spoke to her? She's a talented student who deserves to fly through her PhD rather than deal with horseshit like this.'

Carla saw he was angry but she didn't particularly want to discuss Ashley Jones with him. 'She was as fine as can be expected. You wanted to talk to me about the college societies. I'm not sure how I'll be able to help you given I've not even been here a year.'

Jack sighed and reached into his jacket pocket. 'I suppose it'll be easier if I show you this. It'll save time in explanations.'

He passed her a printout of an email from a reporter at the *Jericho Tribune*, the town's weekly newspaper. Its message was brief.

> We're conducting an investigation into allegations of historic abuse that took place at meetings of the Norseman society. As a current member, we'd love to have a conversation about this matter with you, either on or off the record.

Carla passed back the email to Jack. 'Historic abuse? That's a serious allegation. Do you know what they're referring to?'

'Of course not. It says historic, and given the society has been going since 1935, that's nearly ninety years when I wasn't a member.'

Carla remembered Leda's comment about the Norsemen but had it tagged down as a drinking club for the over-privileged male academics. Her views clearly showed in her face.

'Please don't look like that, Carla. The Norsemen is a small group of friends who meet for dinner monthly to discuss our respective academic interests and raise money for charity. I was invited to join when I arrived and have found it to be nothing more than a convivial dining club.'

'Then simply ignore the email or, if you feel you need to respond, send them a reply saying you know nothing that would help them. I'd recommend the former.'

'Would you.' Jack's tone was sarcastic and Carla was too tired to put up with it.

'If you don't want my advice, why are you in my office?' she snapped.

'Because I've already spoken to the journalist who sent the message. I know I should have just ignored it but I replied telling her I couldn't help. The next thing, she was on the phone, asking me about student societies. One of the fraternities and an environmental one. She said that some had complex initiation rituals that were deeply scarring for the students. At that point I told her hazing was strictly frowned upon and hung up.'

Carla groaned. Hazing was the initiation into a group or society that in some way degraded or endangered the student. There had been well-documented cases of students physically or psychologically injured from these activities and colleges were now on the alert for any forms of abuse. Even benign pranks had now been all but outlawed to ensure the safety of students.

'Is that why you asked me if any students had complained about their societies?'

'Exactly. I thought you might have picked something up, maybe overheard a conversation about the issue.'

'I've heard nothing.' Carla stopped. 'Did you say an environmental society? Was it called SEEC?'

'I think that's who she mentioned. What are they seeking?'

Carla laughed. 'It's S-E-E-C. The Student Ethical and Environmental Club. Lucie Tandy, the missing student, was a member. I really hope it's coincidental.'

'Do you think Lucie might be holed up somewhere feeding this information to the journalist?'

'I don't know.' Jack was another who thought Lucie was alive somewhere, still on her extended time out. The lack of urgency in tracking her down was beginning to depress Carla. In a place that emphasised the student experience, it seemed once you decided to leave, all pastoral care came to a halt.

'I'd like the name of that journalist.'

Jack looked alarmed. 'Don't mention me. I'm in enough trouble already for speaking to her.'

'Trouble with… was that what you and Rafe were arguing about?'

'I apparently should have taken it to the society first.'

Carla pencilled a note of the journalist's name on the email. A Billie Cooper.

'I won't mention you at all.'

Billie Cooper answered on the first ring and invited Carla to Morrell's. Carla, preferring somewhere a bit less conspicuous and desperate to get out into the sunshine, suggested a hot-dog in Suncook Park. As she walked through the campus grounds, Carla was reminded of the beauty and privilege of the college. The sun was reflected off the golden bricks onto the carpet lawns where a sprinkler rotated its droplets into the still air. In the distance, Carla could hear a choir singing in the chapel, the voices lifting into the sky. It was an image of perfection and yet...

At Suncook, Billie was already waiting for her – they ordered their dogs from the stand and stood by the water to eat them, the river snaking away towards the bridge where Rika had last been seen. Carla had very little experience with journalists and Billie was both younger and sharper than she'd expected.

'Who told you about me?' was Billie's first question.

'I can't tell you that.'

'Well, if I were to make an educated guess I'd say Albert Kantz or Jack Caron given you're in the same department.'

Carla took that to mean that Albert was also a member of the Norsemen which was unsurprising given he came from an old Jericho family.

'The reason I've got in touch is that I'm trying to help the brother of missing student Lucie Tandy. I was wondering if your interest in the college's societies might be related to Lucie's disappearance. Dominic Tandy would really like to know if Lucie's OK.'

Billie took a gulp of her soda and frowned. 'If you're asking me whether Lucie is one of my sources then the answer is no. I'm sorry but I've no idea where she is. For what it's worth, I wrote a couple of pieces in April after she went missing but I came to the same conclusion as the cops. Jericho was too much for her and she took off.'

'Where to? Her family have had no contact from her since April.'

'I don't know, but people do just need to get away sometimes.'

She had the callousness of the young, decided Carla, who herself knew the agony of loss. Perhaps that's why she'd agreed to help Dominic when she could barely spare the time. 'Lucie was a member of SEEC. Is that one of the societies that you're investigating?'

'I have heard a story about them that I'm trying to substantiate,' admitted Billie brushing crumbs from her top. 'In order to be initiated into the society you have to prove yourself through an act of militancy – you know, set free animals that have been caged for animal testing or sabotage a digger about to fell a tree. That's all I'm prepared to say as that, at least, is in the public domain.'

'And you have proof of something criminal?'

'I do, but I'm afraid it's nothing to do with Lucie Tandy. It's from three years ago before Lucie arrived at Jericho.'

'Are these rites ongoing though? Lucie clearly wasn't enjoying her time at Jericho and I'm beginning to wonder whether her membership of SEEC might be related to her unhappiness.'

'Could be. I went to Wellesley myself so I know how these things work. If you're a conformer, then you'll be fine, but any attempt at asserting your own personality then you're in trouble.'

'It's surely not that bad,' said Carla.

'Maybe not in SEEC, but it's the tip of the iceberg. The Norsemen, Kappa Beta Rho and two others that I'm digging deep into.'

Carla knew Kappa Beta Rho was a fraternity so probably not relevant to Lucie. 'What about the Owl Club?' she asked, thinking of the card in Frederika Brown's wallet.

'I've not heard anything other than the fact auditions are brutal for admittance into the society. But that's probably a reflection of the acting industry as a whole. Why, have you heard something?'

'Not at all. The club came up in conversation that's all.'

'Hmm.' Billie cast her a sideways glance. 'Information works both ways and I'd appreciate if you hear anything concrete about activities that might constitute hazing, you let me know.'

Carla threw the wrapping into the bin. 'I'm completely in the dark about this but while I have you here, can I ask if you've heard anything in relations to swans? I spoke to a woman who implied that roasted swan might be on the menu at one society. Have you heard of the Norsemen?'

'A little. They only accept post-doctoral students upwards so they like to think themselves a cut above the rest. Roast swan sounds like them.'

'Have you found anyone willing to talk yet?' Carla wiped her hands on a tissue, wondering if she'd ever master the art of eating a hot-dog without making a mess.

'You've got to be kidding but I'm in this for the long game. If I hear any more about swans I'll give you a call.'

Chapter 17

Erin's conversation with Baros had left her with a dilemma. During the exam period, Carla would be overloaded with marking and Erin had already decided not to involve her any longer in the mystery around Fionnuala's death until term was over. She had, however, been moved by Rika's story and Baros's distress that he had been at pains to hide. To have been so young to have had your life laid out in front of you and it then pulled away was heart-breaking for the family left behind. Carla, with her focus on the archaeology of emotion, would be a valuable asset in helping Baros chip away at the years of silence around Rika's death.

Erin could imagine Baros's shock when the wallet with its dirt smeared credit card had emerged from the ground, but he must already have had his suspicions that the body in the ground was Rika's. She wondered if his cousin's disappearance was the reason he'd become a cop and how often he'd scoured the scant files to see if there were any leads he could follow on an official or unofficial basis.

From their conversation, it was clear that the police department had not only been in disarray since Viv Kantz's suspension, but had problems that went much further back than that. The missing evidence bags and files were a depressingly common problem and usually wouldn't necessarily mean that there had been any kind of cover-up over Rika's death. Only this was Jericho, and Rika had been a student at the college. It was an elite, inward looking institution that looked to protect its reputation at all costs. It wasn't beyond the realms of possibility that files had been filleted to protect individuals.

Erin knew that answers often weren't to be found languishing in dusty files but by using advances in forensic anthropology alongside analysis of soil samples found within the grave to suggest how and where Rika might have died. That afternoon, it was clear that Rika had been placed in the grave fully clothed. Although the blue trousers and woollen cardigan were no longer visible to the eye, soil samples had detected the presence of both linen and wool and two small buttons had also been excavated at the site. Not much, but it was a start. What she now needed was Carla's expertise to take a look at Rika's skeleton in the facility.

It was Friday afternoon before Erin was able to take a breath and message Carla asking her to visit. She knew her friend would be intrigued but she felt obliged to tell her that it was nothing to do with Fionnuala but the body found at Wilmington farmstead. Carla replied straight away saying she'd be with Erin in half an hour. In fact she was there in twenty minutes, her face tanned from the sun and her hair windswept.

'There was I thinking I'd rescued you from a pile of marking.'

'I've been eating hot-dogs in the park and trying to discover what happened to Lucie Tandy.'

'You mean the missing student? How the hell have you got roped into that? You need to tell your new boss to give you a break for Chrissakes.'

'Nothing to do with the department. If you want to blame anyone, it'll have to be Patricia.'

Erin listened exasperated to Carla's story. 'You can never resist a mystery. Well, as long as Lucie doesn't end up here, you might stand a chance. Sure you've got time for this?'

'Of course. You know me and bones.' Erin and Carla grinned at each other across the metal gurney.

'Excellent. What I want,' said Erin, 'is for us to look at the remains together.'

Erin opened a box and began to assemble the skeleton that had once been Rika Brown who had been the pride of her family. Baros had promised to drop off a photo of Rika but until then, Erin had a mental image of a small, dark-haired woman with Baros's pale skin. Carla helped with the assembly of the lower limbs and soon Frederika's remains were laid out in front of them.

'Have you heard about the outcome of the post-mortem?' asked Erin.

'Not yet,' said Carla. 'We had a team meeting this morning but there was no mention of it. Were you thinking of sending the report over to the department for comment?'

'Yes, but not for wide circulation. In essence, I'm not at this stage able to ascertain the cause of death. I'm waiting for more lab results and I'd like to set everything in front of a few of you for your opinion. It's probably best I wait until I've assembled all the information I can glean.'

'That seems sensible, so what would you like me to look at?'

'I'm pretty sure that I've extracted everything that these remains are able to tell me,' said Erin, frowning at the skeleton. 'I've already ascertained there's no cut marks on any of the bones that might suggest a stabbing. Poisoning might show up if it was slow acting but unless Rika was held prisoner and then killed, a fast-acting poison shouldn't change bone profile.'

'I can see the hyoid bone is intact. Does that definitely rule out strangulation?'

'Not necessarily, although it does make it a less likely conclusion. Suffocation's still a possibility though. There's also no evidence of gunshot wounds to any of the bones, although of course the damage could have been done to soft tissue.'

'Any evidence of a gunshot in the soil samples?' asked Carla.

'Nothing as yet. I also know Rika went into the grave clothed.'

'But that doesn't preclude a sexual assault.'

'Of course not.'

'Why are you calling her Rika?' Carla's question was casual enough but she'd raised her eyes from the skeleton to stare directly at Erin.

'It's the name her family called her according to Baros who was a cousin of hers.'

'Oh.'

'Yes, "oh" is the right word. I think if Viv was in charge, he'd be nowhere near the case but things have gotten a bit lax there recently.'

'I bet.' Carla bent over Frederika's skull, hiding her own face from Erin's gaze. 'I'm surprised that Baros hasn't claimed the remains yet if the PM has been completed. He must surely want to give his cousin a decent burial.'

'That goes without saying. The problem is that he's not officially her next of kin. That honour goes to her elderly parents living in Germany and a brother, the black sheep of the family by all accounts. Until family politics settle down, Rika stays here.'

'Jeesh. Is he all right?'

'Not really.'

Erin watched as Carla picked up Frederika's skull. 'You've got a brilliant reputation as a pathologist and I'm not sure how I'm going to be able to help you. You must have situations where the PM is unable to give a cause of death.'

'All the time.'

'So however Frederika died, the answer can't be found in her bones.' Carla replaced the skull. 'Did you just want me over here to tell you you're doing your job properly?'

Erin laughed. 'Maybe.'

Carla straightened and pulled off her gloves. 'I can't see anything you've missed.'

Erin experienced a rush of pleasure and then immediately felt guilty. Carla was an expert in death as was, in his own way, Baros who hadn't asked for a second postmortem. He had seen the bones himself and knew what stories could and couldn't be told.

'Oh, shit.' Through the glass partition, Erin saw Baros enter the corridor. There was no time to draw down the blinds and she could see Jenny pointing towards the room. 'Baros is here,' she told Carla. 'Let me speak to him before he comes in.'

Erin slipped out and careered into him in the corridor. He was breathing heavily and his body smelt of soap and sweat.

'I just wanted to run some things by you, Doc. Perez and I are going to visit Step Wilmington who gave permission for the dig on the old farm. He's been in hospital so we've had to hold off interviewing him but we've just had the OK. Do you have any updates for me? I don't suppose you've had the chance to speak to the Prof. yet.'

'She's with me now.'

'Oh, right. Well, I need a statement from her about the man she saw the night of the discovery.' He made to step forward and Erin put a restraining hand on him. 'I've asked her to look at Rika's skeleton in case I've missed anything.'

Baros's expression hardened. 'I don't remember giving permission for her to look at Rika's remains. Have you put in an official request?'

'No, but as medical examiner, I'm entitled to ask in expert witnesses whenever I want. Given Carla was on site when Rika was discovered, she's not seeing anything new. If you've got a problem, I suggest you wait in the relatives' room. The boundaries of this case are blurred enough as it is.' She moved to block his entrance.

Baros stepped back. 'Please, I'd like to see Rika again.'

'Are you sure that's a good idea?'

He didn't answer and Erin relented, going first into the autopsy room.

'Hi,' said Carla to Baros and he answered with a curt nod. His eyes were on his cousin and he closed them briefly.

'I wanted to see if there were any updates before I interviewed Step Wilmington. He's offered to meet me at the site. I've been trying to ring you to interview you about the man from Saturday night.' He looked across at Carla.

'Well, I was around,' she said mildly. 'When are you going out to the Wilmington farm?'

'In about half an hour.'

'Sure Step Wilmington is up to visiting the place if he's just come out of hospital?' asked Erin.

'It was his idea,' said Baros. 'He probably wants a good nose around the site, which is only natural and, in any case, it will help me out.' He glanced again at Carla. 'I suppose you're busy.'

'Yes,' she said. 'But I'd like to come with you. I'm very sorry to hear that Rika was a relative of yours.'

'Thank you.' He looked moved by Carla's words. 'Oh, I've brought you a picture of Rika.'

Erin took a Polaroid snap off him. It showed a dark-haired girl, thinner than Erin had imagined, wearing a cropped top and jeans.

'Was this taken around the time of her disappearance?'

'The summer of '99 so around two months before. I took the photo myself and she liked it so much she wanted to have it but I refused. I'm not sure if I'm glad or sorry.'

'Could I see?' asked Carla holding out her hand. Erin watched as she scrutinised the image. 'She was beautiful. I know this is going to sound like an odd question but did she mention anything about her life here once the course had started? Societies she might have joined, courses she'd taken.'

'She said nothing to me but I was only eight. I only saw her the once after she'd started at Jericho.'

'Do you think you could ask her parents?'

'Is this to do with the Owl Club card that was found in her wallet? You think that's an avenue for me to explore?'

'I'm not sure at the moment.'

Baros shrugged. 'All right, but I'll be looking into it. Shall we go?'

'By the way,' Carla said to Baros as they were leaving the autopsy room. 'Have you had any results from the analysis of the drinking vessel that was found with the body? It might be worth comparing results with Erin's soil samples.'

Baros stopped. 'What drinking vessel? I don't know anything about that.'

Carla frowned. 'The day we found Rika, after you'd all left, a ceramic cup or beaker was found near the body. I happened to be on site and was called over to take a look at it.'

Baros folded his arms. 'It's not in any of the reports. Are you sure about this?'

'Of course. Did you know about the cup, Erin?' Carla asked.

'First I've heard of it.'

Erin watched Carla flush. 'There was a drinking vessel in the grave. Given there was little else in the ground, I suspected it had been deliberately placed there possibly around the time of the burial. I asked the police excavator to take a photo of it and email me a copy. My phone had died by then and I watched him take the image but it never came through to me. I'd have liked to take another look at the beaker.'

Baros frowned. 'Fuck. Let me make a call. Hold on there.'

Baros stepped out into the corridor and Carla shrugged at Erin. 'Where the hell's it gone?' she asked.

'I've no idea.' It was the first Erin had heard of the cup, although it had clearly been discovered after she'd left the site. More incompetence, she thought, but clearly not on Baros's part.

He returned looking angry. 'There's nothing on the evidence sheet at all. Can you remember the name of the man who showed you the beaker?'

'I never knew it. He was medium height with fair hair that was receding but he was no older than late twenties or early thirties.'

'Would you recognise him again?'

'I-I think so.'

'Right. After Wilmington we find out who the fuck has been messing around with evidence. Come with me.'

Carla cast Erin an apologetic glance as she hurried off. Erin listened as the double doors opened and found Jenny hovering in the doorway. Another autopsy beckoned.

'Keep me informed,' she shouted after them. 'Please.'

Chapter 18

Step Wilmington was a surprisingly virile looking man in his early fifties. He had long legs encased in designer jeans but the arms that poked out of his seersucker shirt were unnaturally thin. 'Acute lymphatic leukaemia', Baros had told her on the way over but it was only close up that you could see that he'd been ill. Two dark smudges were visible underneath his grey-blue eyes and there was a faint sheen of sweat on his forehead. He was on his own which suggested he was comfortable with both his body and this remote place. He came towards them as they stepped out of Baros's car, his arm outstretched.

'Well, I live to see another Jericho summer,' he said. 'Detectives Baros and Perez.'

Carla smiled. 'Actually, I'm Professor Carla James from Jericho College. I work in the department that was supervising this dig. Detective Baros asked me to accompany him while we chat about the site.'

'Of course.' Step whipped out a baseball cap from his back pocket and placed it carefully on his head. 'I've already guessed where the young woman was found. It's over there by the trees, isn't it?'

'It is. Do you want to take a look?'

'Already done so. There's not much to see.' Step sounded disappointed. 'You know, I thought about asking for my ashes to be scattered around here once I'm gone. It always struck me as a happy, peaceful place but I think I'll settle for the municipal cemetery now.'

'That's a shame,' said Carla. 'It's still a very beautiful place.'

Step shrugged, unconvinced.

'I believe you gave the college permission for us to dig the site but ownership lies with a number of your relatives.'

'Nine people in total. The house hasn't been lived in since my grandmother died in the early Seventies. There were three sons and a daughter who all inherited a share. Two of the sons are now dead, including my father who was the eldest. Given I was his oldest child and the place is abandoned, the college thought as long as I gave permission after consulting with the family, that would be OK.'

'And did you consult with them?'

'Every single one. My three sisters, the children of Jeb, who's also passed, and my aunt and uncle.'

'And no one raised an objection to an archaeology dig?' asked Baros.

'Not one of them.'

Carla looked around her. If one of the Wilmington descendants had hidden a body on the land, then they'd naturally be concerned about any disturbance that might uncover Rika's body. But raising an objection was problematic. If the consensus was in favour of the dig, they'd be overruled by other family members and they'd also be identifying themselves as prime suspect. There was also the problem that the children of Step's living aunt and uncle hadn't been consulted as their parents were alive to give permission. No, each of the Wilmington family would need to be interviewed, a massive job if they didn't live near Jericho.

'I believe, although the place has been empty for fifty years, you've camped here over the summer,' said Baros. 'Did you set up tents near the old house?'

Step adjusted his hat. 'We didn't like to do that. None of us felt up to maintaining the building; it was falling down during my grandparents' time, but we were drawn back to this place. It has something special about it. Can you feel it?'

Carla nodded although she noticed Baros stayed silent. For him, this place would forever be associated with Rika's death.

'It's an interesting valley which is why we're digging here,' she said. 'We believe settlers have farmed the land since the seventeenth century and have found the location of the old trading barn. I can show it to you.'

Baros sighed but followed Carla as she showed Step where the edifice once stood.

'I wonder why they built the new home away from the barn,' asked Step.

'It's possible the old structure was used as a hay store once the new building was constructed. When it fell into disrepair, it was pulled or fell down and nature took over.'

Step regarded the trenches. 'Found anything interesting?'

'Mainly fragments of pots, some cooking utensils and various bits of rusting farm equipment. We've not been digging for the artefacts but to test the hypothesis that this was an important area of trade. Did your family ever say anything about it? It's possible the barn might have lasted into the nineteenth century.'

'Never heard anything at all.'

Baros was anxious to move on. 'Where exactly did you camp?' he asked again.

Step pointed towards the stream where a small rocky escarpment gave onto flat ground. 'Over by there.'

'But you presumably roamed all over the site. Did you ever notice anything unusual about this place by the trees?'

Step shrugged. 'Nope. I never particularly liked the woods if I was to be honest. I preferred it down by the water. My childhood in the Seventies and Eighties was one of hot summers and swimming in the river and my mother shouting to make sure we bathed downstream of where they gathered the water to make coffee.'

'What about the Nineties?' asked Baros. 'More specifically 1999.'

'I was in my late twenties by then and couldn't get away for more than two weeks at a time. I'd come down here for a few days but I also liked to go away with friends to Europe so didn't spend much time here.'

But he knew the lie of the land here, thought Carla.

'Can you remember where you were the fall of 1999?' asked Baros.

'I was working in New York as a trader. I'd probably been here in July or August to join the camping trip but I wouldn't have come here in the fall. No one would. This place saw a surge of activity in the summer and that was it.'

'So if we say our victim was killed in the fall of 1999, no one would have been here again until the summer of 2000?'

'Sure.'

'*Did* you come back in 2000?' asked Baros.

'I think so. I can't really remember.' For the first time he looked frazzled. 'I'm about to start my fifth line of treatment. Another drug, another hope. Do you know what cancer drugs do to you? They destroy everything

– not just the bad cells but the healthy ones too. My memory is shot. I can't remember what I did last week let alone the late Nineties.'

'I understand,' said Carla. 'Did you have a girlfriend then?'

'Only casual hook-ups and no one I'm in touch with. And I certainly never brought them here, although the atmosphere was pretty relaxed. No one would have minded if I'd brought someone along but I never did.' Step looked around, as if seeing the farm for the first time. 'I suppose you'll be questioning all the family but I can't see it doing much good. Anyone could have come down here in the fall once we'd all gone home.'

'No one mentioned the site looking different, for example?' asked Baros.

'Not that I can remember.'

His gaze stopped on the house overlooking the valley. 'Gracie Oldcastle used to live in that house on the hill. She was widowed young in the early Eighties but I'm not sure who owns it now.'

'Still Gracie,' said Carla, and Step widened his eyes.

'She's still here? I think I might drop by before I leave. It's been a long time.'

'When did the summer camps stop?' asked Baros. 'If they were still taking place in the late Nineties, when did they come to an end?'

'I think around 2003? All us grandchildren were pretty much the same age, in our late twenties and early to mid-thirties. We had jobs elsewhere and made other plans for the summer. Our parents were in their fifties and wanted something more comfortable than camping. To be honest, it also got kinda sad watching the old place fall down.'

'So the last camp was 2003?' said Baros.

'Then or maybe the following year. I spent three years in London during that period and the last camp was about then. No big deal. My folks said they were coming over to visit me and my girlfriend, and the others decided not to come here.'

It all sounded straightforward to Carla even if she couldn't identify with the family bonds that had resulted in two decades of shared enjoyment in the outdoors. Her own mother Sylvia was a devotee of doing interesting things on holiday and Carla had been taken to European cities for week-long trips, sometimes queuing for hours in the Mediterranean heat to get into the Uffizi Gallery or the Museo del Prado. She supposed she had to thank her mother for her interest in history and archaeology, but as a teenager she'd rather have spent her summers being allowed to go away with friends. She wondered what Baros's summers had been like with his cousin missing. It sounded as if he came from a close family and the grief and confusion would have been all-encompassing.

'Can I ask if you ever drank out of pottery goblets during your stays at the camp? Something about this size.' Carla placed her hands apart to show the dimensions of the beaker found in Rika's grave.

Step laughed. 'Plastic and paper cups were the order of things, though I now feel bad about the amount of waste we generated. Definitely no goblets. Why d'ya ask?'

Carla met Baros's gaze. 'Just an idea about something that's all.'

—

After a bit more generic chatter, they watched as Step drove up the track towards Gracie's house. 'I don't feel I was much help,' said Carla. 'From an archaeologist's point of view, the site is no different than when we first found Rika. We have the dug trenches, some of them disturbed by whoever was looking for her body, and then there's her grave over by the trees, nowhere near where we were digging.'

'The working hypothesis,' said Baros, 'is that whoever killed Rika, certainly the person who buried her, knew that she was interred on Wilmington homestead but couldn't remember the exact location. If they dug the grave in the dark, they'd have had only a vague idea of where the burial took place.'

'Surely if they were a Wilmington relation, they'd know the site intimately.'

'Maybe. Places look different in the dark, especially if you're panicking. Perhaps the person looking for the body isn't the person who buried her. I don't know yet, Carla. The thing is, once news of your dig had reached their ears – there was a feature on it in the *Tribune* I've discovered, which may have been the catalyst – they began to look for the body at night.'

'But on the final night they were away from our trench.'

'I'm coming to that. It's a big job carrying a dead person. Unless Rika died here – and I'm struggling to see a scenario where she would have voluntarily come to a place like this – then her dead body was brought here by at least two people.'

'That would make sense. Have you made any headway into who that might be? I heard that Rika was at a party. Have you been able to track down who was there?'

'We're trying but they all were able to alibi each other for the length of the poker game which was approximately four hours. Rika, however, should have been home within eight minutes, ten minutes max. If one of the poker players killed her, where was she for the four hours before they left?'

'You think she was taken within minutes of leaving the party?' asked Carla.

'I think so.'

'She had no boyfriend?'

'Not that we know of.'

'A random pick-up? Jericho must have its sex offenders like anyone else.'

'They rarely hunt in pairs though. We're widening the search to see if there were any similar crimes but we're desperately short on resources. It's me and Perez until we can prove a crime was committed. I spoke to your friend Jack Caron.'

There was something insinuating about the way he said Jack's name.

'Was he able to give a description of the attacker?'

'Male. About his height. That's it, which basically covers half the men in Jericho. You've nothing to add, have you?'

'I'm sorry. All I saw was torchlight and I heard the scuffle.'

'Then we start down the long path of going back to 1999 and piecing together how Rika ended up here.'

'But those students and the Wilmington family. They could be scattered around the country and beyond.'

'Maybe.' Baros kept his eyes on the grave. 'I think the answer lies in Jericho. She died in Jericho and at least one of her killers still lives here.'

Chapter 19

'I've suggested Dominic stay in your old room.' Patricia sounded happy to have a house guest once more.

'What? Oh, OK. That sounds like a good idea.'

Carla was in a rush. She was late for work after oversleeping, probably because she'd collapsed into bed without setting her alarm. Thank God she didn't have any classes, but she'd had to call the departmental secretary to put a note on her door that she'd be late for her one-to-one appointment with a student. She'd fibbed to say her car wouldn't start and the silence at the other end suggested the woman had heard that excuse before. Chatting to Patricia was usually something to look forward to but Carla cut her short.

'I'm sorry, I need to run.'

'You will help him, won't you? He's a nice young man.'

'Of course. I've promised, haven't I?'

Carla rang off and was about to shut the door of her flat when the phone rang again.

'Sorry Patricia, I have to go,' she said into her mobile.

'Who's Patricia?' asked her mother suspiciously.

Oh, Christ, thought Carla, *terrible timing*.

'Look, I'm on my way to work and already late. Can we talk this evening?'

'This evening your time is midnight for me.'

Carla kept her cool. 'I meant evening for you. I could WhatsApp you about eight your time.'

'I heard you might be coming home for the summer. Is that right?'

Carla sighed. She'd sent her brother a brief email in reply to his message saying Carla's mother was looking unwell. She'd promised that she would pay Sylvia a visit while she was back home, little realising he would actually *tell* her mother.

'Nothing's been decided yet,' she said. 'If I'm home, of course I'll come to see you.'

'No "of course" about it,' said Sylvia, who was clearly in a poisonous mood. 'I'll wait for your call later. I'm off to feed the swans.'

'The swans? Hold on, Mum.'

'What is it?' snapped Sylvia.

'Why are you feeding swans?'

'Why not? What have you got against swans?'

Carla was torn between the desire to get going and the knowledge she was already late anyway. 'I've nothing against them, it's just that it's not like feeding ducks. I mean, where are the swans by you?'

Sylvia adopted an offended tone. 'If you came home more often, you'd know they're everywhere on the Thames. Have you never heard of Swan Upping?'

'I know the name. Look, I have to go. I'll speak later.'

Carla hurried to her office, ripping off the note on her door. To her chagrin, the student she'd rushed in for never showed up but it at least gave her the time to search on the internet for 'Swan Upping' and saw it was the annual catching, tagging and recording of mute swans across Britain.

Mute swans again, but she could think of no connection between her mother's harmless pastime and Fionnuala's unclaimed bones. Carla reached into her handbag and pulled out the origami swan given to her by Leda. Although squashed, Carla was able to revive it and place it on her desk. Poor Fionnuala's ending might never be solved but the swan served as a reminder of her brief life.

At eleven o'clock, she had a class on grave markers that Daria, one of Lucie's dormmates, would be attending. It was a course she loved to teach having spent years rootling around cemeteries and burial sites. Carla had been gratified to see her move to the US had provided opportunities to extend this research with families letting their imaginations run riot when arranging headstones for their loved ones. The gothic, the sentimental, the stark – all had a story behind them. As always, it was the emotions behind these that Carla was fascinated by. Why, for example, had the prominent philanthropist, with three official mistresses and probably a lot more unrecognised, built his dead wife a canopied mausoleum at the top of Lawrence Hill?

The class had a lively end of year feel to it and Daria looked surprised when Carla asked her to stay behind for a chat. She was a conscientious student but a little nervy as if constantly looking out for implied criticism.

'Is anything wrong, Professor James?'

'I was wondering if I could have a chat with you and your two dormmates about Lucie. I'm not sure if you've heard but her brother's in town. Has he been in touch with you?'

Daria adjusted her bag, clearly relieved the conversation wasn't about her academic work.

'We've been in touch with Dominic on and off since Lucie went missing but only by email. He paid us a visit last week and I felt sorry for him because we really couldn't help at all. He said he's been putting up the posters around town but I don't think they're going to help.'

'You don't? Why not? Surely a refresh on the search for Lucie is a good idea.'

Daria snorted. 'Yes, but she won't be around town, will she? Getting away from college means leaving Jericho so what good will the posters do? It's as if he's looking for a lost cat that no one else cares about.'

That was a little harsh to Carla. 'Would I be able to talk to you, Ali and June together about her? I could come over to your place. You know, we've been discussing this a lot about Lucie in the department. If you think no one cares about the fact she's disappeared, you're very much mistaken.'

Daria shrugged. 'It would be nice if someone told us that. It makes us worry how much people would care if we went missing.'

'I'll talk to Professor Bauer about it. I know Sabine communicated with you all when Lucie first disappeared but maybe it's time for an update even if we don't have anything concrete to tell you. Could I come around after class tonight?'

Daria looked surprised. 'Tonight? Well, OK.'

—

Carla's first thought when she saw the three dormmates together was to wonder how Lucie had fitted in with the other three. According to Dominic, Lucie was independent and spirited. There was a suggestion of non-conformity about her personality while Carla already knew Daria was anxious to do well in her studies. Ali and June were clearly cut from the same mould, alert and conventional, down to wearing their hair in tight plaits pulled away from their face. They were all sitting around the kitchen table, the three assuming their places as if there was an unspoken agreement who sat where. Carla was left with the uncomfortable feeling that she was occupying Lucie's seat although none of the girls mentioned it.

'The thing is,' said Ali who seemed to have been delegated spokesperson, 'Lucie loved living here when she first arrived. She said it was completely different from her folks' place. I gather there were few books apart from the bible and other improving works.'

'I understood from her brother Dominic that their parents were a little old-fashioned. Jericho must have been a big step for her.'

'Yes, but Lucie is super bright. She told me she spent hours in her town's library and she loved being surrounded by books. When I show you her room, you'll see what I mean. There are books everywhere. Jericho's the perfect place for people like Lucie. It allows you to flourish.'

'I notice you're talking about Lucie in the present tense. You don't think anything terrible has happened to her?'

Ali glanced at Daria. If Ali was the spokesperson, Daria appeared to be the silent leader of the three.

'We think she's disappeared voluntarily,' said Ali finally. 'She wasn't happy here this term at all and I thought she'd have dropped out sooner if I was honest.'

'Can you remember when she started to feel unhappy? If she loved it here when she first arrived, when did it begin to change?'

June wrinkled her forehead. 'I think it was maybe after a month. We enrolled in our classes and all seemed fine but when it came to the add/drop period, she began to get distressed. She went from focused to seriously flaky.'

The add/drop period was the window when students could switch classes that weren't suiting them. It must have been at this point when Lucie dropped Carla's course. 'Did you get the impression that there was something wrong academically or in relation to a personal issue?'

'I don't think she had a girlfriend or anything,' said Daria. 'She was openly gay but I don't actually think she'd ever had a relationship.' Daria pulled at the sleeve of her T-shirt.

'Then what?' asked Carla. 'If it wasn't her studies making her unhappy nor a relationship, why did she go from loving it here in her first month to hating it?'

'We don't know.' June and Ali spoke in unison and smirked at each other. Carla once more wondered about the dynamic of the relationship between these three and Lucie.

'What about the people she met in her first month? Did she ever mention the SEEC organisation?'

'There was Anika,' said June doubtfully, 'but I don't think they fell out as they'd often have a coffee on campus.'

'I'm intending to speak to Anika as well. Was Lucie a member of any other societies? A sorority for example?'

Ali shook her head. 'We're all members of Beta Kappa Rho and we'll be in a sorority house next year. Lucie was fine with finding other accommodation; maybe she was thinking of sharing with Anika.'

'Out of interest,' said Carla, 'is there a reason Lucie wasn't a member of your sorority?'

The three exchanged glances. 'I think the fees were a little expensive,' murmured Daria.

'Fees?' Carla felt a wave of fury wash over her. Lucie, while not a scholarship student, came from an ordinary middle-class background not far removed from her own. How she must have resented being excluded from a society where money and status were more important than her evident intelligence. But that couldn't be the root of her unhappiness, could it?

'Do you have initiation rites in your sorority?'

Carla saw a flash of annoyance in Ali's eyes. 'We can't talk about that. Anyway, anything that might constitute hazing is strictly outlawed.'

Carla looked at the impenetrable stares of the three students. 'Come on, I've heard the stories. Name calling, socially isolating new members, nasty tricks played on newbies. I'm not necessarily talking about your sorority. What about SEEC?'

'We know nothing about SEEC,' said Daria, sounding very much like she didn't care either.

'OK. Was there anywhere else she liked to hang out?'

'I hear she sometimes did some studying in the Edgar Franklin building. She liked the upstairs rooms there,' said Ali, 'even though they were supposed to only be used by grad students. No one actually checks.'

'You think she might have run into anyone from the Norsemen?'

'The Norsemen?' Carla saw to her horror that Ali was starry eyed. 'Why them?'

'I'm just trying to make some connections,' said Carla. 'I know her brother is keen that we explore every avenue.'

'Is Dominic still in town?' asked Daria, trying to sound nonchalant.

'Nice guy,' said Ali, smirking at Daria. 'He's welcome around here anytime.'

Chapter 20

'You think I should be looking into the activities of SEEC,' said Dominic, watching a boat glide past, the rowers red-faced in the afternoon mugginess. Spring was turning into summer, Carla's first in Jericho, and the affluent, tight-knit town was relaxing a little. In the distance, Carla could see the roofline of the college, the older buildings with their tall chimneys dominating the skyline. Carla had called Dominic to give him an update on how little she'd found out. He'd wanted to meet her, Carla getting the impression he was bored at Patricia's, and she'd suggested the river. In the distance was Seeker Street bridge, the spot of Rika's last appearance and where the mute swans could be seen nesting under the old iron.

'I just wanted to tell you I'm still doing some digging and the only lead I have is SEEC.'

'Students for Ethical and Environmental Change? It doesn't sound very threatening, I have to say, unless someone is a billionaire oil field owner and even then, I doubt they care much about a student protest group.'

His tone irritated Carla. 'It's more what's going on in the society that might be of interest, but it's all hearsay at the moment. My colleague Jack Caron told me that a journalist from the *Jericho Tribune* had evidence of hazing activities for some college societies and although these allegations largely relate to activities at the beginning of the year, Lucie didn't appear to settle very well in Jericho.'

'You think something happened when she joined a society that caused her what, seven months later, to disappear?'

'Unless it wasn't voluntary.'

Carla sensed his disinterest. He'd told her he went to university in LA which surely had a different dynamic to elite Jericho. How to explain the stranglehold that some of these societies had over its members?

'Can't you ask around some more?'

Carla shrank from his plea. She had enough on her plate with the discovery of Rika's body, though she'd given Baros and Perez as much advice as she could muster. It was also the thought of the baby in the swan's wing that kept her awake at night. Child-free and career focused, Carla found it difficult to articulate why Fionnuala held her in thrall, but that was the fact of the matter and it was to that strange trailer where neon swan balloons bobbed in the wind that Carla's mind often wandered.

'I could speak to Lucie's friend Anika if you think that would help, although if she refuses to say anything, there's nothing I can do.'

'I just want to find Lucie.'

'I know.' In the distance, Carla could see another boat coming towards them. Were they part of a rowing club? Now she had the initiation rites of societies firmly lodged in her mind, she saw the taint of their trauma everywhere. Perhaps this blonde-haired girl sculling past her with a capable air had, at one time, undergone some water-based ritual as a bizarre baptism into the society.

'Let me talk to Anika and I'll see what she says.'

Anika Bakshi lived in a single-roomed flat in a house not dissimilar to Carla's. It was furnished with Scandinavian furniture and the walls painted dove grey. Anika, dressed in fawn cropped trousers and a thin vest, exuded an air of privilege. Its cause difficult to pinpoint. The girl, after all, was dressed little differently from her contemporaries. It was, Carla decided, Anika's demeanour that suggested a confidence born out of wealth. Beside her, Carla felt hot and grubby. Anika recognised Carla and appeared eager to impress her.

'I've been worried about Lucie ever since she went missing. I was worried it might affect my grades and I've seen a student counsellor to keep me on track.'

Carla was happy to let this go, however self-absorbed it might sound. Almost every student in Jericho was worried about their grades and the hothouse atmosphere made narcissists of many.

'You've been friends since the beginning of term, I believe.'

'Second week,' agreed Anika perched on the edge of a pine-framed chair. No refreshments had been offered despite the heat and Carla's mouth was parched.

'How did you find Lucie?'

'Find?' Anika looked confused. 'I didn't find her.'

'I meant what were your first impressions of her. Was she easy to get to know?'

'She was. She seemed to be on a high – really pleased to get to Jericho. We all were really. It's not an easy college to be accepted by.'

'You met at a SEEC meeting, is that right?'

'Sure. It's something we're both interested in. The US has a terrible reputation in taking action to prevent the stripping of our planet and we're hoping to be the new generation that will effect change.'

'Sounds good. How many are in the society?'

'Around ninety, maybe nearing a hundred now.'

'You said that Lucie was on a high. How long did that last?'

Anika frowned, pulling at her lip. 'A few weeks, I think, maybe not even that. She seemed preoccupied but I assumed it was the pressure of the course. Everyone's an overachiever here and you're suddenly up against peers who are as smart if not smarter than you.'

'Did you ever talk about it?'

Anika shook her head. 'We never mentioned it at all. I got the impression she liked her course but she began swapping subjects which is never a good idea. You come across as a bit flaky and reputations like that can stay with you.'

'Did she mention her dormmates?'

'Sure. She got on best with Ali, I think, but she liked them all. Have you spoken to them?'

'Yesterday evening. They suggested I talk to you.'

Anika frowned. 'Why? I don't know where she is.'

'I had questions about the society you were both involved in. Can I ask, when you joined, did you have to undergo some kind of initiation? Say, undertake a task, in order to join?'

Anika's expression hardened. She hadn't been expecting this question which suggested whatever information was being held by the *Tribune* journalist, it hadn't leached out into college gossip.

'Of course not,' snapped Anika. 'It's just a society, not some weird sorority group. We meet, pay a monthly sub and undergo various modes of activism. There's a demonstration outside a proposed development by James Franklin next week, for example.'

'You're targeting Franklin?' Carla couldn't keep the surprise out of her voice. She'd imagined the group demonstrating against large-scale oil companies or other climate polluters. Franklin was presumably small fry on a global contamination index.

'Housebuilding eschews brownfield sites for building on green pasture. He's raping this historic land for his own profit.'

Carla frowned at the girl's words. Up to now, she'd sounded reassuringly herself but now it was if she were parroting someone else's thoughts.

'Where's the development?' Carla asked.

'Towards the river, which will impede access to this town's most precious natural resource.'

'Right. Did Lucie attend any demonstrations?'

'Of course. We all have to…' Anika trailed off, biting her lip.

'Have to what?'

'It doesn't matter.' Anika began to fidget, not meeting Carla's eye.

'OK, we'll leave that for the moment. Who's the president of the society?'

Anika laughed. 'We don't have presidents. Hierarchical structures are inherently wrong. We prefer the flat management structure.'

'But someone must organise demonstrations, handle finances and so on.'

'There's a management committee that revolves each semester,' admitted Anika.

'And you're sure you weren't asked to do anything to join?'

'I said no.'

'There's just one more thing I wanted to ask you. I understand that Lucie was gay. Were the two of you together?'

Anika's expression tightened. 'No, we're friends.'

'Did you know of any lovers she might have had?'

Anika frowned. 'I got the impression that she was still exploring her sexuality. She used to say these statements like "sexuality is a spectrum" meaning no one is completely gay or straight. I'm inclined to agree with her, but she made everything she said sound hypothetical, if you see what I mean.'

'You're saying you don't think Lucie had, in fact, had a sexual relationship with another woman.'

'Exactly that.' Anika hesitated. 'I'm sure that's right.'

'What about a boyfriend, perhaps before she came to Jericho?'

'She never mentioned anyone.'

'OK. Well, thanks. I don't know if you're aware but Dominic, Lucie's brother, is here in Jericho trying to jog people's memories with an advertising blitz.'

'I've seen the posters.' Anika made a face.

'You don't like them.'

'It reminds me of the type of thing you put up when your dog is missing. It doesn't seem right for Lucie – I actually hate them.'

'Dominic may want to see you. Would you be all right with that?'

Anika shrugged. 'I'll tell him what I told you. I don't know what happened to Lucie.'

'Do you think she's still alive?'

Anika paused, looking down at her hands which were smooth with the nails painted shell pink.

'I'm not sure.'

Chapter 21

Preliminary DNA results for Fionnuala came back from the lab, sequencing the child's genome in an effort to identify her parents. The results had already been run through the state's DNA database and had drawn a blank which left Erin in effect with a string of numbers with nothing to match it to. There was the possibility of requesting access to other state law enforcement databases but unless either of Fionnuala's parents had committed a crime it was a waste of time and resources that was unlikely to be afforded to a dead preterm baby.

Erin sat in her office and rubbed her eyes. There must be a reason why the baby had been found in Jericho. Unlike Rika Brown, the child's near-mummified state suggested it had been kept somewhere dry and warm. Did this suggest an act of love? She doubted it – even a cupboard in a laundry room might have sufficed.

Jenny breezed in wearing an improbably tight T-shirt. Christ, she was beginning to sound like her mother. She was clutching a leaflet and showed it to Erin.

'A guy's on the street corner handing out these leaflets.'

'It's the missing student's brother. Carla knows him slightly.'

Jenny raised her eyebrows. 'He's a bit of a babe. Not my type obviously, but still nice on the eye.'

Erin frowned. 'When exactly did she go missing?'

Jenny glanced at the sheet. '3 April. Why do you ask?'

'I'm trying to construct a scenario where Lucie gives birth to Baby F around that time and leaves town. It would fit in with detectives' view that the disappearance was voluntary. Then for whatever reason, Lucie comes back with her baby and leaves it in the open air for someone to find.'

'A sort of delayed shock type thing?' asked Jenny.

Erin made a face. 'Maybe.'

'Was Lucie pregnant?'

'Not according to Carla but, you know, maybe she wasn't showing. I've seen females at seven months gestation effectively hiding their pregnancies for a variety of reasons. Do you think this brother looks approachable?'

'Definitely,' grinned Jenny with a wink.

—

As it turned out, he wasn't Erin's type. He was too clean cut, almost a product of the plains of Wyoming rather than chilly Seattle. He seemed surprised to see her marching purposely towards him in the street but willingly came back with her to the facility. A swab kit was found and packaged up to send to the lab.

'How long will it take?' he asked her. He had a red flush on his neck as if the procedure had caused him distress.

'A day or so. I can rush it though so you'll know very soon.'

'You really think Lucie might have been pregnant? But that makes no sense at all. She needn't have given birth in secret, as a family we'd have been there to support her.'

'Perhaps the instance of the baby's conception was traumatic.'

Dominic winced. 'Look, I have to tell you no one who knew Lucie thinks she was pregnant.'

'I'd rather eliminate Lucie and then I can strike her from my list of possible parents.'

'Sure.' His face brightened. 'I'll have to tell Carla that I met a pathologist today.'

'No need. I'm seeing her for a drink tonight.'

—

In Morrell's Erin was glad to see there was no Jack and Anna nor Albert and Viv. In fact they had the place almost to themselves at five o'clock. Carla had raised her eyebrows as Erin had recounted the story of pulling Dominic off the street and seemed inclined to treat the whole thing as a joke. She caught Erin's eye.

'Sorry, but I've been stuck reading about the dark depths of hazing. Jeesh, some of the things I've read. There's one society in an English university, I'll name no names, where they all went to a Chinese restaurant and the initiation was they all had to masturbate under the table.'

Erin put down her drink. 'You are kidding me. That is absolutely gross. You know, when I was at Med school, I experienced a kind of hazing.' Erin made a face at being forced to recall a period in her life she would have preferred to leave firmly in the past. 'It was just after the white coat ceremony where we swear to uphold the Hippocratic oath and I had never felt so proud in my life. Just after that, during my first residency, the consultant would regularly yell at all the female students. I think the men got it bad too, but he particularly enjoyed trying to make women cry.'

'Urgh.'

'You never had something similar in your academic discipline?'

'Of course not. Archaeology is fairly egalitarian between the sexes. I'm not saying individual abuses don't go on but I don't think it's endemic. Do you think your experience is common?'

'I'm sure of it. I've since spoken to colleagues over a drink about my treatment and the abuse of medical students is depressingly normal. It's seen as a rite of passage although I'd like to think things are changing. I mean, I can't see my current students at Jericho putting up with that. Hooray for Gen Z.'

'Perhaps it's due to all the work we've undertaken to foster an environment where, if abuse occurs, people feel able to report it.' Carla shrugged. 'You know, I'm wondering if I could help Baros out with Rika's death. There's definitely a link to the early weeks of term. Perhaps she got involved in something untoward and that led to her killing.'

'Until I can ascertain the cause of death, we can't talk of killing,' said Erin.

'OK, death then.'

'It's possible, I suppose. Is that what you're thinking? That what separates the two women across the decades is that Rika and Lucie are both victims of these society rituals?'

'I don't know. I think I might be clutching at straws.'

'The timeline fits, at least with Frederika, who I know more about than Lucie. She came to Jericho full of hope and two weeks later had gone. The problem is that the only society we think she joined was the Owl Club. You think they're worth a look – if she'd been through some weird initiation with them wouldn't it have come out in the initial investigation?'

'I'm not so sure.' Carla stared into her drink. 'Rika was finally getting some freedom, she's not going to have told her family everything she was doing when she arrived at college. I could try to chat to a current member of the club and see what they say but I personally think the burial site is going to throw up the most clues.'

'I know, which is why Baros is being spectacularly nice to you.'

'Me?' Carla laughed. 'I certainly haven't noticed.'

'Take it from me, he is.'

'Look. Sites are more than digging in the ground. It's about context and emotion. You know that's what I'm interested in. The archaeology of emotion – how people felt based on material evidence.'

'Okay, let's focus on that. I'm not sure Baros would be wholly signed up for it but I am. How does looking at emotions help us here?'

'We could first look at the site of the body. I know woodland burials are becoming popular but that's a reaction to the factory feel of municipal cemeteries. In fact, woods are an unusual place to bury a body. Tree roots play havoc with both grave digging and possible maintenance. So maybe we need to look at the emotion behind it?'

'Perhaps the burier had an affinity with woodland, you mean?'

'Well, yes, but also maybe woodland is associated with a sense of safety. Believe me, it would have made life easier if the body had been buried in the more fertile soil of one of the fields. Whoever buried Rika there felt protected there. Alternatively, negative emotion might have played a role in the selection of Wilmington. If it's a member of the family, then perhaps not everything had been rosy on those summer camps and there's a sense of demeaning the land by throwing a body into it. Remember the casual way in which the body was buried.'

'Or,' said Erin thoughtfully, 'we could turn it on its head and say, perhaps the person who buried Rika loved her and wanted her to rest in a place associated with happy memories.'

'It's possible, although there was a lack of respect that I'm finding it hard to reconcile with that.'

'I can see that emotions help us a little but could we also apply it to the initiation ceremonies?'

'Of course.' Erin could see Carla getting excited. 'There are a lot of different emotions at play but it's ultimately about testing the initiate and also engendering a sense of belonging. However the emotions after initiation – shame, fear, disgust – can have a heavy emotional weight and maybe if Rika and Lucie were caught up in it then they experienced those emotions too.'

'Can we extrapolate that to killers, too?'

'Maybe.' Carla tugged at her hair, her mind elsewhere. 'Perhaps it would be better to put ourselves in the heads of not someone who we label "killer" but keeper of the sacred flame. The emotion would be fear of loss of status, of the sense of belonging and perhaps anger that someone has transgressed a written or unspoken code.'

Erin sighed. 'Doesn't give us a suspect in either instance, does it?'

'No, but we've certainly got a lot to think about.'

'I want you to go through all that again.' Erin jumped and looked up at the speaker and then at Carla who looked impassive.

'Pull up a seat.'

Chapter 22

Carla moved over in the booth and made room for Baros. Out at the Wilmington place, he'd only asked her to go through the archaeological elements of the site and how the discovery of Rika unfolded. It was unlikely to be a coincidence that he had happened on their conversation in relation to the case. His demeanour suggested he had been hunting them and would tell them why in his own time.

Carla snuck a look at Baros's face while he was ordering a beer and tried to imagine herself in his position. He had little regard for her – either in relation to her professional life or on a personal level. For him, she had been a nuisance on a previous investigation and she suspected he'd hoped their paths wouldn't cross again. Now he was asking for her professional assessment on what had happened to a young woman who had been a mother figure to him and that must have cost a lot.

When his beer arrived, instead of drinking it he began to fiddle with the label. 'Do you know what I've spent the last forty-eight hours doing? Trying to hunt down any evidence that might have been missed from the original investigation into Rika's death. It's now perfectly clear that the file was not only rifled at the time but has been systematically filleted over the years.'

'You sure about that?' asked Erin.

'I am. In 2005, a cold case team was asked to review the file. It's before my time on the force but I know it took place because I've cross-referenced it to an index that was left in place. The results of that investigation have disappeared.'

'2005?' Carla frowned. 'There must be people still on the books who can talk to you about it.'

'Fortunately, there are, but they drew a blank. The lead investigator's conclusion was that the answers lie within the college. That's probably why the file was removed.'

'Did they say why they'd come to that conclusion?' asked Carla.

'Not so much the context of the investigation – although that was a factor given Rika disappeared within the first two weeks of term. It was more the fact that the cold case team wasn't stupid. They'd spotted evidence had disappeared and they weren't inclined to lay corruption charges solely on the police department.'

'So what you're saying,' Erin signalled for another drink, 'is that the college may have had a hand in ensuring the files and evidence contained nothing incriminating.'

'Yep, and it's still going on which brings me to Carla's chalice.'

'Beaker,' corrected Carla. 'Have you been able to take a look at it?'

'I can't because it's gone missing, in fact it never made it to the evidence sheet. It's why I've been trying to track you down. Jenny said the pair of you could be found in Morrell's but first I want you to tell me why the beaker might have been in the grave.'

Carla took a deep breath. 'OK. Let's start with general observations about where Rika was buried. When we talk about graves, we have the image of what we see in cemeteries, in other words, deep sided excavations around six feet in depth, hence the phrase "six feet under" although in fact cemetery policy for grave depth varies significantly.'

'This looked more as if someone had got a digger and just scraped the top of the soil off.'

'Exactly,' said Carla, 'although there's no evidence of any mechanical work having been undertaken.'

'You wouldn't see tyre marks after all this time. And I'm not sure how you'd get a digger down here without making any noise.'

'There's a rough feeling to the excavation which suggests a shallow scoop method of digging by hand using a shovel with a wide flat blade. I'm afraid that doesn't take you very far as it's the type of tool everyone will carry around with them in the winter to shovel snow. I'm not saying the burial took place in winter but I guess many people leave their shovels in the car all year round.'

'Guilty as charged,' said Baros, wiping his face. 'So anyone with a car and shovel could have buried Rika there. What else can you tell me?'

'As far as I could see, the grave infill is exactly the same material as that which was used to excavate the grave.'

Baros looked at her as if she were a three-year-old. 'And?'

'I'm just mentally going through the process. Not all graves are infilled with the earth that's been removed. People add flowers, mementos, sometimes even soil from a different location. This didn't happen here.'

'And the beaker. Is that a usual grave addition?'

'It was in some communities in Europe but we need to be careful because there have been really odd objects found in more recent burials which might have no significance to them at all.' Carla didn't like to tell Baros about the dissected skull found in Birmingham with a wine glass inside, probably a joke by exuberant medical students. 'But just because it was within Rika's grave doesn't necessarily mean it was placed in some kind of ritual. In fact, I'm wondering if it was any kind of ritual at all.'

'Isn't burying a body a ritual?' asked Baros.

'In archaeology,' said Carla, 'we tend to differentiate between mortuary rites, in other words how we bury a body which in Rika's case was in a shallow scoop grave, and funerary rites, where a degree of ritual specific to the deceased's society is incorporated into say a ceremony. I don't think the missing cup is part of a funerary ritual. It could have been accidentally dropped in the grave or tossed there to hide evidence.'

'Rika might have been drinking from it, you mean, and it contained some kind of poison.'

'Woah,' said Erin. 'You're in my territory now and I've found no evidence of poisoning, so this is completely hypothetical. Maybe you could test the cup though for some kind of residue?'

Carla nodded. 'It's possible if you could find the beaker. I'm fuming still that I didn't wait for the email to come through from the digger on site. He clearly recognised it from somewhere.'

'That fucking guy,' said Baros. 'When I get my hands on whoever removed it from the scene he'll be sorry. I'm sniffing conspiracy which is making my blood boil. You up for looking at the mug shots of all thirty people I think were around this scene the day Rika was found?'

Carla shrugged. 'Sure.'

Baros removed Carla's half-drunk glass of wine from her. 'I need you sober for this.'

—

Baros took her, not to the office but to a small one-storey house on the outskirts of the town. It was a neighbourhood neither rich nor poor. The houses were modest but the gardens well maintained with flowers in pots drying in the sun. Baros adjusted his tie as he walked up the driveway and the door opened to an older woman around five feet tall whose face was the image of Perez's. Baros gave her a kiss on the cheek and walked past her into the front living room where Perez sat at a table with a lace cloth. On it, lay a tablet that Perez was flicking through.

'Just coffee, Mama', Perez shouted. 'No cake.' She raised her eyebrows at Carla. 'She won't pay any attention but I feel I have to tell her. It's my day off. Take a seat.'

Carla realised how tired she was as she sat down. 'I thought you both worked shifts together.'

'We do. It's Baros's day off too but he's doing some unofficial overtime. There's no one to tell him not to anyway.'

'Is the police department really in such disarray?'

'Ever since Viv Katz left, it has been.' Baros sat down and pulled the iPad towards him. 'We're doing this here because I don't want anyone seeing you inside the department. It's my opinion that the drinking vessel was deliberately taken from the site and I want you to tell me who by.'

Carla nodded. 'OK.'

'So we've downloaded photos of as many people we know who were at the site. Perez has trawled through the websites of various agencies, social media posts, online presence and so on. It wasn't just us doing the digging so it's taken longer than we hoped. There are a few still missing but if we wait any longer, there's a chance we'll never recover the beaker. I want you to look through the photos to identify the man you were talking to.'

'It might not be him who removed the vessel from the site,' said Carla, now anxious she might be laying the blame on someone innocent.

'No, but we'd like to talk to him anyway as he has the photo we need. Someone might have been watching your exchange and removed the evidence bag. We need to start following the trail.'

'Have you asked the diggers about the cup?'

Baros and Perez exchanged glances. 'Not yet,' said Perez. 'We don't want to tip anyone off that we're looking for them.'

'OK, makes sense.'

'Given your account of the person you spoke to, I've removed all the women present on site and those of non-white ethnicity. If we draw a blank with the photos we have, we can look at the others but you gave us a good description. I suspect the officer will be in the first ten I show you.'

Perez turned the tablet towards Carla who looked at the first photo. A fair-haired man holding a Maine Coon beamed out from the screen. 'Definitely not, he's too old.'

'OK, next,' said Perez swiping the screen.

'I don't think so,' said Carla. 'It's sort of the right description but not him.'

'Next.'

Carla looked into the blue eyes of a man in an open-necked checked shirt. His slightly thinning blonde hair was swept away from his tanned face. 'That's him,' said Carla quickly. 'Absolutely 100 per cent.'

Perez turned the photo to Baros who frowned. 'He's one of ours, isn't he? I'm sure I've seen him in uniform.'

Perez consulted a list. 'Officer Jeb French. I'll see if he's rota'd today.'

'Don't raise any flags. I want to catch him unawares.'

'I was just going to call Kelly on reception. She'll give me his number.'

Baros grunted. 'Be careful.'

Perez left the room, shooting him a glance of annoyance.

'What are you going to say to him?' asked Carla. 'Surely if you want a conviction, you need to do this by the book.'

'I intend on doing it by the book but I need to think how to approach him and surprise is my best bet.'

Perez came back in. 'I've got his number but Kelly says he's off sick.'

'Since when?' asked Baros sharply.

'He didn't come in yesterday and someone called to say he was sick.'

'Male or female?'

'The voice was male so now she's thinking maybe he's gay. I've sworn her to secrecy about the whole thing.'

'Can we get his address?'

Perez smiled. 'Already got it.'

—

In ordinary circumstances, there was no way they'd have let Carla ride with them to see the officer but given neither was actually on duty, they let her sit in the back seat. Baros's car was immaculately kept although smelt heavily of smoke which was strange as Carla was sure she'd never seen him with a cigarette. She sat in silence listening as Perez searched Jeb's social media accounts.

'I could be wrong but I don't think he's gay. There are a couple of photos of him close up with a woman in her twenties and I'd say they were lovers not friends.'

'Difficult to tell,' grunted Baros. 'How old is he?'

'Not sure but I think he looks older than he is because of his hair. I'd guess late twenties, as Carla said.'

'He wouldn't even have been born when Rika died. What the hell is going on?'

'He might actually be sick,' said Perez mildly. 'Let's see what he has to say.'

They pulled up outside a rundown building near to the Franklin Mall. The front façade was stained a peculiar shade of purple-brown which Carla assumed was some kind of oxide from the paint reacting to the elements. The entry buzzer was broken so Baros rapped on the window of the downstairs flats until an elderly man, his trousers too baggy on him, let them in.

'The address I have is apartment four.'

'Straight up the stairs,' said the man returning to his own place. 'I heard he was sick though. He ordered a pizza but when the delivery boy came, he didn't answer the door.'

Baros and Perez exchanged a glance. 'When was this?' asked Baros.

'Last night. They wanted to leave the pizza with me but I can't stand the stuff.' The door shut with a firm click.

Carla noticed that the pair had tensed. 'I think you'd better wait here,' said Perez.

'I can come to the landing with you.' Carla had no intention of being left behind. 'I don't need to enter the flat if there's an issue.'

'Stay down here,' ordered Baros, motioning Perez to follow him.

Carla watched them climb the stairs. She had the impression the old man was listening behind the closed door, also curious to know what was going on up the stairs. She heard Baros rap hard on the door. 'Officer French are you in there? Jeb, it's your colleagues.'

Carla wrinkled her nose, suddenly aware of a faint acrid tang in the air. Was this why Baros had ordered her downstairs? An expert in ancient death rites, she was innocent of how a recently deceased body might smell.

Unlike in cop shows, Baros didn't try to force the door with his shoulder. Perez hurried down and banged on the man's door again.

'Where can we get a set of keys to the upstairs apartment? Is your landlord nearby?'

'In the trailer at the back of the house. He doesn't own the building, just looks after it.'

Not very well, thought Carla.

Perez disappeared for a few minutes and Carla could hear Baros on his mobile calling for reinforcements. When Perez returned, she brushed past Carla with barely a glance. Some of the tension had dissipated and was replaced by weariness. Perez and Baros knew what they were expecting and it wasn't good news. Carla followed Perez up the stairs. If the immediate danger was over, there was still what was behind that closed door to be faced and Carla's curiosity couldn't be contained any longer. She was ghoulish, her mother had once told her, and perhaps here was the proof. Perez fitted the key into the slot and the door opened. Carla put her sleeve to her nose. The whiff she had smelt below intensified into the reek of a slaughterhouse.

'Jeez.' Perez also put her hand over her nose and followed her partner into the flat, both holding their weapons. If it was a crime scene, Carla needed to make sure none of her DNA contaminated the place and yet she couldn't resist stepping forward. Through the front door, the walls of the entrance hall were painted a drab grey which matched the cord-like carpet. Beyond there was a room with the edge of a sofa in view where a man lay slumped forward as if he was having a fainting attack, except his back was a mass of gore and scoured flesh. The image of a porcupine flashed into Carla's brain as she tried to make sense of the scene, her eyes resting on an arc of red sprayed onto the wall behind. A mass of grey organic-looking material lay on the floor, glistening like offal in a butcher's shop.

'Oh, God.' Carla stepped back and crouched down on the floor, feeling nauseous. Perez was on the phone, asking where backup was and updating the call handler on the situation. Carla heard footsteps approach her as Baros bent down towards her.

'I told you to stay downstairs.'

Carla swallowed. 'Curiosity is the mark of all good academics.'

'Fair enough.' His tone contained none of the sarcasm she usually expected from him. 'Carla, I want you to look at this.'

Carla lifted her face and saw he was offering her his phone. 'What's this?'

'I've taken a picture of the deceased. God knows what they've done to his back but his face is untouched. Can you confirm he's the man you spoke to?'

Carla took the phone off Baros and stared at the image on the screen. Baros must have lifted the man's face to get an image of him and the unmistakeably dead face of the person she'd spoken to at the dig loomed at her. For some reason, Carla assumed his throat had been cut, as surely that was the quickest way to kill someone and would also account for the blood. But the man's face had no marks on it at all although his lips were open as if letting out an eternal scream of agony.

'It's him,' she said. 'It's definitely him. How was he killed?'

'God knows. It's nothing like I've ever seen before. His torso is a mangled mess. This is one for the doc but it's one sick fucker who killed him.'

Chapter 23

When Carla received a call the following morning from Billie Cooper, her first thought was that news had leaked that she'd been present at the discovery of Jeb French's body. As Carla was desperately scrambling for something to say beyond 'no comment', she realised that Billie was calling to give her some information.

'You mentioned when we spoke about SEEC and the initiations students have to undergo to become members.'

'I remember,' said Carla. 'Do you have some news for me?'

'Not specifically about hazing but I've heard there's going to be a demonstration at one of James Franklin's new developments at midday. If you want to see how the group operates, now's your chance.'

'Will you be there?' asked Carla checking her schedule. Anika had mentioned a demonstration and here was the opportunity to see SEEC in action. She had a class at one so her visit would need to be brief.

'I will, but more to talk to Franklin who might make an appearance. I've heard he doesn't like demonstrations on his land. It's the Norsemen who will be forming the focal point of my story as it's the glamour that's otherwise missing.'

'He's a member?'

'That's what I've heard, but even that's difficult to confirm.'

Carla grimaced at the thought of encountering Franklin. 'Can you give me the address?'

As she was pulling together her rucksack with everything she needed for the day, she found the painted stone given to her by Leda who had scrawled her name on the back. She set it on the table, admiring again the naïve but moving portrait of the swan, its wings lifted as if ready for flight.

—

In her work clothes, Carla felt conspicuous amongst the jeans and vest-wearing students, and even Billie had adopted a more casual look for the demonstration. The Franklin development targeted by SEEC was a patch of land where the foundations were being laid for eight houses in huge plots. To Carla's eyes, the land looked no different to any of the other undeveloped lots she saw dotted around Jericho but, according to the woman with the loudspeaker, the place was both a natural habitat for water voles and had links to the Abenaki indigenous group. Carla looked round to see if an Abenaki representative was present but the group seemed to be solely made up of confident-looking students with an air of militancy. Carla, feeling her age, looked around for someone who might be in charge but it appeared that Anika's statement that the group adopted a non-hierarchical structure might be true. Even the girl holding the megaphone passed it on to another student once she'd had her say, a curly-haired male who repeated his predecessor's harangue almost word for word.

Carla frowned. The use of a script suggested a preference for control and non-deviancy which was interesting. Environmental activism was an emotive subject and one felt passionately by young and old alike. She couldn't understand why the group wasn't allowing this natural passion to come to the fore. It hinted that even in a flat structure there would be personalities that dominated to ensure that emotions were channelled correctly.

She kept her eyes on the students, noting Billie seemed relaxed chatting with some members. Despite the relatively modest size of the plot of land, it was a high-profile scheme where you might be able to make a name for yourself halting its progress. Jericho was full of ambitious students with their gaze on future careers as environmental consultants, lawyers, activists. For all of these jobs, you needed an impeccable CV and you'd need to stand out from your fellow activists.

Over by the road, standing next to an orange digger, Carla could see Anika talking animatedly to a group of friends. Anika was handing out placards which looked professionally done – no wonky writing or childlike graphics. Her face then turned towards a black Range Rover that was moving slowly towards the site. The group mobilised, forming a row of people chanting 'eco plunder' and 'save our land'.

'Who's that?' Carla asked one of the students running towards the car.

'James Franklin, the developer. I think there's going to be trouble.'

Carla followed the progress of the car hoping for a glimpse of the town's famous son. Franklin's name was attached to many of Jericho's housing developments, not to mention the shopping mall and college library. Carla had been out for dinner with him the previous year when he'd been on the list of suspects she thought responsible for the disappearance of various Jericho women. His interest in her had since cooled following the revelation that evil sat within the college confines and Carla's department was now down two key personnel.

As the car came to a halt, the driver's door opened and Carla saw Franklin emerge. She'd imagined he had a driver to ferry him around town and she wondered if this egalitarian act was prompted by the need to present himself as a man of the people. She waited and saw no one else emerge from the vehicle but was sure she could see the shadow of another sitting in the passenger seat. Franklin wasn't going to leave himself completely exposed to the mob.

He was wearing black jeans with a white polo shirt. A pair of sunglasses was tucked into his top pocket but Franklin was happy to leave them off as the crowd moved towards him, their chanting getting louder. At least that was what the crowd presented to the casual outsider. But Franklin must know the power he wielded. One word from him into the department head of these students' faculties could have a devastating effect on their futures. Perhaps the flat structure gave them safety in numbers for, as they continued their chant, they kept a respectful distance from the man. No jostling or name calling. Carla moved forward, intrigued by how this was going to play out.

Franklin raised a hand, an action more commanding than anything he could have said. The crowd quietened and then fell silent.

'What you're doing is commendable,' said Franklin in an even voice. 'You're the generation that has to live with the decisions we make today and it's only right that you have your say. However, environmental considerations need to be knitted into technological progress and how we work in the physical environment. People will always need somewhere to live.'

'What about our history? What about the cultural sensitivities of the land?'

'I care about this, which is why a member of the Abenaki people is on the consulting board for this development.'

There was a murmur amongst the crowd. Carla waited for someone to mention the water voles but it seemed they were lacking in advocates.

'I appreciate that you're concerned about what impact the scheme might have on the environment and I'd like to invite one of you to come forward to advise on this particular site. Would anyone like to put themselves forward?'

Carla held her breath. Perhaps this was where a leader might reveal herself, though it might prove to be a poisoned chalice. Franklin wasn't a man to take fools lightly and he was challenging them to field an expert to help negotiate the environment impacts on wildlife.

'I'll do it.' Carla saw to her surprise Anika push herself to the front of the crowd. 'I'll happily advocate for those without a voice.'

Carla tried to remember what Anika was majoring in, pretty sure it was something like accounting. Perhaps she saw it as a chance to get close to Franklin, her eye on a higher prize than the halting of a development. Needled, Carla looked to see the reaction of other students but their faces were impassive.

'Okay.' Franklin smiled. 'If you can give me your details, I'll make sure you're invited to the meeting next week. Work, however, continues on the site as we're on a tight schedule.'

Carla waited for the roars of protest but only the girl she'd seen with the megaphone rolled her eyes.

'I was wondering, Mr Franklin, if I could talk to you about the activities of the Norsemen. I've left a number of messages at your office and I'd appreciate a brief chat.' Billie was standing at the front of the crowd next to Franklin, her mobile in hand to record the conversation.

Carla saw the passenger door of Franklin's car swing open and a stocky man emerge. He had a nonchalant air belied by his gaze fixed on Billie. The man leant down and said something to Billie. Carla leant forward, concerned for the journalist's safety but saw to her surprise the girl start to laugh. Meanwhile, Franklin had swung round and was looking directly at her. He moved away from the car and walked towards her.

'I hadn't realised environmental activism was your thing, Carla.'

Carla flushed and hoped he'd put it down to the heat. 'I'm not with the SEEC group if that's what you mean. I'm helping someone find a missing student called Lucie Tandy and I know she was a member of this society.'

'Lucie Tandy,' Franklin frowned. 'Is she the girl in the posters I see around town?'

'Yes, exactly.'

'You think someone here knows where she might be?'

'I... I'm not sure to be honest. I've heard some comments about their terms of membership and I wondered if she'd fallen foul of group dynamics.'

'Sounds a bit far-fetched. It's usually somebody close to home, don't you think?' Franklin was growing bored, Carla saw.

'I don't know. You see, she apparently changed personality in the weeks after she arrived at Jericho. Went from being fairly outgoing to withdrawing on herself. I'm wondering if she's a victim of hazing.'

Franklin froze. 'You've been speaking to Billie Cooper, I see.'

'It's just one possibility.'

Franklin turned to her, his blue eyes boring into hers. 'And where have your investigations got you to, so far?'

Carla refused to be cowed by the man. 'Nowhere. That's the problem with group dynamics, isn't it? It's impossible for an outsider to work out what's going on.'

'I really don't think Ms Cooper is likely to be continuing with her investigations for much longer.'

'What?' She looked over to Billie and watched the journalist clamber into the back of the Range Rover.

'What are you doing with her? There are witnesses to her getting into your car.'

Franklin's gaze hardened. 'I know what your opinion is of me. Don't think I don't know I was a suspect in the murder of those girls last year.'

'I'm not going to stand here and watch you silence Billie. She has a legitimate story to investigate.'

'I'm not silencing her. She's being offered a job at the *Boston Globe* which is naturally a huge step up from the *Tribune*, no matter how much I admire that particular publication.'

Carla took a breath, her outrage making it difficult for her to speak. 'Then another journalist will take up her story.'

'They really won't, Carla. The paper's current obsession is the body found at the archaeological site which surely you agree is a more newsworthy story than some unfounded accusations against a few benign college societies.'

Carla kept her expression neutral, aware that Franklin was enjoying her outrage.

'You can't keep a lid on things forever, Franklin. Any group has those difficult to control. That's where the weaknesses lie.'

She saw a flicker of dismay in his face and wondered what nerve she'd touched.

'Be careful, Carla. Stay with the students. They're playing at being grown-ups, you won't come to any harm with them.'

She was about to reply when her mobile rang. It was Baros and she wanted to take the call in case he had an update on the missing beaker.

'Carla you'd better come home to your apartment. It looks like you've had an intruder.'

Chapter 24

The post-mortem of Officer Jeb French had been requested as a high priority so Erin reshuffled her morning schedule. The deaths of serving police personnel were considered to be an affront to all law enforcement even if it sounded very much as if Officer French had fallen into bad ways. Erin would have preferred to be working with another colleague as well as having Jenny on hand given the unusual nature of the man's death but the facility head had snapped she was the on-call pathologist and to get on with it. The police department had sent over two senior officers to witness the autopsy. Both wore uniforms and their names were unfamiliar to her. Jenny was beside her looking paler than Erin had seen her as she leant over the body to take photographs.

'Take a break if you have to,' she told her assistant. 'It's grim, I know, and no one here is expecting heroics.'

Together they regarded the victim. Unusually, he'd been placed into the chiller cabinet lying on his front given the injuries to his back were likely to be the main cause of death. To Erin's eye, the only comparison she could make were from post-mortem photos where the victim had been mangled by a bear. But usually with an encounter with an animal there was a haphazard nature to the injuries, the need to piece together injury by injury the timeline of the attack and what had been the fatal blow.

The killer of Officer French looked like he'd been using a manual, ticking off each stage. There were marks of restraint on French's wrists, suggesting his hands had been tied behind his back with rope that had been removed after death. While in a kneeling position, the skin on his back had been scored and peeled back using a serrated knife, probably a hunting or gardening implement. The redness and inflammation on the skin surrounding the knife marks indicated the man had been alive when the first cuts were made as the body sent blood to the wound area to try to clot the bleeding. She pointed this out to the officers present, one clapped his hand over his mouth and stumbled out. The older one was pale but impassive, more used to seeing the worst of humanity.

'It looks as if once the ribs were exposed, the killer moved onto them.'

'At what point did he die?' asked the man, the question anyone would want to know.

'I think he was likely unconscious at this point from the pain, shock and fear. I'm afraid from looking at the ribs, he might have been alive as they were broken.'

The killer had pulled the ribs away from the spine one by one giving the man's back the look of a turkey carcass. By this time, the victim was probably dead from loss of blood which would have been a blessed release. From inside the chest cavity, both lungs had been removed and left at the scene of the crime. They were sitting in a container to the far side of the room, Erin decided to treat them as if they were still in the body – she'd deal with the weighing and observation alongside the organs that were at least still where they were supposed to be.

Erin spoke her conclusions into a recording as Jenny put the camera down and plugged in the saw.

'You ever seen *Game of Thrones*?' she asked Erin.

Erin lifted her head. 'No, but Ethan loves it. Why d'ya ask?'

'There's this character called Beric Cerwyn who's killed by his adversary through a rite called Blood Eagle.'

'And?'

'Well, I mean, it's depicted differently on TV given it's fantasy land, but I'd say the injuries look a lot like these.'

Erin looked up at the police officer whose gaze remained impassive. 'Do you know the reference?'

' 'Fraid not, ma'am.'

—

Back in her office, Erin googled 'Blood Eagle' and read the first half dozen hits. One website was dedicated to questioning whether the practice was anatomically possible and Erin was forced to conclude it was, given what she'd seen from the autopsy. Shit.

'Jenny,' she shouted at her assistant. 'Don't pass on to anyone what you've told me today.'

Jenny came in holding a sheet of paper looking affronted. 'I never discuss my work with anyone. Not even my boyfriend. It's those officers you want to speak to about keeping things quiet. The PD is a hotbed of gossip and that one who puked is going to be the first to blab.'

Erin swung round. 'I'm sorry. I'm sure you don't talk about your work.' She paused. 'You're dating? You kept that one quiet?'

Jenny smirked, trying to hide her contentment. 'Early days. I don't want to ruin it by telling him what I do all day.'

'Fair enough. Look, I think you might be on to something with the *Game of Thrones* reference. I need to talk to Carla though because I think she might be able to help.'

'You might want to discuss this with her, too.' Jenny held out the paper to her. 'I've been checking the emails and this came in.'

Erin looked at the sheet Jenny had given her. 'I don't believe it.'

The DNA that Dominic had provided was a match for Fionnuala. Lucie Tandy was the baby's mother.

Chapter 25

Carla stood in the midst of the wreckage of her belongings and felt visceral fury. A neighbour had spotted the front door to the house open and had called the police. It hadn't taken them long to discover that while her neighbour Nicole's flat remained locked, Carla's own door was ajar and beyond it a trail of destruction. Having someone come into your home is a violation, but to leave it in this state of disarray was devastating. The cushion covers of her coral-coloured sofa were slashed with the white stuffing visible underneath. The ridiculous thing was this was a rented, furnished flat – very little belonged to Carla with the exception of her clothes, laptop and papers, so the damage was to someone else's property. Thank God she had her laptop on her as they'd surely have taken that.

Erin called just as she was wondering whether she should get a hotel room for the night. Carla briefly told her what had happened and Erin promised to come over as soon as she could because she had something she needed to discuss. Erin also told her that Lucie was Fionnuala's mother, a revelation that left Carla flummoxed.

'Don't worry about that one,' Erin told her. 'Because he's next of kin, I need to ring Dominic Tandy myself. I'll also ring Detective Perez to tell her the news. She gives the appearance of giving a shit more than Baros about the baby.'

Baros and Perez were surveying the flat with incurious eyes. Carla supposed compared to a murder investigation this was small fry, but surely there was a possibility it was all connected.

'I can't see anything that's missing. Even my jewellery is still here.'

'I'm pretty sure they weren't looking for anything,' said Baros, casting his gaze around the room. 'Take it from someone who has seen a lot of crime scenes over the years. Some drawers are open, for example, others haven't been touched. That's not what you do in a methodical search.'

'Perhaps they were disturbed,' said Carla. 'They had to abandon the job before they'd finished?'

'Nope.' Baros put a stick of gum in his mouth. 'Look at that set of drawers over there.' He pointed at a pine dresser beneath the window. 'They've pulled the second and fourth drawer open but not the other two. I've opened them and they've not been touched. So the question is why would someone break into your apartment and leave it like this just for the fun of it.'

'How come you two have turned up?' asked Carla.

'We heard it called in on the radio,' said Perez. 'Given you've been assisting in the investigation into Rika's death, we thought we'd take a look.'

'I feel I've only touched the tip of what might have been going on with Rika. The thing is, I'm also helping with a missing student named Lucie Tandy.'

Carla could feel both eyes on her. 'And?' asked Baros.

'I've just learnt that the baby found abandoned in Shining Cliff Wood is Lucie's child so we're talking about conception around September last year. This coincides with the start of term in Jericho. I think Lucie could have been another victim of hazing activities.'

'You mean the same perpetrator as Rika?'

Carla shook her head trying to concentrate. 'No, but I think it's the same issue. Initiations, rites, controlling behaviours – both girls might be victims of sex crimes, for example.'

'What about the father's DNA?' asked Perez. 'If they've managed to match it to Lucie then they must be able to extract the father's profile.'

'They've matched Baby F to Lucie through the DNA of her brother. They've nothing to compare it to in order to identify the father. The whole case has been low priority as the baby died preterm and there's no evidence of a crime. Meanwhile there's no clue as to Lucie's whereabouts alive or dead which leaves us with little to go on. Erin's put in a request for an advanced genetic analysis but unless you intend to sample every male student and those of the teaching staff too, it doesn't lead us anywhere.'

'It's not low priority any longer if there's a connection to Rika's death. How about I demand to speak to the principal about what they know about the activities of these societies?'

'Look,' Carla ran her fingers through her hair, thinking of Billie and her new job. 'We have to move carefully on this. Fraternity and sorority societies, hazing, initiations. They're all part of Jericho culture. You'll get nowhere trying to prise it open like a can of worms. Far better to concentrate on the two women who we feel may have been victims of this culture. We might be able to target individuals if not the societies themselves.'

Baros made a face. 'I paid a visit to the Owl Club yesterday afternoon. It was a complete waste of time. They're rehearsing for an open-air production of *A*

Midsummer Night's Dream and it was difficult to get anyone to concentrate on my questions.'

'Did you get anywhere at all?' asked Carla.

'I discovered the library has copies of old production programmes but they've no idea about membership lists. I have to say the set-up didn't feel particularly secretive. I suspect Rika just wanted to try her hand at acting.'

'Then maybe you want to go through those programmes and track down each student from 1999 and see what they have to say. If they're the person we encountered on Saturday night, then you're looking for someone still living near Jericho,' said Carla. 'I'd help if I could but I feel I'm being pulled in all directions trying to help find Lucie and what happened to Baby F.'

'I'm struggling for resources as focus has moved away from Rika to the death of Jeb French. Although I'm still in charge, I think any conclusions about Jeb's corruption will mean the chief will want this solved quickly. From now on, Rika is only important in terms of finding the killer of French.'

'Do you think the killer is the man who we tried to catch at the dig?'

Baros met her eyes. 'I'm sure of it. French possibly recognised the beaker and tried to blackmail whoever was the owner. We've trawled through French's résumé from the days before he joined the force and he spent time working as a waiter at functions at Jericho College. The Norsemen have that type of thing?'

Carla thought of rumours of roast swan on the menu. 'I'm pretty sure of it.'

Baros scowled. 'This case could already be solved by now if he'd been an honest cop.'

'Then we were lucky, Jack and me. I saw what he did to Officer French.'

Perez was studying Carla's flat. 'It may be you were lucky today, too. Someone's got wind of the questions you're asking and they don't like it.'

Chapter 26

Carla started on her flat clean-up until, on the verge of tears, she rang Dominic asking if he would help her lift some of the furniture that had been moved. He must be brooding on the news Erin had given him about Lucie's baby and would need a distraction. To her dismay, the person she'd really wanted to call was Jack but the thought of Anna's cool judgement if she came to hear about it made her hesitate. Jack's assertion that things weren't going well between him and his wife didn't preclude the possibility that they still exchanged confidences. Dominic was young and fit and she guessed he'd be willing to help. She had thought about asking Baros and Perez to help but they'd seemed anxious to leave, their attention focused on Frederika Brown. Dominic not only came, but brought Patricia who carried in sandwiches and a flask of coffee. She took one look at the mess and said, 'It's not so terrible.'

'But they've shredded my home,' fumed Carla.

'They've made it look worse than it is. Apart from the slashes on your sofa, the rest can be fixed and even they can be covered.'

The three of them worked through the afternoon, straightening, sweeping, trashing and scrubbing until the flat was at least liveable. Carla dashed off an email to her landlord, an academic currently residing in Auckland, and attached pictures of the damage. She felt guilty at describing it as a 'random attack' but unless anyone proved otherwise, she needed to show her landlord she was a responsible tenant.

At four, Patricia dashed back to her house for some old quilts to throw over the sofas and Carla took the opportunity to speak to Dominic who had already been told the news of Lucie's pregnancy. He wasn't as outraged as Carla had expected and she suspected that he thought in Jericho, with its secrets and aura of mystery, anything was possible.

'It gives us a partial answer why Lucie disappeared but it doesn't tell me whether she's alive or dead. If anything, I'm more confused than before because Lucie isn't the type of person to abandon a child by a dumpster.'

'I know.' It reminded Carla that there was a tragedy here that far exceeded breaking into her flat and rifling through her belongings. 'Have you told your parents what happened?'

'I thought that I'd wait until I returned home. I'm resolved to stay here until I find Lucie, and Patricia's said I can stay as long as I want at her home. What I don't understand is how Lucie kept the pregnancy hidden. None of her dormmates noticed it I'm sure. Did Anika say anything?'

'I'm pretty sure she didn't know either, but I can ask her again because I think she's hiding something. Lucie was tall and athletic and although I'm no expert on pregnancy, women do carry their babies differently. It may be that the pregnancy was easy to hide.'

'Someone must have surely known.'

Carla flopped down on the sofa, fiddling with the gash in the armrest. 'We need to keep at it. While the death of the baby was the catalyst for her disappearance it may be that she's alive feeling under threat from the father of her child. My next step is to find out what act of protest she undertook to join SEEC. It would have been early in the term which might fit the timeline.'

'You will keep me informed?'

'Of course I will.' Carla hesitated. 'Look, there's something I need to tell you. When Lucie's baby was found, it was covered in a swan's wing.'

'What?' Dominic looked appalled.

'There's actually a precedent to the practice from an archaeological perspective which Lucie might have known about. Did she ever mention it to you?'

Dominic shook his head. 'Never, but Lucie is well read. She could easily have studied the case. You think it's important?'

Carla shrugged, feeling overwhelmed. 'I don't know.'

They were interrupted by Patricia's return who was followed up the stairs by Erin, her red spiral hair damp from a recent shower. Her eyes fixed on the sofa. 'We're still missing the weapon that was used to kill Jeb French. Has anyone looked at those slash marks to see if it's the same knife?'

'I'm not sure. Patricia — and the police — are of the opinion a lot of the mess here was for show.'

'I'm no expert,' warned Patricia. 'Just my point of view. It's a nasty shock meant to frighten you.'

Erin was kneeling next to the sofa. 'I don't think it's the same weapon. It was a serrated blade used to kill Jeb French while this looks like it's been ripped with a pair of scissors.'

She helped Patricia cover the slice marks with the quilts after which the four of them stood awkwardly in Carla's sitting room. Whatever Erin had to tell her, she wasn't prepared to speak with Dominic and Patricia present. Dominic was inclined to linger, wanting to gain more information about Lucie's baby, questions which Erin was unwilling to answer.

'I've asked for more tests to identify the father but unless he's on a DNA database somewhere, it won't help much.'

'Why Shining Cliff Wood?' he asked. 'Maybe I should focus on that.'

Erin shrugged, her eyes on Carla until Patricia dragged Dominic away, Carla promising to call once she'd spoken to Anika again. Alone with Carla, Erin got to the point. 'I've just completed the autopsy of Jeb French and I feel for you finding him like that. Did anything strike you about the manner of his death when you first saw him?'

'To be honest one glance was enough. He was leaning forward and his back was just this awful, mangled mess. What made me feel sick was that there was this stuff beside his body. Did his killer rip his heart out or something?'

'OK, well, look. I won't show you the autopsy photos as they're bad but I'll take you through the killing of our victim step by step. Jenny's got an idea about something and she's nobody's fool. However, she told me her theory and then I looked it up and I have a horrible feeling I'm now retrofitting my results to fit the possible cause of death. I know better than anyone the power of suggestion so I want you to listen without any preconceptions.'

Carla put her fright and distress to one side. Even the thought of engaging her brain on something other than a stranger ransacking her flat made her feel better. 'Go on, I'm intrigued.'

'I thought you would be. OK, so what I think happened was that the victim let the killer into his apartment. Baros has already told me there was no sign of a break-in and he'd possibly made a date with the killer because he'd kept hold of the beaker that was found in the ground. While French was in the sitting room he was overpowered, possibly with a gun. There's absolutely no evidence of any defensive wounds given what subsequently happened, but his hands were tied behind his back. French probably thought at this point he'd be shot in the back of the head which would have been infinitely preferable to what actually happened to him.'

'I can believe that,' said Carla. 'I saw the state of his injuries.'

'Once overpowered, our victim was turned onto his front and, while still alive, an incision was made into his back and the skin peeled away.'

Carla could feel the nausea rushing over her as the scene came back to mind.

'Sorry – even for me it's a gruesome thought – but I do think he would have become unconscious quickly and he certainly died during the next act. Each rib was pulled back from the thoracic spine and his lungs were removed. That's the mass you saw next to his body.'

'Oh my God.' Carla's mind was whirling. Where had she heard of something similar? Erin had been picking her words and as the image coalesced in her mind, she remembered what image was coming to her. 'The ribs coming out of the spine would have looked like bird's wings.'

Erin took a breath. 'Exactly.'

'Not swans though. It's like a Blood Eagle killing, supposedly undertaken by the Norse. Christ. What a terrible act and all based on thin air. There's only scant the practice ever actually happening and abso- archaeological proof.'

ked on the net once Jenny mentioned it. I think TV has given the whole idea a new currency. actual evidence is there?'

here are references to the killing in skaldic poetry but nought it could either be a mistranslation of an earlier t or literary invention. There's also what might be a piction of the practice on image stones found in Sweden ut the modern view is that it was a Christian myth to fit the traditional view that the pre-Christian pagan Norse were not only bloodthirsty but involved in some kind of ritualistic torture as revenge.'

'You thinking what I'm thinking?' asked Erin.

Carla was beginning to join the dots from the past few weeks. Jack's comments about Billie's investigations into the society and the journalist's subsequent job offer was beginning to have more sinister overtones.

'I am. Don't listen to me denigrating the lack of archaeological evidence. It's my specialism so I'm going to say that. The issue is that it's entered modern currency and if you want to depict the Norse, or Vikings as they're popularly called, in a certain manner, it's a terrifying way of showing an act of brutality. This killing is down to the Norsemen, I'm sure of it. They pick and choose their rituals – beaker burials aren't particularly Scandinavian but someone liked the idea of placing the drinking vessel in with Rika. A selective reimagining of history.'

'But this is nothing I've seen before. Whoever's done this hasn't struck before in Jericho, I promise you.'

'I'm not surprised. The method of killing is going to take police direct to the society's door. It could well be a rogue element responsible for the killing who's taken the code of the society to its extreme. Have you told Baros yet?'

'I wanted to run it past you first. There was a police officer present at the autopsy so it's being fed into the investigation.'

'I think you need to talk to him as soon as possible. It's going to narrow down his pool of suspects for the killing of his cousin considerably if it's the same killer of the police officer. He could have a killer identified within days.'

'I think that's a bit naïve, Carla. We're the ones who know the ways of Jericho College not Baros. You think he'll be able to prise open the secrets of the Norsemen?'

Carla recalled the look in the detective's eyes when he'd surveyed the laid out bones of Rika in the mortuary.

'I don't think Baros is someone to be underestimated.'

'Well, he'll have to be quick. Do you know that there's soon to be a Norsemen dinner taking place at the Edgar Franklin building?'

'Edgar Franklin? But according to Lucie Tandy's flatmates, that's where she liked to go to study. Jesus, I wasn't going mad thinking her disappearance might have sinister overtones.'

'Lucie? I thought we were looking at the death of Rika Brown and Jeb French here.'

'Maybe it's all connected,' said Carla, her mind whirling. 'How did you find out about the dinner?'

'I tried to book one of the rooms for leaving drinks for a colleague but they told me the place is closed Friday as the Norsemen like to hire the whole building for their events. They can certainly afford to do so.'

'Do you know how many are expected? I mean are we talking about fifty plus or a gathering of eight.'

Erin shrugged. 'They were hardly going to tell me that. From what I understand, the big event is at the start of term where new members are initiated. I assume this is one of their more regular gatherings although I have heard...' Erin paused.

'What is it?'

'Well, there's some weird Viking thing going on with multiples of three. Apparently membership of the society is always kept at a number that's divisible by three so when a member dies, they're keen to replace him as quickly as possible.'

'Multiples of three? What the hell has that got to do with Norse mythology? I thought nine was the number that had significance. There are nine worlds in Norse mythology, Odin hung for nine nights and so on.'

'Don't shoot the messenger. I'm just passing on what I heard. You're the one that said they make these things up for their own ends.'

'Hmm. I think three might have some significance too. Odin was dead for three days, for example. OK, so we can expect a multiple of three at dinner – let's hope it's not thirty.' Carla looked around her flat that had a dead feel to it. She was sure there was something missing but couldn't for the moment identify it, a sense of absence.

'Hey,' Erin clicked her fingers at her. 'If you're thinking what I'm thinking, don't. I can't come there with you – I've booked another venue for that evening. Do not, Carla, go anywhere near that building.'

Chapter 27

Carla had decided to watch the comings and goings of the Norsemen from a small opening between the brick building within which the event was being held and a huge hazelnut tree, its branches spiking into the air. Despite the sunshine, the courtyard had a closed, secretive feel to it. The ivy-clad walls of the building opposite darkened the vista and despite efforts to keep the creeper in check, tendrils tapped against the upper windows.

It had still been light when Carla had parked her car and she'd made herself look as inconspicuous as possible, carrying a library book as if she was returning the book to the Franklin building which was open all night during exam time. It wasn't an excuse she'd be able to use as she got closer to the dining room, or at least as close as she could get, but it would allow her to get into her hiding place until darkness.

The group were using one of the college's dining rooms, usually reserved for formal dinners. Carla had hated these at British universities and Jericho was no different. She had once thought they were perfect places to talk about latest developments in archaeological study and exciting new finds. Instead, she discovered faculty liked to talk about their cats or problems with the hired help, all of which she could have got with a ten-minute conversation with her mother.

She messaged Erin to say she was in her hiding place. The image of Jeb French as she had seen him refused to dissipate and Carla had little illusions of the adversary she faced. She would need Erin's help if she was spotted and trouble ensued. A group gathering should lessen some of the danger as the assailant on the dig and French's killer probably worked alone. Erin had wanted to bail out of her drinks early and come along but Carla refused. Although Erin had academic responsibilities at the college, she was inextricably connected with death and Carla didn't want anyone there linking her with either Rika Brown or Jeb French's killings. She was pretty sure now that French had been killed by a member of the Norsemen who he'd contacted after discovering the beaker. She just needed a look at the Norsemens' drinking vessels to make sure.

Once she was ensconced in her hiding place, Carla pulled back into the depths of the tree, smelling its resiny bark. She could hear a squirrel scurrying about in the branches, outraged that its source of food was being disturbed. She checked once more that her phone was on silent and sat down to wait.

Compared to the warm day, the arbour was deliciously cool. At first, there were just the comings and goings of catering staff. Two suited waiters, dressed as Jeb must once have been, followed by a woman delivering desserts with 'Sugar Rush' emblazoned on her van. A smell of roasting meat wafted out of one of the open windows, it smelt like pheasant or another game bird and Carla really hoped she wasn't smelling swan. Carla took a sip of her water and continued to watch.

Finally, in a black suit and bow tie, the first of the Norsemen arrived. He was a small, squat man with a face that as a teenager had been scarred by acne. Carla had seen him around campus but couldn't immediately place him. In her notebook she wrote a short description. The next two arrived together, one whistling as he crossed the quadrangle towards the room. His companion, Carla recognised as Rafe Westphal, Jack's friend, who was straightening his tie as he climbed the stairs. Neither paid her any attention as a door opened and they entered the building.

A group of four walked towards the door in high spirits, clearly well-oiled from some pre-dinner drinking. She noticed that each attendee was carrying a large leather bag. Some had slung it over their shoulder, Rafe had his grasped in his hand. She would have to try to find a way to get Jack to reveal what was in his bag. That made seven in total and Carla wondered if the dinner would stick to the preferred number of nine or be forced to go to a multiple of three. As she was mulling it over, Jack hurried towards the steps, looking distracted as he typed something into his mobile. *Probably texting Anna*, thought Carla sourly.

The final guest came as no surprise to Carla. Franklin was the only one to arrive by car, his driver pulling up in front of the steps as Franklin hopped out. He was the only one to look around him, checking to see if anyone was observing his entrance. Night was beginning to fall and the evening shadows gave the building a sinister, closed look. At the top of the stairs, Franklin looked round again and Carla wondered if he could feel someone watching him. His driver, instead of heading off, pulled into a space with a 'No Parking' sign affixed to the fence and pulled out a newspaper. Shit, that was bad news. Carla's plan, once they were all at dinner, was to get inside the building and see if any beakers or goblets were being used for the gathering.

She waited for ten minutes but Franklin's driver had clearly settled in for the evening. Moving forwards was impossible but she might be able to squeeze around the tree to emerge at whatever lay behind her. She straightened up and used the tree's bark to guide her round its girth. At the back, she met a large rhododendron bush in full bloom. This was more of an obstacle than the tree but Carla persevered through the flowers until she was propelled out onto a small ivy-covered passageway at the side of the building and she could hear the clatter of cutlery and pans. Whatever rite was being practised it clearly wasn't to be conducted in silence.

She could see a side door at the end of the building, propped open with a fire hydrant. Outside, one of the kitchen staff was smoking while scrolling on his phone. Carla decided to brazen it out. She knew the reputation of Jericho. If you weren't part of its culture, you were unlikely to challenge someone who looked like they belonged there.

'Good evening.'

The man jumped. 'Oh, good evening.'

'What's on the menu tonight?' asked Carla, keeping her voice casual.

'Confit of duck.' He moved past her to let her into the corridor, clearly thinking it was her intended destination. Offering up a prayer of thanks to the gods – Norse or otherwise – she slipped into the cool corridor and made her way down to the centre. She passed unnoticed by the busy kitchen door and walked into the central lobby. All was hushed except for the room at the back where muted laughter could be heard. This must be where the dinner was taking place. Carla debated what to do next. She couldn't go into the room, they were doing nothing underhand and who was to say the drinking cups were used throughout the meal. They might be reserved for a toast or another ceremonial purpose. What she needed to do was get into the room after the dinner was finished and speak to one of the staff clearing up, which meant more hanging around.

There was a wide staircase next to the dining room door which she crept up. She'd never been to this part of the building before but knew the rooms were available to grad students for private study. This may be where Lucie liked to hang out when she wanted to work uninterrupted. While she was trying to prove a link between the beaker in Rika's grave and the Norsemen, she had to keep in mind that Lucie might too be a victim.

Carla opened the first door she came to, feeling foolish with the library book still in her hand. She'd decided she would sit out the dinner and wait until the last of the nine Norsemen had left. From the window she could see that she was over the entrance to the building. There was a light over the porch with a sensor that had come on at dusk. It would give her enough light to count them all out after which she'd examine the room they'd left. This room was sparsely furnished but the table lamp had a carved marble base and a bowl of fresh flowers had been placed on the mahogany table. Carla stationed herself by the window in a chair that was too comfy for her tired body, still exhausted after clearing up her flat. Listening to the chatter and laughter below, she felt her eyelids begin to droop as the night outside got darker and darker.

Time slipped by as she dozed, barely conscious of what was going on beneath her until she jerked awake at a sound from inside the room. She turned in the chair and saw a shadow over by the door.

'Sorry, I was just—'

The shape took a step forward leaving Carla rooted to her chair. Nothing had prepared her for the absolute terror that this apparition could induce. He was naked except for a robe made of a rough woollen cloth tied at the neck with a rope. Beneath the robe Carla could see a triangle of hair on the man's chest leading to his groin where his penis sat limp. On his head was an iron mask, the flat metal nose and winged eye sockets obscuring his features.

'What?!'

The figure came out of the shadows and sprang up on her as she desperately tried to comprehend the monster that was bearing down on her. She grabbed at the only object within her reach, a heavy ceramic lampstand. It was impossible to lift as the man's hands came to her throat and she instead threw it to the floor, sickened to realise it made only a muted thump as it hit the thickly carpeted floor. She staggered back against the window, grabbed a bronze statue that rested on a small pedestal and hurled it at the glass. She heard it smash onto the gravel below and a car door open. They'll never get to me in time, she thought as she felt the tip of a knife at her back.

Chapter 28

Carla revived to the sickening reek of expensive cologne which she was sure wasn't emanating from her attacker. The smell made her choke, as if the man's fingers were still at her neck, but when she raised her hands to her throat, she felt her skin hot and red to the touch.

'I'm going... sick.'

'Hold on, I'll get a bowl.'

Carla tried to open her eyes but that made the nausea worse, so she lay on her side, trying to regulate her breathing to save herself from the mounting panic threatening to engulf her.

'Someone... tried to kill me,' she croaked. 'My throat... agony. Strangle.' She couldn't form a complete sentence. 'Where's... bowl?'

She heard the metallic ring of an object placed in front of her. 'It's an ice bucket but it'll serve the purpose.'

Carla tried to make out the owner of the familiar voice. 'Jack?' she asked.

'Not Jack. Franklin.'

She heard his footsteps recede as she vomited into the bowl which made her feel slightly better. She could hear laughter outside, coming through the gap in the window where the glass had once been.

'Your driver... heard the glass?'

'Yes, but Chad was already on alert. He spotted you going in and said you never came out.'

'Saw me. How?'

'There's not much that Chad misses, I'm afraid. He's army trained. Part driver, part bodyguard, part PA. The army is very good at preparing people for all situations, less good at looking after them when they leave the service. Chad said you were hiding in the bushes and then went in through the side door.'

Carla shook her head. 'Never saw him.'

'You're an amateur, Carla, that's why. The question is whether to call an ambulance. It'll create a fuss I'm afraid but the attack might have damaged your vocal cords or neck ligaments. Do you want me to make the call?'

'I... I, no.' Carla didn't like hospitals since Dan's death three years earlier and she didn't want her name out there as the person snooping around the Norsemen dinner.

'Well, all right. I can get you checked out by my physician who's discreet but we need to get you out of here first. Chad, who knows about these things, has told me that if you can get to your feet, you should be safe to be guided to the car.'

'I'm not sure I can do that.'

'Do you want to try to sit?' She felt his hands under her. As she sat up, she began to retch again and he placed the bowl under her. 'Don't mind me.'

After she'd emptied her stomach into the bowl, Carla felt well enough to open her eyes. Franklin was crouching down beside her, his eyes wary. His blonde hair was clipped close to his head as if from a recent cut and set against his pale skin, he looked every inch a Norseman. His aftershave which probably cost a fortune was still cloying but she saw he'd taken off his dinner jacket and was wiping his neck with a handkerchief, removing some of the smell.

'What the hell are you doing here, Carla? Idle curiosity?'

'Of course not.'

'It's not about that missing student, is it? You surely don't think the Norsemen have anything to do with that.'

'Not about Lucie, at least I don't think so. It's something else.'

'Then what?'

'I'm not sure if I can trust you. I mean you are dining here tonight, aren't you?'

'What if I am? It's only a drinking society, a little old-fashioned maybe, a little theatrical for my taste, but it's harmless enough.'

'A man came in wearing a robe and mask. A helmet. He must be one of you.'

'What kind of robe?' Franklin frowned and stood, looking towards the door.

'Wool and tied at the neck. He was naked underneath.'

Franklin swore. 'I need to get you out of here. Can you lean against me and try to stand?'

Carla hated having to rely on him for support. He had none of Jack's solidity but felt remote from her even as she pushed into him to get up. He let her go at her own pace, holding her arm as she stood, feeling the room spin.

'Chad?'

A figure appeared in the doorway, short and muscular, the same man she'd seen at the SEEC demonstration.

'Her neck injuries need checking out. I'm taking her home to call the doc.'

'Can she walk?' Chad regarded her without expression.

'That's the next stage but I would think so.'

'Then I'll bring the car up to the front steps. Who else is still in the building?'

'They all adjourned to the bar but the catering staff will be around.'

'Leave them to me. Wait five minutes then come down.'

—

It was the first time Carla had seen Franklin's house. It was modern as she'd expected, but more modest in size, its oblong exterior clad in a cherry wood where long windows looked onto a small lawned garden that wouldn't have been out of place in the Cotswolds. Inside, a housekeeper gave Carla a curious look and brought them tea while Carla was seen by an elderly physician who said she should go for a CT scan. When Carla refused, he took it in his stride and gave her two of his 'horse pills' that he'd been prescribing for the last forty-five years.

'Brought me into the world so he'll be discreet,' said Franklin. 'This isn't Franklin money talking but old Jericho. There's a huge difference.'

'Maybe my attacker is old Jericho, too. It might explain why he's been able to elude the police investigation so far.'

'Investigation into what?' asked Franklin, nodding at Chad who'd entered the room. 'I want you to listen to this too.'

'Into the death of Frederika Brown whose body was found at a dig. You must have heard of it.'

Franklin gave an imperceptible nod.

'In her grave, was a beaker which a police officer recognised and, we believe, tried to blackmail the person who put it there. The person who killed Officer French used a method known as Blood Eagle which brings the investigation straight to the Norsemen.'

She was gabbling and Erin would kill her for revealing the details. Carla couldn't believe she'd told these two men – she'd have to blame it on her head injury if Erin found out.

'Blood Eagle? What the hell's that?' asked Franklin.

It was Chad who answered and Carla closed her eyes, glad not to have to explain.

Franklin frowned, shaking his head. 'I've told you already, Carla, the Norsemen is a benign college society. We don't re-enact ancient killing rites for our amusement.'

'I think somebody does. I think you've an obsessive in your midst as evidenced by tonight.'

'Are you part of the official investigation into this?' Franklin looked at Carla, scrutinising her reaction. 'No, I thought not. So tell me what happened this evening?'

'There was a man,' said Carla. 'Definitely male and he was wearing a woollen robe. He was naked underneath but not aroused sexually. Do you recognise the description of the robe?'

Franklin screwed up his face. 'In the early days of the Norsemen, there was some dressing up during the initiation event according to the society's history. A robe was worn by the person being inducted but I'd not heard they were naked underneath the cloak. In any case, the practice had died out by the 1960s. Tell me about the mask he wore?'

'It completely obscured his face and, although he sprang at me, I got a good look at what he was wearing. In the car over here, I was thinking about it and I'm pretty sure it is a modern reproduction of a helmet from the Vendel era.'

Franklin narrowed his eyes. 'That's a pretty specific description that doesn't mean anything to me. Can you describe it better?'

'There was metal covering the top of the head. If it's constructed like the original, it will have been made by hammering silver metal plates onto bronze matrices. The covering came down over his nose and the bottom half of his face was uncovered but impossible to identify. There were cut-outs for the eyes that were slightly winged.' Carla shivered as she recalled the sight of the man.

'I've never even heard of anyone wearing that type of thing. Do you think it's someone who maybe wants to join the Norsemen?'

Carla felt herself redden. 'Come on, I was attacked while nine of you were having dinner in the room below. It's got to have been one of your group. Who left the table long enough to attack me?'

'Everyone probably. We don't sit around the table all evening. After the main dinner, it gets a little looser. There's a smoking break before dessert and people were coming and going to use the bathroom. I don't see why anyone would wish to attack you though. Your presence might have been unwelcome but it's hardly the first time someone has tried to listen in on our dinner.'

'It isn't?'

'Of course not. I'm aware that we cast a bit of allure over the college and people try their luck.'

'What about when Chad found me – did he see anything?'

Chad stirred. 'You were alone in the room, ma'am, lying on the floor. If your attacker tried to strangle you, you probably blacked out after breaking the window. I saw no one coming down the stairs and I searched all the other rooms upstairs.'

'So, he must have gone down another staircase to rejoin the dinner below.'

'Getting dressed beforehand,' scoffed Franklin. 'You understand how improbable it sounds.'

'You think I tried to strangle myself?'

'Of course not. I can see you were clearly attacked by someone but I think you're blowing the innocent activities of the Norsemen out of proportion.'

'OK, so tell me something. What do you carry in the black bag you all took to the dinner?'

'Nothing of import.'

'Not ceramic beakers engraved or embossed with an unusual pattern?'

Franklin froze. 'Is that what was found in the grave?'

'Yes and I saw it with my own eyes but only as it emerged from the ground. I'd recognise another copy, I'm sure. So, I'm asking you, what does the beaker mean to you and please don't say nothing. I know groups like yours cover for each other.'

Franklin folded his arms. 'If you remember I didn't go to college here so I'm not natural Norsemen material. It likes to draw its membership from the college – either graduates or dons – because that way people have already been indoctrinated into what is and what isn't permissible.'

'I get the picture.' God knows what medication Franklin's physician had given her but Carla was beginning to feel better although her voice was still raspy.

'So during the initiation ceremony into the society, it's made very clear that any spilling of the Norsemen's secrets or rites will result in "punishment of a Nordic scale".'

'What does that mean?' asked Carla.

'It doesn't specify. If you're like me, you go along with it for fun. Think of the freemasons or Knights of St Columba. To show you how little I take it seriously, I'm happy to share with you what the rite consists of. When the new member has been sworn in, we take a drink of fortified wine from a beaker similar to the one you describe. They're used for ceremonial purposes only. Every member has a beaker and when that member dies, it's broken and their name is scored through on a ledger.'

Carla tried to keep focused but she was suddenly conscious of Franklin's charm. It was if it were just the two of them in the room while he convinced her of the essential benign nature of the rite. 'So, where are the beakers kept?'

'At the homes of the individual. We bring ours along for initiation ceremonies or for dinners like this evening. That's what was in the black bag.'

'Christ. And Officer French would have seen the beakers while working as a waiter at one of your dinners. Is each beaker identical?'

'There's a small number on the underside and those numbers match names in a ledger. It's to stop fakes from being made.'

'How easy is it to match the beaker number to the person?'

'For a non-member impossible, I'd say. The ledger has never been computerised and I've only seen it when their name is scored in front of us when we break the beaker on someone's death.'

'But surely there's a beaker missing and has been since it was placed in the ground back in 1999.'

'I find that hard to believe. Whenever there's a ceremony, the people who are present bring along their beakers to drink from. Unless it's a person who's not been to either an initiation or commemoration ceremony since the 1990s then it's not connected to us.'

'Can I see yours?'

'I don't see why not.'

Franklin rose and Carla was left alone with his assistant. Chad was more affable than Carla had expected, perfectly willing to talk to her while Franklin was away.

'If you don't mind me saying, ma'am, you chose the wrong hiding place to watch everyone enter the college building. Believe me, everyone chooses a tree. You might as well have a big sign saying "I'm hiding here" hung on the branches.'

Stung, Carla bristled. 'There was nowhere else.'

'You shouldn't have been anywhere near the place to begin with. There are cameras, listening devices that could do the whole work for you and send all the intel to your mobile phone. If you really had to be there, you should have walked in like you owned the place and taken your laptop out upstairs. Once that lot get going they don't pay any attention to what's going on in the building. It's the sneaking about that gave you away.'

'How do you think my attacker realised I was there?'

'Did you encounter someone on the way in?'

'Just a boy who I assumed was a member of the kitchen staff smoking outside.'

'Probably him then. He may not have even been staff, just stationed out the side to watch for anyone coming and going.'

'Shit and you're sure you don't know who attacked me?'

'No, ma'am, but it wasn't me nor Mr Franklin. He looked shocked when I told him I'd found you and, if you don't mind me saying, a robe and nothing else on isn't really his thing. He looked like he wanted to punch someone. Of the other eight, I can't help.'

'Do you know them at all?'

'Can't tell you that, sorry.'

Franklin returned carrying a deep navy-coloured display box. He removed the lid and passed the base to Carla. Nestled inside was a brown ceramic beaker, ridged at the rim with a runic pattern embossed into the lower half.

She picked it up. 'This is what was found at the Wilmington farmstead, I'm absolutely sure of it. Do you know what the runes on the cup say?'

'"Man conquers the earth" according to the rite. Is that correct?'

'Possibly. I'm not an expert on runes. "Man conquers the earth"? Not exactly environmentally friendly, not to say misogynist. Can I take a photo of the beaker?' She saw Franklin hesitate. 'It's important. I need to show Detective Baros what is missing.'

'OK,' said Franklin.

'Make sure the number isn't showing,' said Chad. 'Nothing to identify Mr Franklin.'

Franklin glanced towards his employee. 'You think they might come after me? I've known all these men for years.'

'Just looking after your safety, boss.'

Carla snapped the image and put her phone away before she tipped the beaker upside down and looked at the number at the base. Ninety-eight.

'So you were the ninety-eighth member.'

'Apparently. The society has been going since the 1930s so it's hardly surprising.'

'What year did you join?'

'Late 2001 when I sold my first development. My father was a Jericho alumnus so that helped too, although it has become more democratic in recent years. Ancestry is no longer a guarantee of a place in the society.'

'Not very Norse,' murmured Carla.

'I'm sorry?'

'I was just thinking aloud. Ancestry mattered a lot in Viking culture with the family group providing protection and status. How have you become more democratic?'

'Existing members becoming less conservative for one. It's happening in a lot of university societies. The Skull and Bones at Yale in 2021 admitted no conservatives at all. Few descendants of alumni get in there any more.'

Carla weighed the beaker in her hand, resisting the temptation to hurl it against the wall. Boys and their games. 'Frederika Brown went missing in September 1999. We're definitely looking for a number before yours which narrows things down a little. You sure that no one has reported a beaker missing?'

'Not that I'm aware. The chair has access to all the records and I'm going to ensure there's a full but discreet study made of our ledger.'

'Who's the current chair?'

Franklin's blue eyes met hers. 'That would be me.'

Chapter 29

Franklin might have professed a laissez-faire attitude towards the Norsemen but that didn't extend to letting Carla join him in scrutinising its list of members, nor was he willing to discuss any scenarios how a beaker – to be used only at initiation and commemoration rites – might end up buried in the ground at the Wilmington farm. While initially Carla hadn't thought there was a ritual element to the beaker placed in the grave, she was having second thoughts now it was clear the cup was missing, which potentially put suspicion on a fellow archaeologist. The problem was that she was pretty sure that the only person from her department she'd seen enter the building that evening was Jack Caron, but only nine people had been present so perhaps there were others in the past she didn't know about.

If she didn't have access to the membership of the Norsemen, what she could look at was who had been working in the department in 1999. Although Franklin had given Chad instructions to drop her off at her flat, once they were in the car, she asked him to take her to the library.

He sighed. 'If I say no, you'll just make your way over there anyway, won't you?'

' 'Fraid so.'

'Those pills the doc gave you are super strong. You'll come crashing down in a few hours and I recommend you're safely in your bed by then.'

'All the more reason to take me to the library now.' She hadn't mentioned the attack on her flat to either Franklin or Chad and wasn't exactly thrilled about spending the night alone there. But her fear was linked to the man she'd encountered this evening who'd been intent on killing her, she was sure, rather than the damage to her home that had demonstrated an element of showmanship rather than threat.

Chad nodded and turned left towards the college. At the library after she'd climbed out of the Range Rover, he wound down his window.

'If your throat starts to swell or you find it difficult to swallow, call 911. Want me to wait to give you a lift home afterwards?'

'I'll call a cab as I don't know how long I'll be.'

Carla's bravery nearly failed her as she approached the library. Its modern construction, set against the older nineteenth-century buildings, seemed incongruous in the darkness – Carla felt like an alien entering a brightly lit spaceship as the shadows closed in around her. She swallowed, her throat still raw, and gathered all the courage she could muster. Aware it was approaching one a.m. she was surprised to see about twenty or so students at desks cramming hard. She approached the front desk and asked to see the 1999 yearbook for her department.

'All-righty.' It was the same young man who had been drawing hexafoils on her previous visit. He pulled a leatherbound book from a shelf – there was no need to have requested it as it was open access and she took it to a free table. Inside, there was an intro from the then head of department who Carla didn't recognise. One name she did know was that of her old boss Albert Kantz as a young man smiling into the camera. The other professors were no longer in the department, which left only Albert. Christ, his wife Viv had been the target of a serial killer the previous year, surely he couldn't be involved in this death.

Deciding to visit Albert when she could find a free moment, Carla was ready to bail out of the library to get some much-needed sleep. However, watching a student study in the corner at the entrance to the map room made Carla remember her promise to Sabine to follow the trail of Ashley Jones that had led her to the Wilmington place. The student looked outraged when Carla opened the door, probably hoping to have the place to herself in the middle of the night. When Carla went onto the computer and searched for the map that Ashley had discovered, she saw she would need to order it to be brought out of storage. She hovered over the request button wondering if it was a fruitless exercise. In the end, she went ahead wondering why she hadn't seen Ashley around recently. While there was a temporary lull in work on the dig, there was still plenty for a research student to be getting on with. She wondered what Ashley was up to.

—

It was nearly three in the morning by the time Carla crawled into bed. Dawn was only a few hours away and she desperately needed to sleep off the night's trauma. She'd messaged Erin to say that she'd run into some bother but she was safely back home which failed to convey the fear and pain of the night. Chad had been right about her coming down off the pills because, as soon as she hit the pillow, she was asleep, her dreams punctuated by images of the masked man.

She was woken by her alarm which she'd set for ten. Thank God it was a Saturday so no more sarcastic comments from the department's secretary. While she was having breakfast, she formulated a plan of action. If she rang Albert to suggest a visit, she ran the risk of him refusing and that would be that. On the other hand, given that she was responsible for exposing Viv's deception in a car accident and subsequent cover-up, then she most definitely didn't want to run into Albert's wife.

In the end, she wrote a short letter to Albert, explaining that she'd like to see him on a matter that had nothing to do with his leave of absence, which she would post through his letterbox. She got into her warm car and drove the short distance to Albert's house, arriving in time to see Viv driving off with her son in the front seat. She was preoccupied with speaking to the boy and didn't turn her head in Carla's direction. Carla parked up and rang the doorbell to the Kantz house. Albert answered wearing sweatpants, a marked contrast to his usual attire of a tweed jacket and tie. He looked older than Carla remembered, although the spring air had given him a ruddier complexion.

'I wasn't sure if you were going to be in so I wrote a letter. When I saw Viv drive off, I thought I'd chance knocking on the door.'

'Did Viv see you?'

'She was chatting to your son.'

'It's probably just as well. Come on in, Carla.'

The house was messier than the previous time Carla had visited, but had a more homely feel. Whatever Viv and Albert were doing with their time off their respective jobs, it wasn't home improvements. Albert made a pot of coffee and took the tray to the kitchen island where he and Carla perched on stools.

'I hear Sabine is doing a good job of running the department in my absence.'

'She's a good administrator,' said Carla neutrally. The department had a worldwide reputation for excellence but Sabine wasn't in Albert's league. However, she was heartily sick of the fact that Albert's rise to prominence in Jericho was a result of familial influence and his membership of the Norsemen. Perhaps it was just as well the department was being led by an outsider.

Albert's eyes were on the letter she was holding. 'So what did you want to speak to me about?'

'You've heard about the discovery of the body up at the Wilmington farmstead?'

'Of course. I hope Ashley is OK. It must have been a shock to discover that the site you were excavating had a more sinister modern history.'

Was it a good thing that Albert's first thought was of his doctoral student? Carla wasn't sure because most people would have thought of the victim first.

'Did you know Frederika Brown?'

Albert shook his head. 'I knew about her disappearance obviously, and I was actually interviewed by the police at the time.'

Carla went cold. 'You were interviewed? I didn't know that.'

'Surely it's on file.'

'It isn't, but the files are scant with many of the statements missing.'

Albert's eyes met Carla's probably thinking the same thing. It might have been the work of Viv to protect her husband. But she wasn't stupid. She couldn't filch just his statement from the file as it would draw attention to her action so it would make sense to remove all the others. It might, however, also be the tentacles of the Norsemen reaching in to the archives of Jericho PD. Either way, it didn't look good for Albert.

Albert ran his hands across his face. 'If my interview isn't on file, what's brought you here?'

'We think there's a connection between Rika's death and the rites of the Norsemen.'

'This is nothing new. It was a possible link to the Norsemen that I was questioned about and all I could tell the detective who spoke to me is that I remembered virtually nothing of the evening.'

Carla put her hands to her throat. 'Did you have some kind of accident?'

Albert sighed. 'I don't think there's any harm in me telling you about it given I made a statement for the record. It was the evening of my initiation rite that Frederika Brown disappeared but that wasn't the reason I was interviewed. The ceremony took place in the Edgar Franklin building.'

'I know it.'

'It was afterwards that I was at the spot where Rika supposedly disappeared. As part of my initiation into the Norsemen, I underwent a trial by water. Except I didn't know at the time it was going to happen. We drank a lot and then I was driven by two members of the society to the river. There, my head was held underwater for a minute three times.'

'Jesus, if you were drunk, you could have died. Do they still perform the rite?'

'Of course not. There's no way it'd be allowed these days. You know, the society is much friendlier and more welcoming than in my day.'

Right, thought Carla thinking of the previous night. Also, no women, few people of colour, if any. Still a closed shop.

'So what happened?'

'After the third dunking I passed out and ended up in hospital. I was found by some passers-by who called paramedics. I've barely any memory of the evening at all but, of course, it looked a little suspicious when the spot where I nearly drowned was the exact place where Frederika was last seen by a couple heading away from the river.'

'We've never been able to trace that pair.'

'We?' asked Albert. 'What's your role in all of this?'

'I was there the night Rika's body was found. Let's just say I'm invested in the outcome. So you can't recall seeing Rika that evening?'

'I have no memory of anything beyond the initiation rite inside the Edgar Franklin building.'

'Would subsequent members have undergone something similar?'

'Similar but not the same thing. I got the impression both my hospitalisation and Frederika's disappearance put the wind up the chair at the time. I don't think there were any more trips to the river.'

'Albert,' Carla leant forward. 'It's imperative that I know which two members took you to the river that evening.'

Albert looked despairing. 'I don't know. I was asked the same thing and I didn't know then either. The passage of years hasn't improved my memory but in my darker moments, I'm sure one of them was wearing some kind of robe.'

'Christ.'

'What's the matter?'

Carla hesitated, wondering if she could trust him enough to tell him of her experience at the hands of her attacker. On balance, she thought she couldn't and she shook her head. 'Just the theatricality of everything. You didn't attend the meeting the other night?' she asked him.

'I was invited but decided to stay away. I'm on a leave of absence as you know and until it's decided whether I can return, I'm staying off campus.'

'Tell me, Albert, you're old Jericho and I haven't been able to ask anyone else. What's going on? Sometimes I think this town is just a reflection of other rich university towns where tradition, wealth and power allow certain people to thrive and others not.'

Albert stayed quiet, his eyes on her. 'Go on.'

'Other times I think there's something darker going on. The hexafoils from when Max Hazen was killing, the cover-ups in the police department, the smoothing over of student deaths in the media. Is there, I don't know, a powerful group that I don't know about?'

Albert stayed quiet, playing with his coffee cup. 'It's not Orwellian, if that's where your imagination is taking you, Carla. It's just…'

'What?'

'It's just Jericho likes to take care of its own.'

Carla could have screamed. 'But Frederika Brown *was* Jericho. Her family were local.'

'That's not what I meant. Be careful, please. Despite everything, I like you and have a high regard for your intellect.'

It didn't sound like a threat but Albert had proved himself to be a man of changeable moods. She tried a final gambit. 'Can you think of a scenario where Rika Brown might have happened upon your initiation and tried to intervene?'

'I don't know.' Albert stood. 'She would have been a lone woman faced with at least one masked man and me unconscious. Most would move on and report it from a place of safety wouldn't you say?'

Most, but not all. And possibly not Rika.

Chapter 30

Erin was surprised to see Carla push open the doors of the medical facility as she returned from lunch with a salad wrap. Her son Ethan had, to her horror, told her that her 'ass was looking big'. She was as much outraged at the casual sexism as the comment on her body shape but it was naturally the latter that she was focusing on until she could sit Ethan down for a chat. She took Carla into her office and listened in horror to the account of her attack, Carla removing her scarf to show Erin the wounds.

'I knew I should have left those goddamned drinks the other side of college. They were a complete bore anyway and it sounds like you needed a bodyguard. He surely wouldn't have attacked us both.'

'I certainly wouldn't have fallen asleep with you there. That's what makes me mad, the fact I put myself at risk by dozing off.'

'The guy was naked under his robe? It must have been terrifying. I wonder why he didn't get off on the whole thing. Limp penis did you say?'

Carla looked furious. 'I'll be grateful for that small mercy and ignore how like you to focus on the anatomical. If I hadn't broken that window, it might have been me on your mortuary table.'

'But why? All right, you were having a nose around the society, but you wouldn't have been the first. Jeb

French knew the identity of Rika's killer whereas you're not exactly getting anywhere, are you? Unless the killer thinks you have something important and couldn't find it in your apartment.'

'I'm getting too close to the society and the outcome. If I have anything to do with it, it will be to blow its secrets open. Because I also think Lucie saw something while studying in that upstairs room. She might have been attacked by the same man as me.'

Erin saw that Carla hadn't fully recognised how lucky she'd been at the weekend to have Franklin and his bodyguard nearby. It only took on average seven seconds of pressure on the neck to render a person unconscious after which anything was possible, even a death as gory as Jeb French's. Carla's casual demeanour meant she was becoming used to Jericho ways and Erin didn't think that was a good thing. Apart from the bruising around her neck, Carla also had shadows under her eyes which suggested she was becoming obsessed with events both from 1999 and now.

'Let's say Rika did intervene or was even just a passive observer spotted by one of Albert's attackers – yes let's call them that. If they did assault her, I can't see any obvious evidence of it on her skeleton.'

'But what about water immersion?' asked Carla. 'I read about an enhanced forensic test that proved a Neolithic fisherman died by drowning. They test for—'

'Diatoms. Thank you Carla, credit me for knowing my job. When I heard that Rika was last seen approaching the river, it was one of the tests I requested.'

'And?'

'I haven't had the results yet. Labs are overworked and underfunded like everyone.'

Carla groaned.

'Let me go through my inbox while you're here. Jenny's out at lunch too, but she might have spotted something this morning.'

Erin scrolled through her messages to see what results were back but neither the further DNA tests that she'd asked to be carried out on Fionnuala had been returned nor was there an email from a private lab in Maine that Erin had used to send a bone sample from Rika's skeleton for analysis.

'There's nothing back yet but, tell me, if we do confirm Rika died from drowning, does that definitely narrow down the suspects to Albert's two attackers?'

'If I was Baros, I'd definitely want to talk to them both, wouldn't you?'

'Maybe you could tell him now.' Erin drew down a slat of her venetian blind and they watched as Baros climbed out of his car. 'This is beginning to feel like déjà vu.'

Carla rose and grabbed the cotton scarf and wound it back around her neck. 'You know what, I think I'm going to leave before he gets here. There are too many maybes and I'm not sure I'm ready to share what I know with Baros yet. He's also nobody's fool and he'll spot my neck immediately.'

'You want me to stay schtum?' asked Erin. 'Why the secrecy?'

'Because the reality is Franklin is more likely to discover the identity of Rika's killer and I want him left to dig into the society without Baros trying to doorstep him. Can you imagine those two getting along?'

'Good point. I'll call if I get any news.'

Carla knew her way out of the place, and she was gone in an instant, probably hiding in the restroom until Baros entered Erin's office.

'Any news?' His face was set, clearly not in the mood for any pleasantries.

'None whatsoever. I'm waiting for lab results and I've just checked to see if they've come through.'

Baros pulled out a chair and sat down, an indication that all was not right in the world, as he usually liked to remain standing in his interactions with her.

'Seen the Prof. recently?' In a town full of academics, Erin knew who he was referring to.

'Of course. Carla is a friend of mine.'

'She given you any more useful insights from the dig?'

At least Erin could answer this honestly. 'I'm afraid not. What have you been looking at?'

'I think I'm about to become eligible for membership of the National Genealogy Society.'

'I'm sorry?'

'In the absence of anything that might remotely be considered evidence, which incidentally is why I keep hassling you, Doc, Perez and I have been constructing a Wilmington family tree.'

'Ahhh. You don't think that it was just a random piece of wasteland chosen to bury Rika?'

'I don't. It's a lonely place and there are plenty of fields along the road to the homestead that would have made carrying Rika to her grave easier. No, whoever drove there knew the Wilmington farmstead would be deserted and the soil loamy enough to be an easy dig.'

'How are you getting on?'

'It's hopeless. There are cousins, second cousins, third cousins even, that possibly camped at the homestead over the years. Mary Wilmington, the last full-time resident of the farm left a vague will, probably because she didn't know who to leave the place to. Rather than squabble about their inheritance, which is what most families would have done, they came up with an arrangement that everyone owned it.'

'So Step Wilmington has no more of a claim on the place than, say, a nephew?'

'Exactly, although he's become the unofficial guardian of the place since the summer camps stopped. If I could find a way of narrowing the cousins down, that would help as I think that's the generation I'm looking at. I'm concentrating on those who live in or around Jericho but that's not helping much.'

Erin was silent. She didn't much like Baros but she could see his determination, a quality she admired.

'What is it?' he demanded.

'I can't say – I've been sworn to secrecy – but, if I were you, I'd try to work out if any of your Wilmingtons have connections to Jericho College or, more specifically, the Norsemen.'

'Carla,' breathed Baros. 'What the fuck has she found out?'

'Nothing concrete which is why she hasn't told you yet. My advice would be to look at Jericho College as much as you can but don't alienate Carla. She's an insider even if she doesn't realise it yet. She might get there before you.'

After work, Erin had to pick Ethan up from an Escape Room that had opened up near Shining Cliff Wood. God knows how they'd got planning permission for it. It was an old log cabin that over the years had been a video store, bike shop and finally a coffee place. Now it had been repurposed with a neon green 'Escape' light shining above the entrance. Ethan was waiting for her outside. His two friends had been picked up by their mom and were headed out of town for a dinner at their grandfather's. As Erin pulled up, he had ketchup down his top which solved the problem what to make him for dinner.

'Enjoy your dog?' she asked him.

'It was all right.'

Erin turned the car in the parking lot and indicated to pull out onto the road. The evening was warm and fragrant with tree blossom. She wound down the window ignoring the face Ethan pulled.

'Do you mind if we make a quick stop? I haven't been up this way for a while.'

'Sure.' He was sucking on a straw of a huge cup of soda, intent on extracting every last drop.

After a few minutes, Erin pulled into a rest stop at the side of the road near one of the entrances to Shining Cliff Wood. 'Do you want to come for a walk?' she asked her son.

'Nope.'

Erin pulled off her seatbelt. 'I'll be ten minutes.'

She walked over to the dumpster near where Fionnuala was found. She'd not seen the baby in situ. She'd been teaching at the college and had only picked up the autopsy the following morning as part of the rota, but she now felt a sense of responsibility towards Fionnuala despite the other deaths competing for her attention. It was easy to find the spot where the baby had lain. There were three withering bunches of flowers propped up against the tree under which she'd been found at least three yards from the dumpster. Erin frowned. The refuse can felt separate to the scene, simply a marker nearest to the spot where the baby had been placed. Erin cursed the casualness of the police description which had naturally focused on the site as a place where people discarded their trash. If you removed the presence of the dumpster, it was in fact the most accessible part of the wood from the road which suggested another possibility: that Fionnuala wasn't a dumpster baby but a child placed in the woods by someone who only had a moment to lay the child close to a tree. This suggested a completely different implication in relation to Fionnuala's fate. Someone, somewhere, might be grieving the loss of their child.

Chapter 31

'I saw someone hanging around across the road this morning. By the time I opened my window to holler at him, he'd gone. This is making me very uneasy after what happened to your apartment.'

Nicole had grabbed Carla on the communal stairs in their building as she was leaving for the college. In her spiky heels, she towered over Carla, a leather bag over her shoulder reminding her of the meeting of the Norsemen. Carla recoiled, trying to ignore the stab of fear in her chest. She'd left a note in Nicole's mailbox telling her about the break-in, but this was the first time they'd had a chance to talk.

'Can you describe him to me? Did you get a look at his face?'

'He had some kind of hoodie on so I couldn't see him properly, but he had jogging pants on too like he was out for a run. Except he wasn't jogging but standing under the tree watching the building. Do you think he was your burglar?'

'I don't know. If you see him again perhaps you could take a photo, but be careful.'

'Maybe I should call the cops or we could chip in for some private security?'

Carla made a face. 'I don't think my salary from the college will go very far towards that. What about getting a surveillance camera?'

Nicole's face brightened. 'Good idea, let me make some calls and I'll get a security firm to give us a quote.'

Carla nodded, although if the man was intent on accosting her, the campus was probably a better bet. Despite college security, there were plenty of dark corners and lonely passageways that were impossible not to traverse. She wasn't sure that a camera above her front door would keep her safe from her foe.

She was already jittery by the time she reached her office and was dismayed to see Jack standing outside her door, waiting for her. He had on a brown linen suit that crumpled even in the mild warmth of the day but that didn't detract from his attractiveness. God, first Franklin, now Jack. What was the matter with her?

'Carla, we need to have a chat.'

'Sure, come on in.' Carla opened her office that was stuffy after being closed up even for a day. She pulled up the blind and opened a window. 'What's wrong?'

'There are rumours going round about the body we found at the dig. Some of it sounds far-fetched – what's all this about a beaker burial?'

Carla turned round slowly. 'Where are you hearing the rumours?'

'What do you mean? You know what Jericho gossip is like. There's chat about what's going on in relation to the Wilmington site.'

'Chat amongst the Norsemen?' asked Carla now furious. 'Is it your precious society that's sent you here?'

'Now listen, I don't know why you've got a bee in your bonnet about the society but we're just a—'

'I know, just a drinking club, just a group of friends, just a casual network. Well one of you is responsible for this.' Carla pulled down the neck of her T-shirt. 'See what one of your so-called pals did to me on Friday night?'

Jack recoiled. 'Who did that to you?'

'I don't know, because he was wearing a mask. Someone play-acting at being a proper Viking – does that ring any bells?'

Jack moved across to her. 'When did this happen?'

Sickened, Carla shook off his arm wondering, shockingly, if it was Jack who attacked her. Although they'd become close the previous year, they'd not become lovers and she had no knowledge of what he looked like naked. His even temper and academic rigour could mask some deeper passion hidden from view.

'I need to ask you, is there anyone in your group who takes the Norse imagery too far? Someone who considers it more than the gentleman's club you like to believe it is?'

Jack was frowning, trying hard to please. 'It's difficult to say. When I was asked to join, I was happy to have been singled out given its status in the college. Now I think back on it, Anna probably pulled a few strings for me which, although embarrassing from my point of view, isn't exactly unknown here.'

'How are things going between you two?' Carla inwardly cursed, unable to help herself.

'Not well.' Jack looked down at his rumpled suit. 'I stayed in a hotel last night.'

'Didn't go out for a jog, did you?' she asked tartly, thinking of the man Nicole spotted.

'Jogging's not really my style. Look, if you think some serious shit is going to go down with the Norsemen, will you tell me? Things are going badly enough for me as it is without me losing my professional reputation as well. I can find other ways of dining well if I must.'

'Well, talking of dining well...' said Carla. 'Maybe you can answer me this. Have you heard anything about the society dining on roast swan?'

'Roast swan, are you serious?'

But Carla was now thinking furiously. She'd sat on her ruined sofa looking at the coffee table and had tried to identify what had changed about her flat. She remembered placing the pebble with the swan on her table but it wasn't there now. The table had been left intact, just a couple of novels rifled through. So where was the stone?

The missing gift continued to gnaw away at Carla as she taught her final class of the year for the Master's programme. The students were preparing to spend the summer on digs around the world. Two were heading off to Turkey to investigate a newly discovered Greek settlement while another, whose family hailed from Australia, had found a spot on a dig investigating an early nineteenth-century customs house in New South Wales. Carla was keen to give equal weight to the three students who would be picking up the dig at the Wilmington farmstead. Not every student could afford to go to far-flung places – pay was often low or non-existent – and these homestayers would be doing Ashley Jones a huge favour reclaiming its site from its more gruesome past.

Carla's class was interrupted by a knock on the door and Sabine's secretary stood in the doorway. 'Urgent message,' she said, handing Carla a piece of paper.

Your phone's off. Call me. Franklin.

Carla frowned. Of course, her phone was off, she wasn't going to be answering calls while she was teaching. The secretary was looking at her, awaiting a reply. 'I'll call him back once class is over.'

In fact, Carla finished the session ten minutes early, her students keen to leave the stuffy classroom and go out into the hazy sunshine. Franklin hadn't left Carla his number and she only had the contact details for his office. Franklin was busy according to his PA, but had instructed to be interrupted if Carla called, who had to quell the feeling of being absurdly flattered by this news.

'Carla,' Franklin sounded distracted and there was a hubbub of noise in the background. 'I'm in a meeting that I can't leave as it involves a major investor. However, I've got an idea whose beaker might have been discovered on the Wilmington farmstead. I've been trawling through the ledger and there's a member who resigned from the society in the early 2000s.'

Carla experienced a pang of disappointment. Perhaps her attacker and the placer of the beaker were two different people. 'Resigned? You think that significant?'

'I do. The person concerned joined in 1996 which is before Frederika Brown. In July 2000, he left Jericho and joined a private school in Idaho where he was originally from to teach history. He never attended another meeting of the Norsemen and, in 2001, sent in a letter of resignation.'

'You're allowed to do that?'

Franklin laughed down the phone. 'Of course. It's not Hotel California. You can check out any time.'

'This isn't funny, Franklin.'

The silence at the other end of the phone suggested Franklin didn't like being contradicted.

'Do you know if he's still teaching at the school?' said Carla in a more mollifying tone.

'He's now the head and has made a name for the school as a progressive institution. Sends a boy or two to Jericho College each year.'

Carla frowned. 'You've spoken to him?'

'Very briefly. He's got something he wants to get off his chest and he's flying down here this evening. He wanted me to come to him which I can't do, and I'm not sending you there on your own to speak to him.'

'Surely that's my decision to make.'

'I knew you'd say that which is why I bought Warren a plane ticket. He's in the sky now.'

'We don't think he's Jeb's killer, do we? I mean he might have flown here and back and—'

'No, Carla, but it's entirely possible he knows who did. He clammed up when I asked him about the night in 1999 and he says he wants to talk in person. The problem is that while we're in Jericho, and so is the killer, I'm not taking any chances. Chad is picking him up from the airport and will take him straight to my office.'

'Your office?'

Franklin paused. 'Chad believes someone tried to break into my house the other evening. Chad will make sure Warren doesn't come to any harm but I want you to hear what he has to say. I need this recorded and with a witness; the case might be resolved this evening.'

'What about Detective Baros?' asked Carla. 'Shouldn't he be there to hear what your man has to say?'

'Not yet. I'm not sure what his reaction will be given his personal interest in the case.'

'Look, I spoke to Albert the other day and I've discovered that he was rendered unconscious as part of an initiation rite the night of Rika's disappearance.'

Franklin drew a breath. 'You think Albert Kantz might be involved too?'

'If his story is true, he was taken to the river by two fellow Norsemen. That's all he can remember.'

'You think my guy could be one of the men?'

'It sounds like the dates fit.'

—

When Dominic knocked on Carla's flat door an hour after Franklin's call, she cursed the interruption. The plight of Lucie and her baby was fighting against the knowledge that at least one case could be solved and Rika Brown was about to get justice. Dominic, however, disregarded her mood, his face in high colour.

'I think I've got a lead.'

'Come in, but I'm just about go out.'

Dominic's face fell. 'Sorry, shall I come back in the morning?'

Carla looked at her watch. Franklin wasn't a man to be kept waiting and she most definitely didn't want to miss out on the story of the man he was bringing over from Idaho.

'Come in and tell me what you've discovered.'

They went into Carla's small kitchen as she brewed the kettle for tea. Dominic got out his phone and found an image to show Carla. It showed a shaggy white dog, little more than a puppy, gurning into the camera.

'I put a note out on some social media sites asking if anyone had any photos from Shining Cliff Wood around the time the baby was born. I was hoping it would lead me to the person who found the baby.'

'But this is a dog,' said Carla, feeling foolish.

'Look in the background.'

Carla squinted at the phone where two indistinct figures were walking arm in arm. The image was so blurred Carla could only just make out they were both women, one wearing a red coat, the other a yellow mac along the lines Lucie was thought to be wearing.

'You think this is Lucie?'

'I do. It was taken on April third which is the day she went missing.'

Carla looked again, wondering how much to trust Dominic's judgement given how desperate he was to find his sister. The yellow mac was important but what did that tell them about Fionnuala's birth?

'You think she had the baby there in the woods? They just look like they're out for a stroll.'

'I don't know, maybe.' Dominic was also scrutinising the image.

'I mean, it's possible the baby was born elsewhere and Lucie returned to the site of her last walk to leave the baby, but there's still so many unanswered questions. For example, the presence of the swan's wing.'

'Is it important?' Dominic's frustration was clear in his voice. 'The swan doesn't lead me to Lucie, does it?'

'I suppose not. By the way, when you were helping me clean up the flat, did you see a large pebble with a swan painted on it?'

Dominic shook his head. 'I left all the smaller things to you and Patricia to sort. I was helping with the furniture.'

'I haven't seen it since the break-in and I'm wondering where it went.' Carla studied the photo again. 'If this is Lucie, do you know who her friend is in the photo?'

'It's not her three dormmates, is it? What about Anika?'

Carla shook her head. 'It doesn't look like Anika. She's not tall enough. So, there's a friend we're missing? That's a good thing, isn't it? I mean, it suggests Lucie might be alive somewhere.'

'It's a lead. Look, if I send you the photo, would you ask around for me? I'm worried if I put it on the socials, it might scare Lucie.'

'Sure. Send it to my work email.' She was desperate for him to leave and after a few more pleasantries he disappeared, bounding down the stairway two at a time.

Chapter 32

The gate to Franklin's driveway swung open at Carla's approach. There was no need for Carla to announce her presence, Franklin must have got hold of her licence plate number and was expecting her arrival. She parked alongside an SUV with darkened windows, not Franklin's usual vehicle. This one looked imposing with a sense of heightened security. Franklin hadn't been taking any chances bringing his guest from the airport.

The front door opened and the same housekeeper, her manner still inquisitive, welcomed her into the house. She took in Carla's post-teaching look – messy hair and tired make-up – and steered her to the downstairs bathroom. Carla was glad of the time to put some lipstick on and run a brush through her hair. She checked the bloom of bruises on her neck and pulled her collar higher to hide them from view.

The housekeeper steered Carla towards a room towards the back of the house where Franklin, Chad and a small, slim man stood. He wasn't what Carla had been expecting and certainly wasn't the man who'd attacked her. The people behind Rika's death had assumed monstrous proportions in Carla's mind and this man, with his tired face and reserved manner, looked like someone's father. He turned and smiled, although the corner of his eye twitched as he held out his hand.

'Warren Wilmington.'

Carla froze. *Wilmington*. Why hadn't she thought that someone with the surname Wilmington might be a member of the Norsemen? Part of the problem was that Step had presented himself very much as 'town' rather than 'gown'. There was some antipathy between townspeople and members of the college. It had been true in Oxford and was clearly the case in Jericho, and yet there was always some crossover. A Wilmington had been a member of the Norsemen and if Carla had been able to see a membership list, she too would have spotted the name. Well, Franklin could wipe that smug look off his face. He was hardly Sherlock Holmes spotting the name Warren Wilmington.

Carla settled on the sofa. The academic in her told her to wait, listen to his story which would be the mirror of Albert's, but without the abrupt ending where he had woken up in hospital. While he had been rendered unconscious, a monstrous act had been taking place and she would hear the story of that. She also wanted to cut to the end of the story and start with the name of the companion who had been at the river on 26 September 1999.

Franklin was ignoring her which was infuriating but Chad appeared to understand her impatience. 'I heard some of Mr Wilmington's account over here in the car. I said he'd better leave the main bit until we were all together.'

Warren pulled out a handkerchief from his pocket and wiped his face. 'Sorry, I've been waiting for a long time to tell my story and it can't help spilling out now.'

'That's OK. I don't know if Franklin has explained who I am but I'm an archaeologist who was on site when the body of Frederika Brown was discovered.'

Warren looked shocked at her forthright manner. Christ, she wasn't Erin who was blunt to a fault. Carla looked across at Franklin and tried again. 'I've been trying to discover what has being going on recently and the trail led me to the Norsemen.'

Warren nodded and took a sip of the fizzy drink in front of him. 'I've heard that a lot of the fraternities have changed now. I certainly hope so because it was a dog-eat-dog world when I was a member. I've completely banned secret societies in my school and I give all the graduates the same talk before they leave. Be kind, moderate your drinking and don't follow the pack. If I'd respected those rules myself, I wouldn't have been in torment for the last twenty-five years.'

Carla noticed he was addressing her and wondered if it was because Franklin was still a member of the group he was about to blow apart. 'I've spoken to my boss Albert Kantz so I have a pretty good account of the initiation ceremony and the drinking afterwards, as much as he can recall. What he doesn't remember is who took him down to the river.'

'I've heard Albert isn't doing so well at the moment which is a shame. He had a lot of promise as a younger man. Well, in answer to your question, we drew lots and I won or lost depending on your point of view along with another member. We took an unresisting Albert down to the river. You were supposed to dunk his head under water three times as a kind of cleansing ritual. You know, shrugging off the preoccupations of your previous life and entering a new state.'

Carla resisted the temptation to roll her eyes. 'There's nothing to suggest the Vikings had such a rite. It's a made-up ritual designed to frighten people into conformity.'

Warren flushed. 'You're preaching to the converted.'

Carla couldn't contain her impatience any longer. 'If that's the case, why all this "me and another member". You're still protecting each other. I need to know the name of the person who was with you that night. Who accompanied you to the river?'

Warren looked at Franklin, the chains of the Norsemen code still running deep. 'He was a post-doctoral student like me. His name was Rafe Westphal.'

'Rafe,' Carla swallowed. 'Isn't he too young to have been a member back in the late Nineties?'

'He joined in January 1999 as a freshman. Rules were bent in return for a large legacy from his father who was also a member.'

'Did you know this?' demanded Carla, turning to Franklin. The identity of the man was not news to either him or Chad, Carla could see. Either Chad had lied to her when he said he'd asked for Warren to wait to tell the story, or the name had spilt out in the car from the airport. Whichever it was, Franklin showed no surprise at Rafe's name.

'I wasn't aware of how Rafe came to join the society. Why should I be? Perhaps we should listen to Warren's story as to what happened on that night back in '99.'

'As I told you, we drew lots and Rafe and I got picked for the cleansing. Albert was pretty drunk so we had to haul him into the car. I just wanted to get the whole thing—'

Warren stopped as Chad stood, his phone clamped to his ear. 'I gotta take this call, Mr Franklin.'

Franklin nodded. 'Carry on, Wilmington.'

'We dragged Albert to the river and found a spot next to the bridge at Seeker Street. It was a bit quieter there than downtown, although I realise now we should have gone further upstream to be completely out of sight.'

Carla realised that most of Warren's account would be accompanied by regrets which was probably his way of dealing with the trauma.

'We'd already dunked his head twice when we heard a scream from the bridge and a girl came hurtling at us, shouting at us to stop. My heart nearly stopped – I was desperate to get out of there, but Rafe kept shouting: "The third time is the one that counts, it has to be three times" and—' Warren stopped. 'And then he hit her. I can remember the look of shock on her face as she went down into the water. I—'

Chad returned looking tense. 'We've got a problem,' he said to Franklin. 'Did you tell anyone, Mr Wilmington, that you were coming down here?'

'I… I… of course not.'

'Did you tell Rafe?' asked Franklin. 'What's the matter Chad?'

'The security detail you had tracking Rafe tell me he's headed out of town and has purchased an airline ticket on his credit card.'

'How do you know that?' asked Carla. She could understand Franklin paying for someone to keep an eye on Rafe once he knew the identity of Rika's killer but knowledge of the airline ticket suggested something bordering on the illegal.

Franklin briefly glanced at her. 'Does it matter? He's leaving Jericho and I'd really like to know how he's aware we're on to him.'

Carla climbed to her feet aware Rika's killer was slipping away from them. 'Then you need to call Baros. Rafe can be stopped before he leaves the county but only by law enforcement.'

'You'll need to do that, Carla. It'll save needless explanations if he gets a call from you.'

Carla pulled out her phone and with shaking hands rang Baros's number.

'Yeah,' he said, back to his old greeting.

'Are you on duty?'

'Yeah, why what's up?'

'The man we think is responsible for Rika's death is heading out of town, possibly towards the airport. We think he's making a run for it. James Franklin has been looking through records of the Norsemen and has identified him as Rafe Westphal.'

'Shit, Jesus.' Carla heard a yowl of pain.

'Are you OK?'

'I've just spilt hot coffee on me. Perez, pass me a napkin. What's his full name and licence plate number?'

'I don't know but I'm going to pass you over to Chad, Franklin's assistant. He knows all the details.'

As Chad spoke to Baros, Franklin yanked Warren out of his seat. 'What the hell did you call him for? You're not even a Norseman any longer. Why tip him off?'

'I told you, I couldn't help myself. Once I knew I was coming here, I wanted to talk about that night and get the facts straight. Look, it was a mistake me coming here – I think I'll book a flight back this evening.'

'You won't.' Chad had cut the call. 'You're staying here. Rafe is currently refuelling at the gas station north of Jericho.'

Franklin already had his car keys in his hands. 'Want to see the culmination of your hard work, Carla?'

'I don't think you should go without me Mr Franklin,' said Chad grasping Warren's arm.

'I need you to take care of our star witness. It's all circumstantial without Warren's evidence. Stay here with him. We'll save explanations for later.'

Chapter 33

In the car, Franklin typed an address into his satnav and set off, his expression hard to read. It was a different Franklin than Carla had seen previously. When he'd spoken to members of SEEC, Carla had the impression that his 'man of action' had been all show for the protestors, as had the clearly capable Chad in the passenger seat. Now it was just the two of them headed towards a killer who'd shown no mercy to Jeb French and probably Rika too. Perhaps Franklin felt safe in the knowledge that Baros and Perez were also heading to the scene, hopefully with reinforcements.

'Do you have a tracker on his car?' asked Carla, holding tight to the strap above her window.

'It's better you don't know.'

'At what point did you realise it was Rafe?'

'In all honesty, I suspected Rafe before I spoke to Wilmington. When you were attacked at the dinner, although any of us could have slipped out, I definitely remember Rafe leaving the room and only getting back in time for the toast. He was my number one suspect so I asked Chad to do some digging into his background. This included credit card statements, and one purchase from 2015 was of particular interest. An item made by a company called Dexter Armory. They make reproduction fighting equipment including the Vendel helmet.'

'Jesus, Franklin, what the hell are you playing at? That's enough evidence against Rafe for—'

'For attacking you, yes, but not for the killing of Frederika Brown or Jeb French.'

They were overtaken by a car, its lights flashing. 'I think Detective Baros will be way ahead of us from now on. Chad is continuing to feed them information about the location of the car.' Franklin handed her his phone. 'You can read out the updates.'

'Heading east on Route 125. He'll soon meet the highway.'

'Definitely going to the airport.'

'What do you think he'll do when he hears the siren behind him?'

'He won't outrun a police vehicle but he's reckless. There's a possibility he might be armed despite not being able to carry it through airport security.'

'Where's the airline ticket for?'

Franklin made a face. 'Iceland.'

Carla turned in her seat. 'Iceland?!'

Franklin shrugged. 'Odd destination given it leaves you right out of options, it's not like fleeing to Central America where you can flit between countries. He might be trying to make his way to Greenland.'

'Greenland? Jesus. What is it with Rafe? We're not in the Viking era now.' Carla had heard stories about wild, inhospitable Greenland where the polished Rafe would surely stick out a mile.

An alert came up on Franklin's phone. 'The car's come to a stop in a town called Jacquesville. According to the map, we'll be there in ten minutes.'

Updates continued to stream through as the interminable seconds ticked by. Now the car they were chasing had come to a halt, Chad couldn't provide any more location information but urged Franklin and Carla to stay in the car. Finally, they came upon the sign to Jacquesville, population 3,480, and Carla surveyed the landscape.

'Over there,' she shouted as she spotted an empty squad car. Two uniformed officers were leaning into a green Mercedes, one rifling through the glove department, the other checking under the seats. They straightened when they saw Carla's companion.

'Mr Franklin,' one said respectfully.

'Do you know the direction the suspect was headed?'

'No one saw him take off. Detectives Baros and Perez are doing a circuit of the town now.'

Carla looked around. The main street consisted of a single strip of stores with a hinterland of houses spreading into the surrounding countryside. The name continued to nag at her. Jacquesville. She was sure she'd never visited the town before but she couldn't place the reference. In the distance, she saw Baros's car slowly approach.

'No sign.' He looked exhausted, his face badly shaven although his eyes were hidden behind mirrored glasses.

'Why did he pull over here?' asked Carla. 'It's a town, but small. There can't be that many hiding places.'

The uniformed officer made a tut of annoyance but Baros kept his eyes on her. 'Go on, Prof.'

'The name of this town means something to me. Jacquesville. What's it famous for?'

'It's famous for nothing,' shouted Perez from the seat next to Baros. 'Let's do a circle again, he'll be hiding out in a yard somewhere.'

Baros had got out of the car and shouted to a huddle of three women, who'd exited the grocery store and were staring at the vehicles with undisguised curiosity. 'Hey. What's Jacquesville famous for?'

The women shook their heads.

'Told ya,' said Perez.

A man had come out of a shop and was watching them, his arms folded. 'We're famous for a lie. A hoax.'

'Oh my God.' In a flash, Carla remembered. 'Jacquesville was the place where runic stones were found and a hypothesis formed that the Vikings had travelled outside Newfoundland to New England.'

'Hoax,' shouted the man.

'When was this?' asked Franklin.

'The 1970s if I remember correctly, but there's a group of people who still believe the stones to be genuine. Not archaeologists, but—'

'Rafe isn't an archaeologist. Where were the stones supposedly found?' Franklin asked the shopkeeper.

'In a field down by the river.'

'Get in the back of the car and direct us,' shouted Baros.

'I can't, I have to keep a delivery—' He took a look at Baros's face and nodded, pulling the door to and locking it. They made a strange convoy: Baros's vintage Mustang, the squad car and Franklin's Range Rover. This time there were no lights, just the steady roll of tyres over the asphalt. The town was eerily quiet although Carla could see faces at windows and half ajar doors watching them as they passed.

'What do you think he's doing down there?' asked Franklin.

'I suspect he knows the game is up. He was never going to Iceland or maybe this is Plan B.'

They turned off the main road and down a dirt track signposted to the river. In rainy season it'd be a nightmare to pass down but the dry weather had hardened the ruts on the road. In the distance, the river shimmered, wider than at Jericho. Carla shivered. The stretch of river at Suncook Park had been the location of the drowning of her former colleague while upstream Rika Brown had met her end. She dreaded what the river would next bring.

They juddered to a halt, forced to a standstill by the two cars in front.

'They've obviously seen something,' said Franklin. 'Stay in the vehicle.'

Carla saw the doors open of both police vehicles, Baros first out of the car with his gun out. 'Raise your hands in the air,' he shouted.

'What can they see?' wailed Carla. 'I need to take a look.'

'We stay here,' ordered Franklin. 'The windows are reinforced if shots are fired.'

Carla unbuckled her seatbelt and leant over Franklin to get a better view of the river. 'What's that?' she asked pointing to a shape in the water.

'You mean who. It looks like Rafe is in the river. If you open the dash, there should be binoculars in there.'

Carla found the glasses and trained them on the figure. 'Christ.' Rafe Westphal was naked, the water swirling up to his thighs causing him to list and stumble. To her horror, she saw that he was wearing the Vendel helmet, the sight as terrible in the distance as it had been the evening she was attacked.

She passed the binoculars to Franklin. The group of law enforcement all had their guns trained on Rafe. 'Why don't they shoot him in the leg or something? He won't be able to stay on his feet for long – the river will sweep him away.'

Franklin snorted. 'It's hard to be that accurate when you aim at a moving target. Those kind of shots are for the movies – once they fire, it'll be the end for Rafe. If I were in Baros's shoes, I'd want him alive to answer questions around Rika's death.'

'He's unarmed,' said Carla, unable to contain herself any longer. 'I want to see what's happening.'

'I told you to—'

Carla ignored Franklin, opening the door and stepping out onto the track. A draft of hot air hit her face, and she could smell the grassiness of the river reeds, a contrast to the electric tension crackling around her. Even the shop owner was standing by Baros's car, his gaze fixed on Rafe.

'Get out of the water,' she heard Baros roar at Rafe. 'Or I will come and get you.'

She moved a step forward, desperate not to draw attention to herself. She felt Franklin at her side, holding her arm. 'Leave it to the professionals, Carla.'

'Why?' she whispered, not sure who the question was directed at.

'I'm not sorry,' shouted Rafe at them. 'There is a force mightier than all of you. Power to the Norsemen.' He lurched, and Carla realised the weight of the helmet was fighting against his attempts to stay upright in the water. He took a step back, the water now to his waist and lost his footing.

'Shit,' said Carla.

She saw Baros move forward, ploughing into the water, and her last glimpse of Rafe Westphal was the metal of the helmet before that too sank into the water's depths.

Chapter 34

Rafe might have been a self-taught expert on all things Norse but he hadn't banked on the currents of the Alford River if he was hoping to be swept away to join the gods of Odin and Thor.

'Look over there.' The shop owner was pointing at a spot a hundred metres in the distance where they could see a shape hitting the reed bed.

'I'm on it.' Baros, soaking from his plunge into the water, ran down the riverbank followed by Perez while the two uniformed cops got into their car, bumping over the ground towards the stricken man.

'I don't think we should let Baros get to him first,' said Carla. They watched as the patrol car overtook the running detectives and reached Rafe, the taller of the two patrolmen hauling him out of the river.

'I'm calling an ambulance,' said Franklin tapping into his mobile phone as Carla watched Perez pull back Baros from the prone figure.

'Is he alive?' she shouted at the figures but received no reply.

—

Three hours later, Carla was making coffee for the group piled into her sitting room. Erin was fresh from the medical facility and had a scrubbed look, probably jumping in her car straight from the work shower. Baros and Perez were sitting next to her, squashed onto Carla's ripped sofa although Baros was perching on the edge, keen to get the explanations over with. Rafe was in hospital, under police guard, his condition uncertain. Franklin, the first to arrive, had taken the big armchair and looked unembarrassed that the others weren't enjoying the same comfort. Carla had grabbed the only stool from the galley kitchen and was perching on it, glad of the extra height.

Baros looked at his watch. 'I'm only giving you this time because I owe you, Prof., and my bosses aren't letting me anywhere near Rafe so I've currently got nowhere to go. Let's get on with it.'

Carla nodded. They'd soon enough be going their separate ways – Franklin back to his world of empire building, Baros and Perez to policing the crimes of Jericho aided by Erin's forensic autopsies. Rika deserved this long-delayed wake. 'In September 1999, Rika came to Jericho on a scholarship. She was a talented scholar and did what most freshmen do and made friends, went to parties, joined societies – the Owl Club in Rika's case. Within two weeks, she had disappeared and as the last sighting of her had been at the bridge, this led to the assumption that she had drowned.'

Baros, she saw, was pale, his eyes boring into hers. 'Which the family never believed.'

'Of course not. We know that Rika was in a grave on the Wilmington farm but we've been perplexed how she got there. I was convinced it was something to do with her group of friends from the poker night and initially thought it might be due to the activities of the Owl Club. However, Baros could find nothing untoward in relation to its activities and we now know that she died because of what she saw on that walk home.'

Franklin folded his arms. 'It makes a hard listen,' he warned Baros, who brushed the comment away with his hand.

'Rika left the poker game and should have been back home within ten minutes. The walk was straightforward although in the fall, there would have still been a lot of overhanging branches from the trees lining the river. It's no longer possible to discover the identity of the couple who saw Rika but given the time of year, there would have been students out on the streets.'

'Which is nothing new,' said Erin.

'Exactly. What we now know is that an initiation rite as called by the Norsemen, or hazing as it is known today, took place that night. Albert Kantz, the grad student initiated into the society, had his head submerged in the water as part of the rite. He passed out and remembered nothing from the evening except he had crossed the milestone and been accepted into the society.'

'Pathetic,' said Perez. 'Boys playing games.'

'Rika caught Rafe and Warren in the act and screamed at them to stop. She clambered down the path where she was hit by Rafe and stumbled into the river.' Carla stopped. 'That's as far as I'd got when we got the call that Rafe was fleeing to the airport.' She looked at Franklin. 'You need to take if from here.'

Franklin took his phone from his shirt pocket and laid it on the table. 'Perhaps it might be easier if you heard it from Wilmington himself. I got Chad to record what happened next.'

They watched as he fiddled with the recording, snippets of Warren Wilmington's voice filling Carla's flat until he found the place where Carla had left off.

'*I waded into the water but I was so drunk the girl kept slipping away from my grasp. I finally managed to drag her out but I realised she wasn't breathing.*' There was a pause before Warren's cracked voice continued. '*I pulled her under one of the weeping willows so that no one could see what we were doing and began CPR. I tried for about ten minutes until it was clear she'd gone.*'

'Ten minutes?' Baros was appalled. 'If they'd called an ambulance they might have revived her. There are cases of drowning victims who are revived up to ninety minutes after the accident.' He looked across at Erin who nodded her confirmation.

Franklin, who had stopped the tape at Baros's interruption, pressed the play button once more.

'*We then started to panic. I wanted to leave the girl there and call the cops anonymously but Rafe said that we might have left evidence at the scene and it was important to hide the body. He was so matter-of-fact it was unnerving and I was so addled that I agreed with his plan. I knew the Wilmington farm would be empty after the summer vacation so I suggested there. There's no way anyone would spot us once we were down by the old farmhouse.*'

'Do you believe this crap?' asked Baros.

Erin looked up. 'I'll be able to corroborate the story once bone analysis confirms death by drowning. It sounds like he was pressurised to find somewhere fast to bury Rika's body.'

'I personally think you're going too easy on Warren,' said Perez. 'He's no nice guy and will be arrested for being an accessory after the fact.'

Carla thought back to the white-faced man she's met earlier in the day. 'If it's any consolation he's lived a blemish-free life since the incident which isn't the case for Rafe. The killing appears to have been a catalyst for Rafe becoming more extreme in his embracement of Norse mythology. He must have been delighted when he drew the lot to give Albert his dunking in the Alford River.'

'Can we get back to Rika?' demanded Baros.

Franklin, who had clearly listened to the tape already had decided not to put Baros through the ordeal of listening to the mechanics of Rika's burial. 'They took Rika to the farm and buried her near the trees, an area that Step said was rarely visited. When they had finished digging the hole, while Rafe was looking away, Wilmington threw his beaker into her grave. It was a symbolic act of saying goodbye as he never again attended a meeting of the Norsemen. In 2001, he wrote stating he wished to resign.'

'Two weeks,' said Baros. 'She had two weeks of happiness before it was taken away from her, for what? A dunking in the river for some bullshit ceremony. Please tell me that the Norsemen have learnt something from this tragedy.'

'I wouldn't know,' said Franklin. 'I tendered my resignation yesterday evening. They responded to say they accepted my decision and that they'd be electing a new member in the coming weeks.'

Carla thought of Jack. Would he also resign? While married to Anna, she doubted that very much. Unlike Franklin, his place and standing at the college depended on him being part of the establishment.

'I know the chief is keen to brush the killing of Jeb French under the carpet,' said Perez. 'We think Jeb contacted Rafe when he discovered the cup. He had no way of knowing who it belonged to but he was hoping Rafe, with a reputation for protecting the interests of the Norsemen at all costs, would cough up some funds to line Jeb's pockets.'

'Jeb had no idea of the extent of Rafe's fanaticism,' said Carla. 'Do you think Rafe will confirm Warren Wilmington's account?'

'I don't think he'll be able to stop,' said Baros. 'He's a fanatic and they're usually the blabbers.'

'I just wish that I could find a connection between what happened to Rika and Lucie Tandy.' Carla said, staring at the empty table where the swan stone had once rested.

'It's probably just coincidence,' said Baros. 'You're conflating two cases. We're looking for Lucie especially as we now know she's the mother of Baby F. I still think her disappearance is voluntary. When she wants to be found, she will be.'

Carla thought of Dominic on his computer away at Patricia's house pleading for photos from visitors to Shining Cliff Wood. 'There's a family like yours trying to discover what happened to their child. I'm not letting go of this one.'

Baros sighed. 'Try to keep out of trouble if you can, Prof. It's not too much to ask, is it?'

–

After everyone had gone, she texted Jack and asked for a meeting away from college. Erin wanted to take her for a drink but there was unfinished business she needed to thrash out with Jack. They met at a small French restaurant he'd taken her to previously. It smelt of mussels and fried fish, a speciality of the place, and it was only when Carla started to eat that she realised how hungry she was.

'When you offered to keep watch with me at the Wilmington farmstead, did you actually care that an archaeological site was being disturbed or were you more concerned about maintaining the reputation of the Norsemen?'

To his credit, Jack didn't look affronted or adopt a fake outrage. It was a perfectly legitimate question and, feelings aside, Jack's answer would influence Carla's decision whether she could ever work with him again.

'I promise you, Carla, that I was as intrigued about the whole thing as you were and I wanted to discover what was going on. No one put it into my mind that I volunteer. The watch wasn't even my idea, if you remember.'

'But Rafe must have been desperate to know what was going on at the Wilmington dig. Did you mention it to him?'

'I don't think so, but if you remember there were notices all around college asking for volunteers to dig the site. He probably spotted the news there.'

Carla took a sip of wine. 'So why was he so angry that day I came into your office?'

'We were arguing about that journalist, Billie Copper, who was trying to contact me for information about the Norsemen. I told him to leave it to Franklin who had a plan.'

'Oh, I know all about that.'

'Look, I know you've got everything to despise me for but I'd never put you at risk or anyone else in the department. I didn't know the extent of Rafe's obsession with the Norsemen. It seems he was determined to join the society as soon as he arrived at Jericho but he's never had the influence to steer it in the way he wants, so he's got deeper and deeper into his own view of Norse mythology.'

'Hazing is illegal both in this state and at Jericho College. You had a responsibility to call it out when you heard about Billie's investigation.'

'She was talking about historic cases. I didn't know anything about what went on in the 1990s. No one coerced me into any weird initiation rite when I joined. I thought these things were firmly in the past.'

Carla shrugged. In the past, and yet Jack had proved surprisingly easy to lean on. A weakness in character maybe, but also a demonstration of the insidious power of these societies. The Norsemen. Urgh. Everything about the title was repulsive right down to its far-right connotations. A group of privileged white males acting out some half-baked fantasy of ancient initiation rites.

'Does Anna know about everything that's happened?' asked Carla.

'I've spoken to her a little about it. If I want to keep my job, and believe me I do, then I'll need all her influential friends to continue to advocate for me. It's how it works around here but it's not like the old days. For Anna, I'm becoming a bit of a liability.'

He must have caught sight of her face. 'I'm truly sorry, Carla. The whole thing has been the final straw for my marriage, and Anna and I have split up again. I suspect it might be for good this time.'

Despite herself, Carla's heart jumped at the thought Jack was single again. She turned away from him and looked around the restaurant. 'No wonder there's such a distance between town and gown. How Detective Baros must hate us with our secrets and disdain. It's him who kept Rika's flame alive all these years. And you're sure that you had no idea that Rafe had threatened me or raided my flat?'

'Of course not. Only…'

'Only what?'

'I'm not sure if it could have been Rafe who broke into your apartment. You describe a man in a hoodie and jogging bottoms watching your place and that doesn't sound like him at all.'

'And you've not heard of any connection at all to Lucie Tandy?'

'I've not heard of anything. I don't think you can lay the blame for her disappearance at the Norsemen.'

'Well, someone's been watching my place and a gift went missing from the flat the night it was burgled.'

'What gift?' Carla saw that he'd pushed away his food, his appetite gone.

'It was a present of a stone with a painting on it. In value terms it's inexpensive but I can't find it anywhere.'

Jack looked unhappy. 'Take care of yourself, Carla.'

She nodded. 'You could actually leave the society, you know.'

Jack nodded. 'I know,' he replied but Carla saw he made no firm promise.

Chapter 35

Erin was feeling left out of things. News of the chase and capture of Rafe Westphal was all over the college and the medical facility. She was ecstatic, of course, that Rika's killer had been found and even corrupt Jeb French would get his justice. But Erin couldn't shake off the feeling that she'd missed out on the action given it was she who Baros had opened up to at the beginning. She busied herself with the autopsy of a man dead from carbon monoxide poisoning, the result of a faulty gas heater at a trailer park. Not Deerbrook Terrace, this one was a small makeshift park with a reputation for addiction and criminality amongst its residents. Cause of death was straightforward to record but once she'd showered, Erin's thoughts turned to Leda and her quirky cabin that she'd visited with Carla. She pulled out Fionnuala's file, still depressingly brief, and began to read through her notes again. With nothing new jumping out at her, she circled the name of the person who'd first identified the swan's wing and made a call.

Doctor Mei agreed to visit Erin at the facility, professing a desperation to get away from the college and her exam paper marking. Half an hour later, she arrived wanting to talk about Carla.

'She's getting a reputation for herself. She wants to be careful.'

Erin bristled at the criticism of her friend. 'She helped catch a killer. Anyway, Carla will thrive wherever she is. Unlike us, she's not rooted in Jericho so she's the freedom to push the boundaries a little.'

Doctor Mei pursed her lips. Erin knew a little of the woman's story – she'd come to Jericho on a scholarship but her parents had returned to China after decades in Chicago and considerable pressure had been put on Mei to go with them. The doctor had refused and was currently estranged from her family according to college gossip. It was a shame she had little good to say about Carla who was a rebel in her own way.

'Remember I got you down here a few weeks back to look at some feathers and bones that needed identifying?'

'The mute swan.'

'Yes, exactly. I've been reading through the file again and I'm wondering if I drew as much on your expertise as I should have.'

Mei was flattered and softened. 'I told you everything I could. Mute swans are a non-native species introduced to North America in the late nineteenth century so they're sometimes referred to as invaders. They were brought into the country to populate lakes and ponds but, as often happens, it had a devastating effect on the local wildlife.'

'So, they're pretty easy to find around here. Are there any culling programmes to ensure they don't become invasive?'

Mei shook her head. 'All swans are protected and the Jericho wildlife code doesn't differentiate between indigenous and non-native species.'

'Damn. I'm trying to work out a way by which someone would procure a swan's wing. How many birds are we talking about in Jericho?'

Mei shrugged. 'Between twenty and thirty. I can give you the exact figure if it's important.'

'So, if a swan dies in, say, an accident, what happens?' Erin decided to put aside Carla's obsession with roast swan for the moment.

'It depends. Sometimes they're taken to veterinary practices for disposal or there are private animal waste companies. Sometimes we're called to ask for advice but the college wouldn't get involved in the actual removal of the animal.'

'I suppose I could call around the veterinarians in Jericho to see if anyone's taken possession of an injured or dead swan.'

'In cases where I'm not sure what to do, I usually refer people to Mrs Campion. She knows the laws around swan protection and who could help with an injured animal.'

'Mrs Camp— you mean Leda?'

Mei rolled her eyes. 'I think that's how she refers to herself but it's a terrible name. Do you know what happened to Leda?'

'I do, unfortunately. The thing is, I've already spoken to the woman.' She didn't mention that Carla had come along too. 'She says she knows nothing about a swan's wing.'

'That's bullshit. One time I visited her, she had an injured swan in a sort of cupboard at the back and she told me it wasn't the first time.'

Christ. Why hadn't Mei told her this before? Maybe she hadn't been asking the right questions because the previous time they'd met, Erin had been stunned by the revelation of what the child had been wrapped in. It also opened up the possibility that Leda hadn't been truthful when she and Carla had talked to her. Christ, was there anyone in Jericho who didn't have a secret?

'Maybe I should pay her another visit,' she said.

After Mei had left, Erin was preparing for her second autopsy of the day when a call came through, taken by Jenny. Her assistant came into the autopsy room, her hands trembling with agitation.

'There's been a death. It's all my fault.'

Chapter 36

It was an exam day and the corridors of the archaeology department were as hushed as the oak-panelled room on the other side of the quad where the examination was taking place. Carla passed Jack's office and saw that, uncharacteristically, his door was ajar. He had his head in his hands but rather than an expression of despair, Carla saw that he was reading a single sheet of paper laid out on his desk intently. Carla hesitated and rapped lightly on his door, making him start.

'Is everything all right?'

He turned over the sheaf of paper and smiled across at her. 'Not really. It's a letter from Anna's attorney. I'm trying to digest it all.'

'She's surely not laying the blame of everything that happened at your door. I mean, I may have been harsh with you but I do appreciate that the Norseman isn't the only closed society operating at the college.'

Jack shook his head. 'Anna doesn't care about what happened. Sorry to be brutal but that's the reality I'm dealing with. The letter is about what happens to the embryos we've had frozen during our various IVF attempts. Anna's asking for permission to use them in the future.'

'What?' Carla tried to hide her shock. 'Even though you're separating. How do you feel about that?'

'I'm not sure. Part of me thinks it's academic as we've had no success at all during any of our procedures and we've been told the embryos aren't particularly of good quality. In fact, the consultant recommended against freezing them but Anna was adamant.'

Carla bit her lip. It was an ethical minefield not least because of the impact any decision might have on future relationships. Anna's desperation for kids was palpable, she wondered how much the letter was about Anna retaining residual control over Jack. No wonder he was conflicted.

'What do you think I should do?' Jack asked her, looking slightly ashamed.

Carla took a step backwards. 'I'm not sure I'm the best person to advise you, except I would say don't reply immediately. It's an emotional time for you both and I don't think it's the best frame of mind to make decisions like these.'

Jack made a face. 'Her lawyer has given me until next Friday but I agree, I'm not going to be rushed into this one. What are your plans for the day?'

Carla looked at her watch. 'I'm hoping to catch up with Erin and then meet a friend for dinner.'

You're not the only attractive man out there, she silently told him.

He stood, pushing his hair out of his eyes. 'If Erin is on duty, she might be otherwise engaged. Did you hear about the woman who died up at Deerbrook Terrace?'

Carla reached out a hand to steady herself. 'A death?'

'Apparently one of the local eccentrics who lives up there, goes by the name of Leda, was found dead at the bottom of the cliff, a suicide maybe. The security officer at the gate told me this morning.'

Carla felt the room tilt and right itself. She began to dig in her pockets, looking for her mobile.

'What's the matter?' Jack was at her side in an instant, his hand on her arm. 'Are you ill?'

'I need to find my phone. If Erin has heard about the death, she'll be trying to call me. We spoke to the woman named Leda, her real name's Maureen, about the baby found by the dumpster at Shining Cliff Wood.'

'You think she was responsible for it?'

'We thought she might have some clue as to who had wrapped the child in a swan's wing.' She saw Jack's eyes widen. 'I know, shades of the Vedbaek burial, but we came away with little except mementos. Christ.' Carla gasped for breath. 'The stone she gave me was taken from my flat the night of my burglary. Her trailer was full of swan artefacts – some kitsch, others a bit more macabre.' Carla turned. 'I need to speak to Erin or maybe Baros.'

'I'm not sure if the death is suspicious. I'm only passing on what I heard this morning.'

Carla found her phone in her bag and saw she had a single missed call from Erin. She hesitated, wondering how much to tell Jack. She supposed it didn't matter now. There was nothing to link Lucie with the Norsemen.

'The baby is almost certainly the child of the missing student Lucie Tandy. I'm sure that Lucie is also the victim of a hazing incident. The dates certainly match. It seems the Norsemen aren't the only society members desperate to protect their secrets.'

'Rafe wasn't representative of us, Carla.'

Carla shook him off and grabbed her car keys from her bag. 'Someone is dead all the same. That's what happens when you try to protect secrets. Someone dies.'

On the drive out to Deerbrook, Carla tried to call first Erin, then Baros and finally Perez. None of them answered and Carla guessed they must be busy at the trailer park. It must be a suspicious death. Leda had shown no signs of being depressed or anxious so why else would she climb to the top of a cliff and throw herself off. An accident? Leda most definitely wasn't the active kind, although she had admitted to visiting Shining Cliff Wood on occasion. There was a big difference between catching a bus up to a local tourist spot and climbing the escarpment behind the camp. Carla remembered the stick propped against a chair in the trailer. Leda wouldn't have attempted a climb unless it had been forced upon her and yet Carla couldn't imagine what information Leda might have had of interest to a killer. She'd known of the Vedbaek burial and had been moved by it but had pointed out to Carla that there were differences, not least the gender of the baby. It had felt an innocuous enough conversation and yet Leda was dead.

She rang Dominic who answered immediately.

'Still on for later?' he asked. 'I thought we could go for a Chinese—'

'I'm not sure. Look, I don't want you to panic but a woman that Erin and I questioned about Lucie's baby has died.'

'Dead?' His voice rose a fraction. 'How?'

'I don't know, but I'm heading over there now. I'll be able to update you later but I doubt I'll make it to a meal.'

'Where did she die? I'll meet you there.'

Carla hesitated. Dominic was determined and resourceful but a distraction when she needed to concentrate.

'Look, I'll—'

The decision was made for her as she lost the signal. On balance she'd have warned him to stay away until she knew exactly what had happened to Leda. She switched her mobile on silent to give her a chance to think about Leda. The entrance to the park was strangely quiet, no sea of patrol vehicles that she had expected. Parking up at the same spot that she and Erin had taken on the previous visit, Carla approached a group of women who were talking in hushed tones.

'I've heard about what happened to Leda. Can you point me in the right direction?'

They didn't want to talk to her, moving their gaze away to a point in the distance where she could see three vehicles parked close together.

'Is that where Leda died?' Carla asked.

'She was called Maureen,' said one of the women. 'Maureen.'

'When I saw her in her trailer, she had a walking stick – I mean cane. How would she have got up to the cliff?'

'No one is saying she fell from the cliff. Talk to the cops if you're that interested.' It was a different woman this time, her voice more hostile. Carla returned to her car and drove slowly up the hill. She could see a patrol car outside Leda's trailer where more people huddled to watch the investigation. Further up the hill, the trailers petered out to be replaced by bare scrubland. Carla spotted Baros's car and drew up beside it. He peeled away from the woman he was talking to and came towards her.

'Surprised to see you here, Prof.'

He was wearing aviator shades and Carla saw her red face reflected in the glass. 'Erin and I met Leda when we were trying to discover what happened to the baby in the swan's wing.'

'Erin told me.'

'She's been here?'

'Briefly this morning. She wanted to look at the body in situ but she wasn't here long. She said she'd do the autopsy this afternoon as a priority. She seemed upset.'

'I missed a call from her. Was Leda killed?'

Baros took off his sunglasses. 'How you doing, Carla? Maybe you should be resting after all the excitement of the other day.'

Carla folded her arms. 'I'm all right. So, what happened to Leda?'

Baros sighed. 'Someone trying to make it look like she fell off the cliff. Doc is pretty sure she was, in fact, attacked around the head with a heavy rock.'

'Here?'

'Judging by the blood, I'd say yes. Forensics have finished and they say there's evidence of two sets of footprints. One approximately the size of our vic's and there are cane marks accompanying the prints, the other larger, probably a man's. No evidence Leda was dragged up here so she came this far willingly.'

'Do you have any suspects?'

'Nope. You?'

'You know, you might want to talk to the Student Ethical and Environment Club, known as SEEC. I'm pretty sure something went on at the beginning of term to upset Lucie which may have resulted in an attack.'

'Christ. What's that got to do with our vic? You think she wrapped the baby in the swan's wing? I'll go for that, given how fucking weird Leda's trailer is, but why would anyone want to kill her for that?'

'Maybe two of them dumped the baby – Lucie and the child's father. Perhaps Leda saw who he was and could identify him, or maybe Lucie was there when Leda discovered the baby and she told her what had happened.'

'Woah!' Baros put his shades back on. 'That's a lot of maybes. Too many. My guess, if you think this is all connected, is that she finds the dead baby and wraps it in the wing and brings it back to her caravan. Right?'

'Maybe. Those caravans are roasting hot so maybe that accounts for the mummification of the child.'

'Her killer knows that she has the baby, but doesn't realise that she never actually met Lucie. Maybe the killer knows Lucie is still alive and is trying to find her?'

Carla blanched. 'Then Lucie's in terrible danger. Her brother's in town looking for her and this is the scenario he's dreading. That Lucie is out there somewhere terrified.'

'You know, the person she's hiding from doesn't necessarily have to be the baby's father. What about her dormmates? Perhaps one of them has a secret to protect – they might know for example the identity of Lucie's attacker if we're assuming the conception wasn't consensual.'

'I don't know.' Suddenly parched, Carla reached into her bag and took a swig of water. 'Maybe Anika, her friend, knows something she's not telling. When I spoke to her, I got the feeling she was holding something back. Maybe I should talk to her.'

'Perhaps there's a friend you haven't yet discovered.'

'You know you might be right. When you start at the college, the first term is a blaze of new people. Some friendships stay, some disintegrate within weeks. You think I should look again at who she knew?'

'Maybe. Leave Leda's death to us. If you want to carry on tracking down Lucie, I can't stop you. Don't want to stop you, in fact, but be careful. Someone else is trying to find her too.'

—

On her way out of the development, Carla couldn't resist stopping at Leda's trailer. Crime scene investigators had left, but a lone officer was pulling a reel of tape to seal off the door. Thank God someone had switched off the grotesque flashing lights.

'I'm a friend of Leda's. Could I go in? Baros said it would be OK.'

The officer paused. 'He said to expect you. You've got five minutes and he said to tell him if you spot something important.'

Embarrassed at being so easily read by the detective, Carla opened the door and stepped inside. Again, the heat assailed her along with the sour smell of curdled milk. On the side sat a carton of yoghurt that Leda must have been eating when her visitor called. There was white powder everywhere and a sense of order destroyed and Carla was sure Leda would have hated her precious trinkets disturbed by this mess. Carla continued into the room where she and Erin had listened to Leda's assurances she knew nothing of the story of the dead baby. Perhaps she had played them, emphasising her ignorance of the child's conception and birth.

Carla opened drawers and cupboards, following the trail of detectives but if she'd hoped to find a wing to match the one covering Fionnuala, she was disappointed. She opened a desk diary and flicked through the pages.

There was nothing to suggest a visitor and most of the pages were depressingly blank.

If Leda had found the dead baby, might she have kept it somewhere safe in this trailer? She'd hinted at trauma and exile and perhaps she'd identified with the abandoned child. Carla shook her head. It was impossible to tell. As she shut the door, she shouted over to the officer.

'I didn't find anything but did Baros tell you to look for the remains of a swan?'

The officer nodded. 'Already covered.'

Chapter 37

Anika was at home in her flat revising for an exam, wearing a silk dressing gown in a shade of crimson. As before, her nails and hair were immaculate but the flat was a reeking tip. The smell of stale pizza hung in the air, a result of the grease-stained cardboard boxes lying open on the table. Anika spotted Carla's glance.

'I had friends around last night and I haven't gotten around to clearing up yet.' Anika pulled the collar of her dressing gown tighter. 'Anyway, I needed the company as someone tried to break into my room yesterday afternoon.'

'How do you know?' Carla looked around, wondering how the girl would be able to notice if anyone had entered the flat.

'There was a broken pane of glass when I got in after my exam. They'd tried to use the gap to reach the window latch but it's got a lock on it.'

'Have you reported the attempt to the police?' asked Carla, the details of the break-in uncomfortably close to her own experience.

'I've not had time yet.'

It was nearly two in the afternoon and Carla had to remind herself that she'd been a student once herself, although lazing around in nightwear had never been her style. She found the girl's languidness irritating which she tried to hide, needing to get Anika on her side for the questions she was about to ask.

'Have you been to any meetings with the Franklin group yet?' she asked, remembering the demonstration and Anika's selection as student rep.

'Last week there was a meeting but James Franklin wasn't there.' Anika sounded put out, reinforcing Carla's opinion she'd offered herself for the role to enter Franklin's milieu.

'I'm sure he'll come to meetings in the future. He comes across as hands on regarding his developments.'

Anika shrugged. 'Maybe.' She regarded her nails. 'That would be nice.'

'It's not what I've come here to talk about though. Look, I know you've been trying to protect Lucie but I believe the danger to her is now more real than ever before. If you have any idea of where she might be, I need you to tell me.'

Anika played with her hair, winding one long tress around her forefinger. 'I don't know where she is. We liked each other and hung out a bit but I didn't know what made her tick. I've told you all of this before.'

'OK, you weren't that close, but you were nearest to a best friend that I've been able to find for Lucie. Even her flatmates don't know her well so I suspect you more than anyone might know what was bothering Lucie.'

'That's not true,' Anika burst out. 'I never knew she was pregnant. She never told me that. I found out from someone in class. When she told me she needed some time out, I never thought that there was a baby involved.'

'We have secrets from even our best friends.'

'I wish you'd stop calling her that. She did have a best friend but it wasn't me.'

Carla held her breath. 'She did? Who was it?'

'I don't know. I only saw them together twice but they were holding hands. That makes her a closer friend than I was.'

Carla realised Anika's voice was tinged with jealousy suggesting a relationship more complex than the one she was keen to portray.

'Was it one of her dormmates? Daria, Ali or June.'

'Definitely none of them. I met them a couple of times when I went back to her place. This was a different girl.'

'You told me when we last met that she wasn't seeing anyone.'

Anika shrugged, refusing to look Carla in the eye. 'I didn't think it was important.' Again that suggestion of jealousy. Christ. Carla swallowed her fury. If Lucie and another girl were holding hands, it suggested a sexual or at least romantic relationship. Lucie had been at odds to keep her relationships private but had nevertheless felt comfortable enough with a new partner to bring the affair into the open.

'When was it you saw this?'

Anika frowned, pulling at her lip. 'February, I think. Maybe March.'

'Which time – the first or the second time you saw them together?' Carla's annoyance showed in her voice she knew but this could have changed everything if Anika had mentioned it earlier.

'I saw them twice on the same day,' Anika huffed. 'The first time was in the morning and then I was walking back here and I spotted them going into a bar.'

Carla groaned now not sure of the sighting's significance. It could have been a casual fling that flared and died, yet it didn't sound like Lucie at all.

'What did she look like, this girl you saw? Do you think she was a student?'

'Of course. I think I've seen her since but it's hard to say.'

'Can you please describe her?' Carla had endured enough of this languid girl's toying with her. 'Otherwise, I will have to call the police and ask for a formal interview with you.'

The threat was hollow. She was no authority on police procedure and she doubted she could persuade either Baros or Perez to immediately question someone who was essentially an innocent witness.

'They looked like twins,' spat Anika, her relaxed manner gone. 'Long blonde hair, long legs wearing tiny jeans and a vest. Just like Lucie.'

Carla frowned at the description. Buried deep within her a memory was awakening. 'Was she muscular, strong legs and arms?'

'Probably.' Anika was making an attempt to calm down. 'Why?'

Where could she get a photo of Ashley Jones? She had been right to believe that there was a connection between Rika Brown and Lucie Tandy and the link was Ashley. Carla opened her phone. On the department's homepage there was a list of current PhD students but no photos. However, there were photos of the summer dig, filed under 'current projects' and in one of them, Ashley could be seen standing over one of the trenches, her hands on her hips.

'Do you think this is her?' she asked Anika, showing her the image.

Anika needed glasses which she fished out of the pocket of her dressing gown. 'Looks like her,' she admitted. 'Who is she?'

'Someone I need to speak to quickly. Please, Anika, go and pack a bag and stay with some friends. Someone is trying to find Lucie.'

—

Ashley had told Carla she lived in Exeter House post-grad accommodation. Carla had learnt that these small rooms with shared bathrooms were highly coveted, not least because someone came in everyday to clean for you and you get to eat in the college dining rooms with the faculty. The warden at the accommodation knew the exact movements of his residents and said that Ashley was currently running a lab skills class, an extra way for postgrads to earn money. Despite the urgency, there was no way Carla could interrupt the students and was about to loiter outside the examination room when she pulled one of Dominic's posters from her bag.

'Do you recognise her?'

The man pursed his lips. Another of the rules Carla had heard about was that no overnight stays were allowed for guests of the students unless permission was given by the warden. The implication was that members of the opposite sex were unlikely to be granted permission. It was an old-fashioned rule and must be a nightmare to enforce in these enlightened times.

'She stayed over in Ms Jones' accommodation a few times, I believe.'

'Is she there now?'

The man shook his head. 'I haven't seen her for weeks now.'

Carla's heart jumped. 'Weeks? Can you remember the last time you saw her?'

'I...' Carla saw the man knew a great deal he wasn't telling her.

'The girl in the poster is missing. Haven't you seen them pinned on trees around Jericho?'

He shook his head and Carla realised this small complex of rooms was his world. Nothing beyond had any significance for him. It was to his love of the college and students that she appealed.

'I'm anxious not to disturb Ashley. She's got a lot on after everything happened at the archaeology site. I'd really like to get this sorted out without involving the college.'

It was the right tactic. The man had probably guessed at the relationship between Ashley and Lucie — there was no reason to keep it quiet after all — and disapproved of it.

'One day a few weeks ago, the girl in the poster was crying. Ashley was leading her to the car, supporting her I think, and they drove off.'

'A few weeks ago? How many are we talking about here? Two, five?'

The man's face changed. Despite not knowing about the posters over town, he must have been questioned by college security when Lucie had first gone missing. It seemed incredible that he was only now putting two and two together.

'More than five,' he admitted. 'I never thought anything of it until now.'

Covering his arse, thought Carla. 'Do you know where they were headed?'

The man reluctantly shook his head. 'I don't know. They were gone for a few hours. Ashley came back on her own.'

'When you say a few hours, do you mean two, three, four?'

The man considered. 'Three,' he decided.

So, Ashley had driven Lucie somewhere at most an hour and a half away, possibly nearer if she'd spent some time with her friend. The man had more to tell her. He coughed.

'She was on the phone to her mom, I heard her address her, asking if she'd already arrived at her holiday destination.'

'She was checking if her folks were away?'

'That's what it looked like to me.'

Carla could have kissed him. 'I don't suppose you have an address…'

'Not allowed to give it, sorry.' He folded his arms. 'I'm sure you have a next of kin for your digs though, don't you?'

I do, thought Carla, *I do*. 'Look, if you see Ashley—'

'I'll say nothing,' he promised.

—

Carla rang Dominic as she rushed to her office to find the address of Ashley's parents.

'I've got a strong lead on where Lucie might be. Shall I go to her first? It might look a bit heavy-handed if we arrive together and I promise you I'll tell her you're in town.'

She could hear Dominic tapping something, maybe a pen on a table, as he considered her proposal.

'I'm not sure. I'm worried she might be distressed given everything that's happened, especially if she's got wind of the woman who died today. Can I come with you?'

'I don't mind,' said Carla. 'You could always stay in the car if we decide on a different tactic when we get there.'

'Where do you think she is?'

'I believe she was in a relationship with a graduate student named Ashley Jones. Does the name ring a bell?'

'Ashley Jones? No, I've never heard of her. Where does she live?' His insistence was beginning to jar with Carla.

'Here in Jericho but her folks are away. I'm picking up her address now and then I can swing by wherever you are.'

'I'm at Patricia's catching up with her.'

'Hi, Carla,' Patricia shouted in the background.

'If you come and pick me up, I'll meet you on the front steps.'

The departmental secretary called up Ashley's address in an instant and Carla scribbled it down on a piece of paper. The place meant nothing to her, newish to Jericho there were no surprises there, but maybe Patricia would be more familiar with the area. Dominic was waiting in the sunshine as promised. Carla always felt a pang when she saw the house that had been her refuge for her first few months at Jericho.

'Is Patricia around?' she asked Dominic. 'I should at least say a quick hello.'

'We're in a hurry, aren't we?'

Carla frowned at his curt tones. 'Look, maybe it's better if I go alone.'

He made an effort to relax. 'Sorry, ignore me. I'm fired up that I might see Lucie again so I've forgotten my manners. Go and say hello to Patricia if you like.'

He was already in the car, breathing deeply and Carla shook her head. 'It doesn't matter. I'll see her afterwards when we have something to tell her, even if it's nothing.'

'It didn't sound like nothing.'

Again, Carla frowned at his tone and was beginning to wish she hadn't suggested he travel with her. Lucie was going to be upset, devastated, and brothers, as Carla well knew, could be overprotective.

She got in the car and started the engine, turning to the steps where she expected Patricia to be watching them depart. Odd she wasn't there. The satnav told her to head to the main highway north of Jericho, where she'd pass through three towns before taking a road west to a small cluster of houses. 'Does the name Silent Falls mean anything to you?' she asked Dominic.

'Nothing. It's just another New England town, isn't it?'

It was Lucie's place of safety though, thought Carla, *Shouldn't we be at least grateful for that?*

They drove in silence through the shimmering landscape. Carla hadn't thought late May could be so warm and she was glad she'd soon be leaving the heat behind for a more uncertain British climate. As they turned off the main highway, towards a hamlet marked on the map, Dominic pulled down the car's sun visor and began to check his face in the mirror. A creeping feeling that something was off began to take hold of Carla but she kept her eyes on the road, trying to hide her mounting anxiety. A house appeared in the distance, a white two-storey structure, imposing and sterile. She was used to these types of places in Jericho and it said a lot about Ashley's personality that she hadn't turned out to be a privileged brat.

Carla stopped the car and sat in silence. 'If she's in the house, she'll have heard the car approach.'

Dominic unclipped his seatbelt. 'This has gone on long enough. Let's go.'

Chapter 38

Erin completed the autopsy of the woman who had been born Maureen Campion but had adopted the name of Leda despite its tragic association. She sat down heavily in her office chair as Jenny placed a cup of coffee in front of her, not one from the vile machine at the end of a corridor but from Starbucks across the road from the facility.

'Must be tough when you know the victim. It's never happened to me.'

Erin made a face and took a sip of her coffee, enjoying its warmth trickle into her chest. 'I'd met her once and I was struck by how honest and kind she was. I'm struggling to understand why someone would want to kill her.'

The autopsy had been straightforward. Although Leda had a raft of health issues: enlarged heart, fatty liver disease and diabetes all caused by her weight, she wasn't outside the system. She was taking medications for both her diabetes and angina and could have lived another ten plus years. What had killed her was a blow to her head by something square-ish, probably a brick her assailant might even have picked up from the trailer park. The edge of the weapon had caught Leda's temple and Erin suspected she'd been turning to say something to him or her before she was surprised by the blow.

Erin had read more about the mythical Leda before the autopsy and had noted that after being raped or seduced by Zeus, Leda bore him two children in addition to two by her husband. The woman known as Leda had also given birth to a child or children although it was impossible to guess how many. A complicated life that had ended tragically.

Erin took another sip of her coffee and pulled Fionnuala's file from the stack on her desk. Leda had been an expert on swans and now she was dead. There must surely be a connection with Fionnuala's death. The file was depressingly thin, containing little more than the baby's autopsy report, Jenny's post-mortem photographs and the DNA results. It was this final report that Erin lingered over. She'd been able to DNA match the baby to Lucie Tandy but had got no further and certainly not in relation to identifying the child's father. She glanced down and remembered she'd ticked the box for more DNA work.

'Hey, Jenny,' she shouted. 'Did we get any more results back on Baby F?'

'I think an email came in overnight. I've not had a chance to sift through the messages yet.'

Spring had heralded a series of staffing cuts and they'd lost one of their PAs. Managers, without a single medical qualification between them, had decided that pathologists and their staff should share the load of monitoring their inboxes given that only they could decipher the information contained within the body of the messages anyway. Jenny took the brunt of this work but she was often as busy as Erin.

Erin located the email and opened the accompanying attachment. As she read the results, she rubbed her forehead, trying to make sense of the words.

'How much do you know about DNA, Jenny?' she hollered to her assistant,

Jenny appeared in the doorway. 'Not much. I know the procedure, how to harvest samples and send them off to the lab. Why?'

'I asked for more information about Baby F's DNA in an attempt to identify her father after she was matched to the missing Lucie Tandy. The lab has analysed the genome, in other words the map of their whole DNA, and found an absence of heterozygosity.'

'What does that mean?' Jenny came into the room and shut the door.

'The test scanned the baby's genome to look for missing or duplicate sequences of DNA code called single nucleotide polymorphisms. It's important because a missing sequence could account for the death of Fionnuala, sorry that's what I've called the baby.'

'I've been calling her Fiona.'

Erin could have hugged her goth assistant. 'In her case, however, an absence of heterozygosity means her DNA contains large chunks where the mother and father's contribution are identical.'

'Oh, fuck,' said Jenny, always quick on the uptake. 'We talking about incest or something? Hold on, didn't you say that Carla was friends with Lucie's brother.'

'She is. Shit, let me ring the lab and check I'm reading the results correctly.'

The lab assistant who answered the phone was emphatic. Fionnuala parents were first degree relatives either father and daughter, mother and son, or brother and sister. While the assistant was talking, Erin was frantically dialling Carla's number but the phone must be on silent. She checked her text messages and found a single one.

> Tried to call. On my way to Silent Falls where I think I'll find Lucie.

Erin typed in a reply.

> Are you alone? Pull over and wait for me. Don't trust Dominic.

Erin called up the place on the map and saw there were ten houses in total. She'd keep trying Carla and hope to God Dominic wasn't with her. Worried about her own safety, she messaged Jenny her destination and called Baros. The phone rang to voicemail but she told him as much as she had discovered.

'I could come with you,' shouted Jenny.

'Stay here – I've left your number with Baros. There's a possibility that Dominic's not with Carla and is at Patricia's. Can you find a way of checking? She lives on Hoyt Street. I can't remember the number but there'll be a daffodil yellow car in the driveway.'

'I'll head down there now and pretend I'm looking for Carla. I'll ring you if he's there. It'll take some of the danger away from you.'

'Be careful. Remember, the autopsy we've just completed is probably his work.'

—

In the car, Erin tried Carla again but the phone still rang out unanswered. If she was like Erin, she would have the phone permanently on silent to stop it ringing unexpectedly in lectures. She was sure Dominic was with Carla as the two had become close in the last few weeks, although Erin had hardly paid him any attention. He was nice looking enough, although a little too clean cut for her type. The thought that he might have fathered a child with his sister turned her stomach. She knew incest occurred, of course. A recent US study into sick children had revealed a higher-than-expected rate of absence of heterozygosity but she'd never expected to see a case in well-to-do Jericho. More fool her.

She'd reached the outskirts of the town when her phone rang. 'Carla?'

'It's me, Jenny.' Her voice was ragged. 'I've got to Patricia's and when I got to the front door, I could hear moaning coming from inside the house.'

'Is it Carla?'

'I managed to look through the window and there was a lady on the floor, it's not Carla. I broke a window to get in and I'm waiting for the ambulance to arrive.'

'Is Patricia all right?'

'I think so. She said he hit her when she reached for her phone to get a family member over. She was worried about his reaction when he took Carla's call and she was going to tell Carla to go without him. He's definitely with Carla.'

'Christ.' Erin put her foot on the accelerator. If she was stopped by the cops, she'd tell them her friend was with a killer being hunted by Jericho police.

'Come on,' she willed her ageing Buick. 'Come on.'

Chapter 39

'Hello, Lucie'.

Lucie turned, pulled the buds from her ears, her eyes widening in shock. They had first rung the doorbell and knocked but there had been no answer. However, they could hear the sound of someone moving around inside the house and, on turning the doorknob, had found it unlocked. The spacious hallway had a vaulted ceiling from which bounced the sound of someone humming in the room to the right. As they entered, Lucie had her back to them as she fiddled with a coffee maker. She sensed their presence before she saw them, her back stiffening before she spun around. Lucie's fair hair hung in limp tendrils around her face in the heat and Carla was struck by the air of vulnerability the girl gave off.

'It's Professor James from Jericho. Please don't be afraid, we're just here to check you're OK.'

Lucie's face turned from surprise to fear. 'We?' she queried. 'Who do you have with you?'

Carla realised Dominic had hung back behind her. He came from out of the shadows, his eyes on his sister. 'We were desperately worried about you,' he said, moving forward. 'It's thanks to Carla here that we realised you'd been sheltering with Ashley.'

'Keep away from me.' Lucie turned to Carla, her expression pleading. 'For God's sake don't let him come near me.'

Carla looked to Dominic aghast. 'What's the matter?' Dominic had gone very still, his eyes fixed on his sister's face. *Oh, Jesus*, Carla thought. *I've trusted the wrong person. I've brought trouble, terror even, to Lucie.*

'I understand you're upset, but I've come to take you home.'

'I'm not going.' Lucie screamed. 'I've had enough of you pawing me. Leave me alone.'

Dominic looked at Carla. 'I think you should let us chat in peace. Lucie is clearly upset.'

Carla took a step forward. 'I'm not leaving her. I'd like you to leave me on my own with Lucie while we have a chat.'

'What?' Carla saw Dominic's eyes narrow in fury. He hadn't expected her to argue with him and some of Lucie's terror was now seeping into Carla's skin.

'I think you should go.' Carla's voice was firmer than she felt. At six foot to her five-two, he towered over her, most men did. She knew in her heart of hearts that he would never go. Her mobile was in the car – if she could get to it, she might call Erin, Jack even, but it would be too late.

Dominic seized Carla's elbow and pushed her towards the door. 'This is between us two and I don't want you here.'

Carla was propelled out of the front entrance, her feet tripping on the floor as she heard the door slamming behind her. She hit her head on the stone steps, and a white heat of pain shot through her brow. What the hell was happening inside the house? On her hands and knees, she pulled herself up and crawled back towards the house. Dominic had allowed her to go first through the door to provide fake reassurance to Lucie, but as she moved towards the steps, she discovered she couldn't stand, the blow having sapped all her energy. She lay on the tiled doorstep, her cheek resting against the cool tiles. Her eyes narrowed as she followed the tessellated pattern. It was of the old type, put down in Wales and beyond, an intricate pattern designed to entrap the devil from entering the house. And yet, Carla thought, he's already there.

Carla tried to stand again, using one of the front pillars to pull against. From inside, she could hear shouting – Dominic's loud and commanding, Lucie's near hysterical. *He's going to kill her*, thought Carla, still trying to make sense of how she had got it so wrong. Was Dominic angry because Lucie had got herself pregnant? If it had to do with the initiation of the SEEC, Carla had found nothing to suggest anything untoward had gone on. And yet, Lucie must have been forced to have sex without her consent to have fallen pregnant. Dominic could not surely blame Lucie for an unwanted sexual assault unless… she'd mentioned Dominic pawing her.

'Oh, God.' Carla stood straight, her head still in agony. 'What have I done?' she shouted to the empty garden, the bright rhododendrons like those found at the Wilmington farmstead making a mockery of the dark thoughts in her head.

Inside, there came a crash. A table or heavy vase falling to the floor and there came a piercing cry that echoed throughout the house, seeping through the cracks and into the hot summer's day.

Carla leant against the door, hammering as hard as she could. 'Lucie! Are you OK?'

The silence was all-encompassing. Carla turned and stumbled towards her car, trying to remember if she had left it unlocked. Her bag was inside the house and she would break a window if she had to. All to get to her precious mobile phone.

The door opened. In her haste to get to Lucie, she'd left the car unlocked. She took her phone from the side pocket and saw twelve missed calls from Erin. She dialled 911 first telling the operator that she thought a domestic incident was going on inside the house and then rang Erin.

'Oh, God, Carla,' shouted Erin, her muted voice failing to disguise her panic. 'Is Dominic with you?'

'He's inside Ashley's house with Lucie. I think… I think… there's something terrible about him.'

'Call the cops,' said Erin. 'I'm in the car and coming out to you.'

'They're on the way. I just don't understand what—'

'I'll explain what we've found when I see you, but please don't go in there yourself. Dominic is incredibly dangerous and I don't want to see you injured.'

'I can't just sit here, I've got to do something. Oh, God.'

Carla looked up towards the house to see the door opening. 'I think he's coming out here. I— Oh, no.'

A figure, tall and slim came onto the porch, their features hidden from the mass of blood covering their face. Carla knew at once it wasn't Dominic but Lucie, though it did little to ease her terror. In Lucie's hand was a carving knife, its blade at least six inches long. Carla had a fear of knives. She knew what destruction they could wreak and she was alone in this desolate place. But was Lucie friend or foe? If it was Dominic who had let off that piercing scream, then God knows the turmoil that was going on in Lucie's mind.

For a moment, Carla thought of locking the door and driving away. Even in her dazed state, she'd surely get to the end of the drive and onto the main highway. But as Lucie approached, she saw the girl drop the knife and stumble forward, her knees sinking into the parched grass. She let out a howl into the air that froze Carla – a wail of mourning raw and grieving. Carla opened the door and, squatting next to Lucie, pulled her into her arms.

Chapter 40

They were far out of Jericho so there was no Baros and no Perez. The patrol car that pulled up while Carla was holding on to Lucie revealed two female cops, one of whom went into the house. When she emerged, she looked briefly over to where they sat on the lawn and called for an ambulance walking towards the bloodied knife as she spoke into the phone. Her partner was tending to Lucie, checking her over until it was clear that the blood that covered her arms didn't belong to her.

'Is he all right?' Carla asked the officer after she cut the call.

'I'm afraid not, ma'am,' she replied. 'I'm calling for backup. I need to ask if either of you have a weapon.'

'A weapon?' Carla was shocked. 'Of course not. I'm the person who rang in the emergency. We came looking for Lucie – she's a student missing from Jericho – and I brought along her brother Dominic who'd been looking for her. I hadn't realised it was he who Lucie was hiding from.'

Carla was gabbing and the officer laid a hand on her. 'The vic is this woman's brother? I thought it was a domestic abuse call.'

'It was. I believe it to have been an abusive relationship but I'm only guessing. You need to speak to Lucie.'

Carla wasn't allowed to accompany Lucie as she was taken away by ambulance but they offered to call another to take her to get her head checked out. Carla refused and while she was making her statement to a detective who had arrived on the scene, Erin drew up in her car. Her eyes widened when she saw Dominic's blood, transferred onto Carla's clothes from Lucie and Carla hastened to reassure her she wasn't injured.

'It was never about hazing.' Erin sat down on a garden bench besides Carla as they watched the blaze of blue lights as various agencies went about their business. 'The problem is that we conflated Rika's death along with the problems Jericho has been having with the Norsemen society. Lucie's disappearance and the death of little Fionnuala were to do with something even darker.'

'I can't believe I missed it,' said Carla. 'I fell for Dominic's assurances that he was desperate for news of Lucie simply because he was her brother. Is Patricia all right? I hate to think of Dominic attacking her.'

'I think she'll be fine. Like you, she's mortified to have been duped by Dominic. He clearly joined her church to get access to any Jericho gossip and when that didn't unearth Lucie, he persuaded her to introduce him to you.'

'Could we have prevented Leda's death? It maddens me to think I laid the trail for her killing by firstly mentioning how Fionnuala was found and then leaving the swan stone in my apartment. The gall of the man that he helped me clear up the mess he created.'

'I don't know. Maybe we are responsible. Maybe bringing justice for Fionnuala came at a price.'

It's what Carla most liked about Erin, her ability to confront unpalatable truths head on. Carla would have to live with the knowledge that she led Dominic to Leda as Patricia introduced him to Carla.

'There's evidence of swan remains in Leda's caravan according to preliminary forensic reports. That's hardly surprising given Leda's obsession, but it's proof that she might have had access to a swan's wing. Unfortunately, they're even available on certain quarters of the internet. We'll never find out how she got hold of it but it's possible she bought it once she discovered the baby.'

Carla groaned. 'This place. Which reminds me there's something I want to show you.'

Erin shook her head. 'No more now. I'm going to take you to the ER to have your head looked at. You should have got into that frickin' ambulance when you were offered one.'

Carla could feel a reddening behind her eye and was secretly grateful that it was going to get checked out. However, she did need Erin to see what was preoccupying her. Leaning against Erin, she limped over to the front door and pointed at the interconnected pattern.

'What do you see?'

Erin frowned. 'What do I see? The floor of a front entrance.'

'But what's it made of?'

Erin huffed. 'Tiles in a series of interconnecting lines.'

'*Exactly*. It's a form of ritual house protection and I think it's much older than this colonial style house we're looking at now. I think it's the site of a much older building where they've retained the original entrance.'

'Jeeesus, Carla. We've a dead body in the house which isn't my responsibility, thank God, and you're looking at the floor.'

'Unless,' Carla continued, frowning, 'someone laid older stones at the front of this newer house. Do they do that over here?'

Erin, got up, huffing. 'People do what the fuck they want here, so yes that's possible. I think we need to get that head sorted out before I seriously think you've lost the plot.'

Carla allowed herself to be led away and into Erin's car and she resisted the temptation to look back at the floor. She was sure she was right but she couldn't for the life of her think why that stone floor was important.

Chapter 41

Ashley pulled an e-cigarette out of her back pocket and sucked on it furiously, surrounding them both in a cloud of vapour. She'd tried to gain access to the ER room where Lucie was being checked over but her lover was under police guard with no one allowed access. Ashley was looking more vulnerable than she usually presented. She'd pulled the sleeves of her cardigan down over her hands and her leg jigged up and down as Carla tried to calm her nerves.

'Lucie's parents are coming from Seattle and, as next of kin, they'll be given first opportunity to speak to her. Do you know what her relationship with them is like?'

It would be every parent's nightmare to speak to their child who had killed a sibling. There would be some difficult conversations to be had around Dominic's obsession with his sister and how much of this they'd turned a blind eye to.

'I've never met them, of course, but according to Lucie they are kind-hearted but naïve. Small town people whose life revolved around church and running their local grocery store.'

'They must have been proud when Lucie got into Jericho College.'

'Very but they had high aspirations for both of their children, it's just that Dominic had chosen to study closer to home.'

'To keep an eye on Lucie.'

'It looks like it, doesn't it?'

A nurse padded towards them and Ashley glanced up at her, hopeful for more news. The nurse glided past them, causing Ashley to sigh.

'When did Lucie tell you about the baby?' asked Carla.

'As soon as we got together in February. She was clearly pregnant when she took off her clothes. I didn't mind, I mean some girls are bi and mistakes get made, but after we had sex the first time, she told me what had happened.'

'That Dominic had raped her?'

Ashley looked embarrassed. 'That Dominic was the father, certainly. She told me the sexual assaults had been going on for three years since she was fifteen. The problem is she didn't see it as rape. Unwanted attention she called it.'

'Christ.'

'I know, but at least she could see he was obsessive. She became pregnant the final time, which happened the night before she flew to Boston en route to Jericho. Once she knew she was pregnant she had to decide what to do and one thing she was sure of was that she wasn't going home for Christmas.'

'Dominic hadn't made any attempts to visit her before that?'

'He'd emailed saying he was intending to see her but she told him her living arrangements and that she'd expose his actions if he tried to visit. He'd decided to wait until she came home for Christmas but she never went.'

'She spent it with you?'

'Yes, exactly, although we weren't together at that point. I met her in a bar and she told me she was staying put for the vacation so I invited her up to my folks. They weren't bothered – they were too busy planning their next cruise.'

'So, when did you get together?'

'End of February. The twentieth to be exact. We then spent Easter together which had been more difficult to arrange. Because her folks are religious, they were putting more pressure on Lucie to come home and Dominic was obsessively emailing her about her plans. Everything unravelled after the Easter break. We needed to work out what to do about the baby but things weren't going well. She'd begun to have contractions and she was sure it was coming. She decided she'd have it and leave it in a safe haven. There's one at the fire department and we'd come up with a plan to get it there at night when on the second of April, the baby was born.'

'Fionnuala?'

Tears sprang in Ashley's eyes. 'I heard that's what you'd called her. It's a beautiful name.'

'Did Lucie think so too?'

'I couldn't talk to her about it.'

'So, what happened on the day Fionnuala was born?' *And died*, thought Carla.

'We were visiting Shining Cliff Wood and the cramps became heavy. It was early evening so it was quiet and Lucie turned to me and told me the baby was coming. She was wearing a skirt and she took off her underwear and squatted near a tree. I was panicking but also struck by the primaeval nature of what was happening. It was a posture our ancestors would have adopted.'

Ashley was going to make a very good anthropologist.

'Was the baby alive when it was born?'

Ashley shook her head. 'No.'

'You're sure?'

'Positive. I've looked up ramifications of what we did and Fionnuala never took a breath.'

Carla exhaled. Police would be questioning Ashley closely about the events, especially given Erin's conclusion that the baby had most likely taken a breath. She wondered if Lucie would tell the same story.

'Then what did you do? Leave it by the dumpster?'

'Of course not.' Ashley looked appalled. 'We put her in a shallow grave and covered her with leaves. I'd told Lucie about sky burials in Tibet and she liked the idea. I've no idea how she ended up by the dumpster.

'Leda must have watched Lucie give birth and you bury the child. She either marked the spot somehow and later returned with the swan's wing or she took the baby down to the trailer with her and returned to the wood a month later. She didn't leave it by the dumpster, she left it on a bench for people to find.'

Some might think that she showed more compassion than the two girls, but that wasn't Carla's judgement to make. That act of kindness and caring — also primaeval in its essence — had cost Leda her life.

'After the baby was born, Lucie had a complete breakdown and I moved her to my folks. We couldn't tell anyone she was safe because that would have led Dominic to her.'

'It must have been a shock when you saw the posters up on the tree.'

'We'd kind of been expecting it, but it meant Dominic was in town which upped the danger considerably. Then the body was found at Wilmington farm and I couldn't believe it. It was as if my professional and love life was in ruins. Christ. Do you think Jericho will have me back after this?'

Carla wasn't sure. The college had the fallout from the Norsemen to deal with but there were powerful people determined to deflect attention away from the college. Who was Ashley's ally? Not for the first time, the injustice of it all made her mad.

'I'll do what I can,' she promised, noting the look of disdain Ashley gave her.

Chapter 42

Fionnuala's ashes were scattered by Lucie and Ashley in the garden of the Wilmington farmstead near to where the family had camped. Carla was taken aback when Ashley told her of the plan. Wilmington had its own dark heart but it was Ashley's passion and that had rubbed off onto Lucie. The final resting place of her baby would be in that wild and beautiful field. Lucie was still awaiting a decision by the District Attorney's office on what charge, if any, she was facing in relation to Dominic's death. Her lawyer was arguing self-defence. The knife had been taken from the block standing on the kitchen counter which, he argued, ruled out premeditation. Carla hoped that Fionnuala's DNA results would be enough to convince the DA that Lucie was victim rather than perpetrator.

It was a blazing hot late June day as Carla packed to join a dig in Wales, where she'd offered her services not for the pursuit of research but just to get the feel of soil under her fingertips again. She was tidying up her workstation in case it was needed over the summer, even though Sabine had indicated that there wouldn't be the usual office merry-go-round and she could leave her stuff as it was. Nevertheless, Carla wanted any personal items out of the college and into her flat. Her part in helping Dominic locate Lucie had left her violated and she wanted no one else accessing her life while she was away.

Jack did not come to say goodbye, although he'd left a card on her desk. On the front was an Edward Hopper painting of a white building with a lighthouse attached. Inside he had written, *You're a beacon of light, Carla. Don't give up on me.* Carla looked at the message for a moment, opened a drawer and placed the card face down inside. There was no mention of the Norsemen and whether it would continue to meet.

Baros had also dropped by to say goodbye to her. It was a surprise to see him – he looked better, as if a weight had been taken from his shoulders – but he was still curt with her. Carla decided to focus on his actions rather than demeanour. He was there, they had a coffee together, and Baros told her the family was making plans for a memorial service to celebrate Rika's life. Carla liked the sound of that but she'd never be able to pass the Wilmington place without thinking of the long years Rika had lain in the ground. If Baros knew that Fionnuala's ashes now lay on the plot of land, he mentioned nothing of it.

As she was leaving the college, conscious of her cotton dress sticking to her damp limbs, she heard the toot of a horn coming from a dark Mercedes. She looked around her, wondering if they were trying to attract the attention of someone else, but the window wound down and the blonde head of Franklin leant out.

'Can I give you a hand with that box?'

On cue, the driver door opened and Chad came over and took the box from her which he deposited in the boot of the car. He opened the back passenger door and Carla slid in beside Franklin. The inside had an unusual smell. She'd expected expensive male cologne or possibly leather polish. Instead, it had a muted fragrant tone, possibly juniper berry.

'Back to your apartment?' Franklin asked.

'Please,' she said. 'How many cars do you have?'

'Too many. Don't tell your friends at SEEC.'

The first minutes of the journey were spent in a companionable silence, Carla gazing out of the window glad to be in the icy air conditioning.

'I hear you're spending the summer in England,' he said finally.

'Wales. What about you?'

'Me?' The question amused him. 'I'm in negotiations to purchase a plot of land on the edge of town and I hope to complete that sale soon. That will keep me occupied for the summer.'

'More houses?' asked Carla.

'A biotech research facility is planned for the college. I'll be providing the land and supervising its construction. It's no secret.'

'More contracts for the Norsemen?' Carla was unable to help herself but Franklin's face remained impassive.

'You could live here all your life, Carla, and the inner workings of Jericho would remain a mystery to you. Did you know, for example, that Albert Kantz is set to be reinstated in September?'

Carla turned to him. 'I've not heard any talk about this at all.'

'Of course not. Sabine hasn't even been told that she'll be stepping back into her former role but I can assure you that the decision has already been made.'

Carla wondered where the white-hot heat of anger came from. Sabine's role had only been a temporary appointment pending an internal investigation into the extent of Albert's knowledge of his wife Viv's cover-up of a fatal road accident. That had already been completed and

Albert, fundamentally a decent man, would be returning. What made Carla's blood boil was that Franklin, who knew Jericho inside out, had been the one to tell her. A complete lack of transparency.

She swallowed her outrage. 'It will be good to have Albert back. What about Viv?'

'Viv's position isn't looking so good. What people need in Jericho is a champion and she doesn't have many, if any. Even her staff are lukewarm about her possible return.'

Carla was unsurprised when it came to Baros. The cold case investigation into Rika's death had been allowed to wither and die under Viv's reign although she was hardly responsible for the failings of the initial investigation. But it wasn't Baros's pay grade where Viv needed her champions and Carla wondered how the dynamic would work in that marriage where Albert retained his high-profile career and Viv didn't.

They had reached her flat and the car slowed to a halt. For a moment, Carla thought that Franklin would get out to say goodbye but that clearly wasn't his style.

'Well, so long Carla. Enjoy Engl— Wales and, while you're there, have a think whether Jericho is the place for you.'

Carla went cold. His tone wasn't threatening and if anything, she detected worry in his voice.

'You think I've rattled too many cages?'

'Not just you. If I knew Doctor Collins better, I'd be saying the same thing to her too. But, then, Erin's not going anywhere – her son Ethan is still at school – but you have other options.'

'I'm used to rarefied academia. Don't worry about me.'

'But the problem is, I do. You turn up for a fight which I like and admire but misogyny runs deep in this town.

Don't look so surprised, Carla. I have sisters, an ex-wife I still care for. I want to see women on equal footing.'

'Then running away isn't the answer, is it?' Carla opened the door and stepped out. Leaning back through the door, she said, 'I appreciate the warning though.'

'Then if you ever need help, give me a call.' He hesitated as if to say something else and shook his head. 'Enjoy your summer.'

Carla watched as Chad deposited the box on her front stairs. 'Would you like me to carry it up to your apartment?'

She shook her head. 'I'll be fine.'

She didn't turn round as the car drove off, although the temptation was nearly too great. Her flat felt stuffy and she would be glad to leave this continent behind and revel in the uncertain and changeable Welsh climate. Would she come back? She had no other job to go to, so the answer was almost certainly yes. She also had unfinished business, but for the life of her she couldn't work out what or who it involved. Time, she decided, would tell.

Acknowledgements

I'm grateful, as ever, to my agent Kirsty McLachlan at Morgan Green Associates for the continued support of my writing. Thanks to Siân Heap for editing Quiet Bones, her last task before departing Canelo for pastures new, and to Louise Cullen and Alicia Pountney for picking up the baton and their enthusiasm for this new series. Thanks to publicist Kate Shepherd too for her hard work.

I couldn't do without the support of Tony and Judith Butler who are my keen-eyed first readers. Marion Todd, Sheila Bugler, Rachel Lynch and Jeanette Hewitt provide much needed moral and writing support and I've appreciated the welcome I've received at bookshops, libraries and festivals as I've launched Carla out into the world. Thanks to Sarah Tarlow for her perceptive comments and guidance and to Crime Cymru pals Philip Gwynne Jones, Gail Williams, Bev Jones, Alis Hawkins and Louise Mumford. My local independent bookseller Gwisgo Bookworm run by Karen and Niki are always a delight to visit and you can always request a signed copy of any of my titles from them. We have a lovely community talking about books each Saturday on Facebook. Do come over and say hello if you have a chance – https://www.facebook.com/SarahWardCrime/.

Thanks to Dad for always reading and promoting my books and the rest of the family especially Adrian, Ed and Katie, Heulwen, Gareth, Pete and Jo, and Anita and Anwen. Finally, thanks to Andy for all the support and encouragement. It wouldn't be the same without you.